Hot Valley

Hot Valley

James Lear

CLEIS
PRESS

Published in the United States by
Cleis Press Inc., P.O. Box 14684, San Francisco, California 94114.

Printed in the United States.
Cover design: Scott Idleman
Cover photograph: Louis LaSalle, www.louislasalle.com
Text design: Frank Wiedemann
Cleis logo art: Juana Alicia
ISBN-13: 978-1-61664-090-3

Thanks to Mark and John for
New England hospitality.

This book is dedicated to the memory
of Richard Amory (1927–1981)
author of *The Song of the Loon*.

PART ONE:

Trouble Comes
to Vermont

I

Unlike most young men, I never longed for glory or adventure on the field of battle. The outbreak of hostilities between the North and the South in 1861 meant nothing more to me than the interruption of the long, hot, eternal summer of my adolescence—a season that had already long overstayed its time. At the age of 21 I was still behaving like a boy of 17, interested only in my own pleasure, unwilling to face the fact that I was now a man. Manhood meant responsibility, and responsibility meant work, and work meant an end to my diet of lotus flowers.

When war was brewing, I simply ignored it. Even when the fighting began, I thought of it as something far away, like the action in one of the novels I loved to read. But the war would make a man of me—even me, the spoiled son of a prosperous New England family, a pampered dilettante who exploited his social position for the most ignoble ends. It would find me in my comfortable backwater, it would pull me out and knock me off balance and throw me into the fire. It would change everything about me—so much so that

I hardly recognize my 21-year-old self now, viewed from a distance of five years.

Much to my parents' disgust, I had little interest in the family business, the grandly named Hydropathic Establishment, which my father had built up from a modest little bathhouse to a major New England visitor attraction. I had no desire to learn bookkeeping, or contract law, or any of the other dreary subjects that would make me into a useful, dutiful son. I had some vague idea that I wanted to be a writer, for which I could hardly be blamed, having been educated at great length (and no little cost) in the finest schools the East had to offer. And so I spent my days with my nose buried in a book, or sleeping, or staring out the window, or swimming at the lake, or daydreaming about a glorious future, crowned with laurels and lionized in the literary salons of New York, London, and Paris.

Such were my days. My nights were very different. At the age of 19, I discovered the workingmen's bars and rooming houses on the wrong side of the tracks—literally on the wrong side of the tracks, as the railway that arrived in 1849 had carved the town of Bishopstown in two. On our side were the quality stores, the town square, the nicer hotels, and the pleasant residential streets that fanned out into the woods beyond. Beyond the tracks were the run-down boarding houses, the dubious bars, the obvious whorehouses, and a crazy assortment of buildings, some of them old and decayed, others new and already falling down, where dwelled the workers and drifters to whom I was drawn. The Irish arrived with the building of the railroad; some of them settled and became prosperous, even moving to the nice part of town, where they were tolerated for their money. Others drank and gambled, wasted themselves and their wages, and put up with visits from well-intentioned churchwomen and preachers who tried, without much success, to win them over to righteousness. Added to that was an indigent population of salesmen, engineers, and others of no apparent occupation at all who sat in the bars awaiting opportunity.

In a town like Bishopstown, it was hard for men of that class to meet women; even the whores who worked in the two rival houses were beyond their reach. Most preferred to spend their money on liquor, rather than saving it up for a loveless half hour with one of our downtown demoiselles. And this was where I saw my chance. I would do all the things that the professional women would do, and more—much more— without a dollar changing hands. In fact, as some of the better looking laborers quickly learned, I was willing to spend a little of my own cash if I felt it would increase the yield.

My first real foray was on the night of my 19th birthday, after a dreary dinner at home with family friends and relations. There was much table talk about my future, about the glorious career I would make in the Bishopstown Hydropathic Establishment and Mineral Spa Center, the pride of the town (said my father) and foundation of the Edgerton family fortune. "Jack," my father said, downing another of the endless toasts, "make me proud, make me rich, make me happy." To which my mother added "and make me a grandmother!" which caused a great deal of giggling among my sisters and the daughters of a neighbor whom we'd known since we played together as infants. I nodded and smiled and drank more than I should have.

When the plates were cleared I announced that I was going into town to meet some school friends. "Go ahead, son!" my father said. "Raise a little hell!" My mother tutted and shushed, but I could see by the indulgent smiles around the table that they were happy to think of their young man making his way in the world, sowing a few wild oats before settling down as a fine upstanding member of the community. Little did they know that the only fine upstanding members in which I was interested were encased in dirty corduroy work pants in the downtown bars where I was headed. I had promised myself that, after months of fantasizing, I was finally going to take advantage of the opportunities available to me. It was my birthday present to myself.

The town center was about 20 minutes' walk from the house, and by the time I got there the cool evening air had taken the edge off my bravado. I sauntered with my hands in my pockets, I whistled a merry tune, but my stomach was turning over and I thought I was going to piss my pants. Why hadn't I relieved myself in the woods before I emerged into town? Oh well, it was too late to turn back now—I knew that my courage would fail me—and so I pressed on and crossed the railway tracks, letting my feet lead me, trying not to have second thoughts.

I'd already identified the bar that would be my first port of call, an establishment in an unremarkable clapboard building, called the White Horse. The dirty first-floor windows bore the legends "imported wines" and "Kentucky sour mash," while the upper story advertised "clean rooms." I knew from earlier reconnaissance missions that there was a steady traffic of workingmen in and out of the White Horse, and judging by the state of some of them as they wove their way unsteadily from the bar at night, they shouldn't be too difficult to befriend.

Without breaking the rhythm of my stride—I knew that hesitation would be fatal—I walked straight up the steps, across the shabby porch, and through the swinging doors of the White Horse. The first thing that hit me was the smell—stale whiskey, tobacco smoke, and the sharp tang of unwashed bodies. It was too dark to see anything much at first, but gradually my eyes, watering from the smoke, made out the lights above the bar and a few tables illuminated by lamps. Twenty pairs of eyes looked up at the newcomer, registering little more than faint surprise. I was obviously out of place—but the drinkers in the White Horse were too wrapped up in their own problems to care much about anyone else.

12

A lone customer in the far corner, a heavyset man of about 40 with a thick yellow moustache and a denim work shirt, raised his glass in acknowledgment of my presence. That was the only welcome I received at the White Horse.

I might have turned on my heel and run home, but for the fact that I was now desperate to piss, and so, once more using my nose rather than my eyes, I found the unsanitary lean-to that passed for a bathroom. Pushing through the battered wooden door that separated it from the main bar (but which did nothing at all to contain the smells), I found two buckets, some torn-up newspaper, and a three-legged stool with a hole in the seat. At home we prided ourselves on the latest word in sanitation; this was like a return to the Dark Ages.

I unbuttoned my pants and pulled out my cock, and within seconds I was pissing like a horse. The noise as it hit the metal bucket was tremendous, but all I was conscious of was a relief to the sharp pain that had tormented me since I got to town. I was so engrossed in "making myself comfortable," as we said at home, that I didn't hear the door open behind me. I sensed the presence before I saw it—and some instinct told me that it would be the man from the corner table.

"Guess you needed that, son," he said, leaning against the wall.

"Er...I guess so..." I was still pissing, and found it hard to make small talk.

"I could hear you way out in the barroom."

"Oh. How embarrassing..."

"No need to be shy," he said, making no pretense of being there for any reason other than to talk to me. "Sounds like you got a healthy constitution." His voice was low and gravelly, a smoker's voice. I couldn't yet turn fully around to look at him; my sidelong glances caught the blue of his shirt, the yellow of his whiskers, the glint of belt buckle caught by the light of the single guttering candle that illuminated the pisshouse.

"Well, I've finished now," I said, hating the prim tone of my voice. I started to put my cock back in my pants.

"Now you hold on a minute there, boy," he said, stepping up to the bucket beside me. "Don't do nothing in a hurry. Make sure you shook it dry."

I made a halfhearted effort to obey him—but, even now as my most feverish fantasies were coming true, materializing beside me, so close that I could smell the whiskey and tobacco on his breath and feel the heat from this thick arms—I wanted to bolt.

"You can do better than that. Come on, show me that it's nice and clean and dry."

I continued to shake it as he made gruff sounds of approval.

"That's better. Don't want piss stains on those pretty pants, do you?"

"No."

"Well now, all this talk of pissing has got me thinking I need to take a leak myself. You don't mind, do you?"

"Of course not." I stepped back, thinking he meant for me to vacate the room.

"Well, that ain't friendly," he said, "seeing as we've only just become acquainted." With one hand he unbuttoned his fly; the other he extended toward me. "My name's Mick. What's yours, boy?"

I shook the offered hand. "Jack, sir."

"Sir. Ain't been called that for a while."

He must have seen me staring down at the hefty piece of meat he'd just hauled out of his pants; it looked like a gourd.

"Big, ain't it?"

"Yes...sir."

"Too big for those railroad whores."

"Oh..."

"Bigger than yours, I reckon."

I suddenly remembered that my own cock was still hanging out of my fly. I must have looked ridiculous as I stood there with my mouth open. Thank God the lights were low, and Mick couldn't see me blushing.

"It's heavy, too. Want to feel it?"

He took my hand, which he was still grasping, and guided it down to his prick. I had an urge to run, to tell him that he'd got me all wrong, that I'd just come into the White Horse to make myself comfortable, nothing more, that I must be getting home... But then my hand made contact with the silky-smooth skin of his huge, fat cock, and I knew that I would never really be able to go home again.

"Hold it for me, then, Jack." He put his hands on his hips, pushed them forward, and started pissing into the bucket—a few drops at first, but then a torrent. I could feel the vibration of it passing through his prick as I held it. My own cock became hard without me even noticing, it happened so quickly.

Before he was even halfway through, Mick grabbed me by the back of the neck and drew my face toward his. The skin on his cock was smooth as satin—but his face, whiskered and weather-beaten, was like a combination of leather and sandpaper. The first contact was like an electric shock. At first I flinched, but his hand prevented me from pulling back. And then his lips opened and found mine, and we kissed. It was my first kiss, outside the chaste pecks of the family circle, and it was wet and hot and tasted of whiskey. I staggered a little, my grip on his cock faltered, and the ebbing stream of his piss went all over the floor and both our legs. It didn't seem to bother Mick, who kept kissing me with the greed of a starving man. I guess he didn't get too much affection in his line of work, whatever it might be.

Eventually we broke apart, and two hard cocks faced each other in the stinking gloom.

"I got a room upstairs," he said. "Want to join me?"

15

I needed no second invitation. Hardly bothering to dress ourselves properly, and making no effort to disguise the damp patches on our pants, we entered the bar. To my astonishment, we were greeted not with suspicious stares or frosty dismissal, but with a gale of bawdy laughter. Mick acknowledged it with a wave of his hand, and led me by the hand through the bar.

"Got yourself a piece of ass," the barman said, a swarthy-looking man with a bald pate and thick black eyebrows. Mick clacked his tongue in response. He took a key from a hook above the bar and led me up a flight of dark, unlit stairs. He seemed to know his way.

"Long time since I had company like yours," he said, lighting the lamp in the small square upper room. It contained a single bed, a washstand, a chair, and a chamber pot, and that was all. A piece of muslin was tacked across the window.

"Do you work in town?" I asked.

"Yeah, sometimes. I come and go. Laboring work's scarce. I go where I'm wanted. Bishopstown's as good as anywhere," he said, casually unbuckling his belt and drawing it through the loops. "What brings you down here? Don't often see a face as pretty as that down here."

I had never been called "pretty" before, although I thought, in my vanity, that I wasn't bad looking, with my wavy blond hair and my regular features, and the smooth pale skin that I had often inspected in the mirror, alone in my room at night, longing for company. My mother's friends sometimes said I was "a fine young man," and my arrival in a room was often heralded by a certain amount of twittering from girls of my sisters' age.

"Oh, I just thought I'd look in..."

"To the White Horse? Your sort don't belong here. You go to the fine hotels on the other side of town." He was sitting on the chair, unlacing his boots.

"I wanted something different."

He laughed. "Well, you certainly got that." Then he frowned, concentrating on a knotted bootlace. "God damn. Can't see a thing."

This was my cue. I knelt at his feet. "Here, let me."

He leaned back, extended his legs, and rested his heavy-shod foot in my lap. "That's a good boy. Your eyes are sharper than mine. You sort it out."

I quickly unraveled the knot, unlaced his boot, and pulled it off. The thick wool sock underneath smelled of leather and fresh sweat, but wasn't too offensive. I pulled it down, eased it off his foot, then rubbed his foot as I'd seen my mother do to my father after a hard day's work.

"Oh, that's good," he sighed. "You're a good kid."

"Thanks," I said, freeing his other foot.

"Jack, ain't it?"

"Yes, sir."

"Jack. You ever been fucked up the ass before, Jack?"

His directness took my breath away.

"No, sir."

"Well, that's what you're going to get tonight. Think you can take it?"

"I don't know."

"Want it?"

I hardly knew. I looked down, still rubbing his feet.

"Yeah, you want it, boy, I can tell. Why else would you be here with me? You want this, don't you?" He squeezed the mighty mound at the front of his trousers.

"Yes, sir."

"You want it bad."

"I want it bad."

"You got it, boy. You got all of it, all night, any way you want. Up your ass, down your throat. You ride it any way you like."

"Th-thank you."

"Now git up." I stood before him as he sat, legs splayed, shirt unbuttoned to reveal the thick hair on his chest, bare-footed. "Undress yourself."

The thought of being naked, vulnerable and exposed, in front of this powerful, confident man only a few years younger than my own father excited me to the point of faintness. My hands shook as I pulled off my necktie, threw down my jacket, and fumbled with my shirt buttons. Soon I was topless.

"Stop there."

I stood still.

"Come here."

I stepped toward him, standing between his open legs.

"You got a skin on you like a woman's." His rough hands ran up my sides, feeling the ribs, across my back. "So smooth and fine. But just here"—he ran the back of his knuckles from my belly down to my belt, where a bush of darker hair was growing thicker by the month—"that ain't like any woman I ever seen. Well, maybe there was one girl in Chicago. Hairy Mary they called her. She had a tail like a brown bear." He leaned forward and started kissing me on the belly while his hands explored my ass. Again, the rough-ness of his whiskers caught me off guard.

"You're going to be red and raw all over in the morning, boy."

"I don't care."

"Now let's see your ass."

Thank God he took control; without his guidance, I might still have lost my nerve. Instead I turned around and dropped my pants. I was wearing silk underclothes, a gift from my parents.

"Wooh!" hollered Mick. "We got some fine French draw-ers on!"

"They were a birthday present," I stammered, blushing like the virgin I was.

"Nice," he said, letting a hot hand wander over my silk-covered cheeks. "Very nice. Now let's see how fast you can take 'em off." The underpants were soon around my ankles, bunched up over my boots and pants.

Mick whistled. "That is the finest piece of ass I've ever seen in all my days," he said. "You sure you want me to fuck it? Almost seems a shame."

"I... I want you..."

"You got me, boy, any way you want me." He stood up and put his arms around me from behind. I felt the hair on his chest tickling my back, the hardness of his groin pushing into my bare ass. He kissed me on the neck, on the ears; my arms hung limply by my side. He was in control.

He pushed me forward till my knees made contact with the cold metal of the bedstead, and I fell forward. The blankets, when they hit my naked body, felt as rough as his beard, as if he was kissing me all over at once. With my ass exposed and pointing upward, he started to undress my lower limbs, quickly removing each boot, pulling off my clothes till I was completely naked.

"Fuck," he said. "Am I dreaming?"

"No, sir," I said, and to convince him that he was very much awake I reached around and pulled my butt cheeks apart. That was all the reassurance he needed, and suddenly I felt that hot breath on my hole, felt the sandpaper of his face against my buttocks, and then—oh, brave new world!—felt his tongue lapping at me, licking me, caressing me where I had never been touched before.

For years I had dreamed of what it would be like to be with another man, to have his body at my fingers' end, to feel him and explore him with all my senses. Now that it came to it, however, I could concentrate only on one thing—the sensations that were happening to me. My entire body was on fire, tense and yet more relaxed than it had ever been, as Mick's tongue worked around my ass. His rough hands pulled my cheeks further apart, and then, when he dived in and forced his tongue past my ass ring, where I had never imagined a tongue would go, I gasped and jerked my legs back. He came up for air for a moment, saw that I was not about to cry out for help, and got back down to work. The sensations were so intense that I had almost forgotten about my cock, which was rock hard, pressed down against the edge of the bed, pointing back between my thighs—but when Mick grasped it, still lapping at my ass, and jerked it a few times, the sensations were suddenly doubled, tripled, multiplied to a crazy infinity. I felt as if I was falling into a chasm, I called out and struggled, and then, before I knew what was happening, I was spewing hot white sperm all over the dusty floorboards.

Mick kept holding and squeezing my cock, reluctant to let it go, and lay forward so that his body covered mine, the rough cloth and wiry hair against the smooth, sweaty skin of my back. The heat felt good; without it, I might have started to shiver. I felt weak, I felt helpless, I felt like crying.

After a while—maybe a minute, maybe 20—he pushed himself up and stood. I rolled over, flexed my legs, rubbed my face. For a moment, I didn't know where to look, I felt awkward and bashful. I suppose he sensed this.

"You'll be leaving now, then," he said, picking my shirt from the floor and holding it out to me. I took it and held it limply. I felt disappointed. Obviously our encounter was at an end.

"Can I see you again?" I asked.

He looked puzzled. "What do you mean?" His voice was suspicious.

"I mean—can we do this again?"

His eyes met mine. "We can do this anytime you want." He stood over me, looking down hungrily at my still naked body. I could see from the bulge in his pants that he hoped it would be sooner rather than later.

"How about now?"

"You mean it? You want more?"

"I want you. I want to see you, touch you."

He smiled. "Boy, it's all yours." He pulled his shirt over his head, bunched it up and threw it over the chair. His body was massive, bulky, far from graceful. There was a deep scar from under his left armpit down to his abdomen. There was thick, browny-yellow hair all over, from the razor line right down to his belt, over his shoulders, all over his arms. His waist was thick, his arms long. I stood up—we were the same height, almost—and pressed myself against him, reveling in the touch of his skin, his hair, his hands. We kissed, long and deep, and my cock stirred back to life. His grasped it, and it grew quickly to full hardness.

"How old are you, Jack?"

"Nineteen today."

"Yeah," he said, squeezing my dick. "I remember nineteen. Always ready for more. Well, I ain't got much to give you for your birthday, Jack, but take whatever you can find."

I dropped to my knees and buried my face in his crotch. It still smelled of piss, where our earlier efforts had splashed his pants. I could feel how hard he was, how big. I undid his belt, let his pants fall around his ankles, and fished around in his drawers for my prize. I drew it out of the fly with difficulty, as it was rock hard and inflexible—and it stuck out from the faded white cotton, thick and dark and heavy.

"Happy birthday, Jack."

I may have entered that room a timid virgin, but by the time I left it I was a fully committed, cock-hungry slut. From my first taste of Mick's cock, with its mixture of sweat and piss and precum, I was hooked. I grasped it by the base and kissed the tip, then tentatively licked it; Mick stood there with his hands on his hips, watching my first steps with amusement.

"Come on, Jack. Open your mouth and suck it."

21

I didn't need to be asked twice. I took the head between my lips, then moved down an inch or so. It was too much—I gagged—but not enough. With tears running down my cheeks, I worked my way down. I wanted him to fill me. I wanted to possess him.

"That's it, boy. Suck my dick."

He moved one hand to the back of my head, caressing me and gently initiating an up-and-down, back-and-forth movement. With each stroke my lips were stretched further, my mouth was fuller, and my throat protested. But I would not be defeated. I breathed when I could, sucked and stroked him with a greedy vigor.

"Take it easy, Jack. I don't want to come just yet. See, at my age it takes a little longer to get ready again."

I sat back on my heels and watched him undress. Finally he stood before me, fully naked, his thighs like tree trunks, his great prick and balls hanging there, swinging with each movement, throbbing. I did not know what to do. I wanted him, all of him, I wanted everything, I wanted to be annihilated, to be completed.

Fortunately, Mick took a more practical approach to achieving the same ends.

"You ready to be fucked, Jack?"

"I guess so."

"It's gonna hurt like hell."

"I don't care."

"I'll stop if you want me to."

I sniffed and tossed my head defiantly. "I won't."

He laughed. "Get up on the bed. We'll take it easy to start with. Lie on your side."

At first he held me, kissed me on the neck, caressed my cock. Then his fingers started probing into my crack, still wet from the tongue bath he'd given it earlier. If fucking was anything like that, I thought, I was in for a good night. He pushed and rubbed my hole, and slipped one wet finger in up to the first knuckle. It felt strange, but not so strange; I'd done as much and more at home alone with my fingers and one or two inanimate objects, such as candles. The finger worked its way in, and it felt good; I pushed against his hand, wanting more.

"You're ready."

"Yeah."

"You sure about this? You ain't gonna run to Daddy?"

"No, sir."

"You promise?" Maybe Mick had had bad experiences before; maybe that was why he led this drifting life. Maybe that explained the scar down his torso; I had visions of vigilante groups, knife fights, leaving town in the dead of night... I knew what I was doing was dangerous, unspeakable, criminal. Did I care?

"I promise. I want you to fuck me. I want you to fuck me hard."

"Okay, Jack. Don't say I didn't warn you."

He pulled his finger out of my ass and then, before I could get used to feeling empty again, hawked some saliva into his hand and smeared his prick with it, pushing the head against the target. I pushed back in response—and, to my astonishment, he slipped inside me. His dick was so much bigger than his finger. It felt as if someone had pushed a hot potato inside me. There was no pleasure, but neither was there particular pain.

"Go ahead. I'm fine."

"Slow down, horsey. You need to be broken in slowly." His hand played around my dick, which, unknown to me, had suddenly become limp. "I'm going nowhere till this is hard again. You'll thank me later."

And so, resting the head of his cock inside me, controlling its position like an engineer, he resumed kissing my neck, murmuring obscene endearments in my ear, and playing with my prick. Within two minutes, I was harder than ever and felt like I was ready to come again. My ass was working around his cockhead like a wringer.

And then he began to fuck me. I thought I was ready for him, but nothing could prepare me for the sensations that were to follow. He pressed another inch, another inch, another inch into me, and suddenly, where there had been nothing but pleasure and appetite, there was pain.

"Hey!" I shouted.

"Hurts, huh?"

"Hurts like hell."

"Let's just wait a second. Hold it there. Just breathe in and out for me. Take it easy." He kissed me again, he played with my cock. At first I couldn't understand why he didn't just take his cock out of me, as it hurt so much—but then, after a few moments, the pain began to slip away and the pleasure returned. And so we proceeded, cautiously, stopping and breathing and waiting when necessary, until he could push no further.

"That's it, Jack. You got all of me."

I reached around behind me and felt his stomach pressed against my back. I felt my ass ring stretched around the thick base of his cock. I grabbed his balls and pulled them toward me.

"I can't get them in as well, you greedy little bastard."

And so the fuck began, slowly at first, gaining momentum. My body was focused entirely on the sensation of cock and ass—and yet, to my surprise, my mind was floating free, wandering from subject to subject. I thought of my schoolmates, my family, my prospects, my future. I thought of the things I had studied, I thought of how my life might unfold. In all these thoughts I was impressed by one overwhelming idea—that here, now, at this moment and in this room, my life was really beginning at last, and that whatever happened to me in the future would be defined in some way by the pleasure that Mick's cock was giving me as it drove into my asshole.

And then he pulled out.

"How you doing?" he asked, sitting up beside me.

"Good. Why are we stopping?"

"You'll see. You think that was what fucking was all about? Oh, boy, you have no idea."

And so, for the next half hour, he fucked me in every conceivable position. He had me up on my hands and knees, ramming into me from the back. He had me sitting down on his cock as he lay back on the bed. He spun me around, he flipped me over, he rode me and supported me and possessed me. Finally, I lay on my back, my legs resting on his shoulders, as he braced himself with his powerful arms and fucked me harder than I believed possible. And yet I took every stroke, I met every thrust, and I wanted more. I could not tell if I had come again or not; my belly was wet with slippery, sticky fluid, and yet I was still as hard as could be. Finally, he doubled the rate and vigor of his thrusting, stuck his tongue down my throat, and spewed his load up my hole.

I thought this would be the end, but he quickly rallied and, leaving his cock firmly lodged inside me, sat back on his heels, pulling me toward him.

"Let's see you come again, Jack. This time with me inside you." He grabbed my dick, jerked me gently a few times—and it was enough. The feeling of his hard prick invading my guts was enough. My dick was just the trigger. This time, I came with my whole body, and spilled a massive load across my chest and stomach. It ran down my sides and soaked into the thin cotton sheets.

We lay together for an hour or two, drifting in and out of sleep, listening to the heavy footfalls along the corridor, the creak of floorboards, the banging of doors. In the silence of the night, every sound was amplified; God knows how loud our revels had been. Everyone in the White Horse must have known that the young man in the stylish suit who wandered in off the street was no longer a virgin.

It was getting light when Mick roused me. "You better get home. People will be asking questions."

I did not want to leave. I wanted to stay with him forever, and I told him so.

"You do as I say. We'll meet again if you want to."

In answer, I dived down into his groin and started sucking his cock. It started to rouse itself in my mouth.

"Not now, Jack. There's a big wide world out there and we have to be on our guard."

"Fuck me again."

"I will. I promise you I will. But now you get home. We don't need that kind of trouble. Go on. Get dressed."

I walked home in the gray dawn, listening to the chickadees stirring in the pine trees, and climbed in through my bedroom window, as I always did when I'd been out exploring at night. The house was silent, and I slept until nine. There were a few jokes at my expense, good-natured raillery about how seedy I was looking, how they could smell whiskey on my breath, a suggestion that I must have a sweetheart down in town. I laughed and kept my own counsel.

II

FOR TWO YEARS, BETWEEN MY 19TH BIRTHDAY AND THE outbreak of war, I dedicated myself to the art of fucking with an application that, had I brought it to my working life, might have made me a rich man. I grew stronger in my body, thanks to swimming and riding and running and the regular exercise I took in the bedroom. My body became harder. The hair on my head became, alas, a little thinner; at the age of 21 I already had a pronounced widow's peak, and was receding at the temples. But the hair on my body spread and grew thicker, creeping up from my belly to my chest, around my nipples. It was never as thick and wiry as Mick's, and it was several shades darker than the hair on my head—but there it was, extending down my thighs and over my ass, filling the crack that once, when Mick first tasted it, had been almost bare. I became a man—in my body, at least, if not in my mind.

I returned often to Mick at the White Horse, and he became my tutor, my mentor, and a more admirable moral guide than you might have thought. He taught me to observe the conventions of New England life, to behave like a gentleman, to take my pleasure discreetly and with consideration for others, to run no unnecessary risks. He had learned by painful example just how badly wrong things could go for the likes of us, and he told me, one night as we lay naked together after he had fucked my face, of how he came about that deep scar on his torso. A young man in another town, a jealous wife, an angry father-in-law, an ugly brawl in a bar, a knife, a desperate flight on horseback, still bleeding, infection, a fever, near death... Mick had learned the hard way just how dangerous the love of men could be.

It had not, however, put him off, and in the White Horse he'd found friends who would support and protect him. The barman shared his tastes, and on more than one occasion joined us for the night. I took them both, at both ends, alternately, together. One evening, when business in the White Horse was slow, the barman locked the doors with just himself, Mick, another rough laborer called Scott, and me inside. We fucked on the bar, on the tables, on the floor, upstairs and down. I took them all—and, that night for the first time, I learned what it was like to fuck another man, sticking my prick up the barman's hairy ass as he leaned over a beer barrel sucking on the two hard cocks in front of him.

And it wasn't just in the White Horse that I took my pleasure. With the confidence of extreme youth, I had my own adventures. I assumed, like a fool, that any man who took my fancy would be happy to accommodate me. I lay, shamelessly naked and erect, on the sunny rocks at my favorite swimming pond, daring other bathers to come and join me. I worked my way through several of the cleaners, engineers, and clerks at the Hydropathic Establishment. Seldom was I turned down, and even if I was, nobody would have dared say a word against the boss's son. I even seduced family friends who came to visit, "accidentally" stumbling into their rooms after everyone had retired for bed, ready with some foolish story about looking for a book, and often stayed till dawn, tasting forbidden fruit.

But it was always to Mick that I returned, and I never tired of his loving. Our appetites matched perfectly. There was nothing I could dream of doing that he was not already expert at. His cock was always hard, always ready for me. And, more than that, we became friends. We talked. He advised me, warned me, encouraged me. When he wasn't fucking me, he was like a father to me. In return, I helped him out with money when work was scarce, and, to keep him in town, I even found a job for him at the spa. He impressed my father with his knowledge of boilers and water-heating systems, and he replaced the old chief engineer, whose idea of modern technology was a coal fire. Mick moved out of the White Horse and took a cabin in the woods, where we could fuck as loudly as we wanted, with only the occasional moose or bear to hear us. I do not know if my family wondered about this unlikely friendship, or if talk reached their ears of my inappropriate associations; if it did, they were far too polite to mention it.

Reluctantly, I took a job myself at the Bishopstown Hydropathic Establishment and Mineral Spa Center, largely to silence the mutterings about "earning my keep" and "preparing for the future" that were becoming far too frequent for my liking around the family table. I was placed in the accounts department, apprenticed to Jasper Windridge, my father's "right hand," as he liked to call him, an unlikable man of middle age who took great pleasure, I thought, in pointing out my shortcomings. I suppose I cannot blame him, as I was an unwilling student, interested only in the clock, my mind on my next debauch. It was all I could do to add up a column of figures without error; the complexities of double-entry bookkeeping were a mystery to me. The only double-entry I was interested in took place in the White Horse, when I managed, with concentration and a hell of a lot of butter, to accommodate both Mick and the barman in my painfully stretched asshole.

I worked with an ill will, doing as little as possible, antagonizing Mr. Windridge to the point that he would threaten, once or twice a week, to "speak to your father." I dared him to do it, and went back to doodling winged cocks on my notepad. Somehow or other I learned the basics of accountancy, but it was more in the way that a tree soaks up rain than by any positive effort on my part. In years to come, I would thank Mr. Windridge for that grounding he gave me in dollars and cents; at the time, however, I regarded him as little better than a troll from a fairy tale, barring the gate to the garden of delights.

And so I might have continued, wasting my youth in pleasure, heedless of the future, burying my head in a book (or a hairy crotch) every time there was talk of politics. When Abraham Lincoln was elected in 1860, the town was alive with talk of trouble to come, with cheers and boos and rallies and counterrallies; the papers carried nothing but stories of secession and abolition and constitutions and conferences. It meant nothing to me—a background hum, the wind in the trees, the gurgling of a stream.

Even Mick was shocked at my lack of interest in current events. "This is history in the making, Jack," he said to me one Sunday afternoon when we had headed off for a walk in the mountains, looking for secluded places where he could fuck me in the open air. "You should pay attention."

"There's only one thing I'm interested in," I said, hauling his half-hard cock into the dappled light of a forest clearing. The subject was quickly dropped as I sucked him to a full stand, and wasn't resumed until his dick plopped out of my ass an hour later.

"There's going to be trouble, Jack," he said, as we washed ourselves off in a clear, fresh pond. "Not just for you and me, but for the whole country. Father against son. Brother

30

against brother. Friend against friend."

"Gloomy old man," I said, splashing him. We wrestled ourselves dry on the forest floor.

But he was right. Trouble arrived one day in February 1861, and with it came Aaron Johnson.

At home, over breakfast, we read about the secession of six more states from the Union, the adoption of the Confederate constitution, the threat to military establishments in the South. There were dark looks, pregnant silences, and my father mentioned the word *war*.

"Don't talk like that," my mother said. "You'll frighten the girls." My sisters, in fact, looked far from frightened; they were much more interested in the troubles than I was, and found the prospect of war exciting.

"I'd go and fight for Lincoln right now if I was a man," said Margaret, older than me by two years—and she looked as if she meant it.

"I'll not have that talk at this table," my mother said, fussing with plates and napkins. My father sighed and rubbed his eyes. I'm sure he'd have preferred it if the fighting talk came from his son, rather than his daughter.

"Jack," he said, "I want you in the office early this morning. Remember?"

"Oh, father..."

"We have a new employee starting in the accounts department and I particularly asked you to look out for him. Or have you forgotten already?"

"Let Windridge take care of him." I imagined another little accountant, a sort of miniature Windridge, crouched at his desk, scratching away at his figures. Perhaps I would have more free time for fucking...

"*Mister* Windridge," my father said, "has enough to do sorting out your mistakes without having to take on extra responsibilities that I have already delegated to you, John."

I knew that whenever he called me John rather than Jack I had better act the obedient son.

"Yes, sir. I'll get there right now."

"Who is he, this new gentleman?" asked my mother; she was always interested in arrivals at the spa, hoping, I suppose, to find a husband for one of her daughters.

"His name is Aaron Johnson," my father said, puffing out his chest. "He comes to us from Virginia. And he is a Negro."

Time stopped for a moment, forks poised halfway to mouths, teacups held above saucers. My sisters' eyes—and I suppose mine—were as round as dishes.

"A black gentleman!" Jane, my junior by two years, said. "Here in Bishopstown? Oh, how wonderful!"

"And we are not to treat him any different from anyone else, do you hear?" my father said. "He's an educated man, he comes with the most impeccable letters of recommendation, and he will be, I hope, an important citizen in our community. A hardworking, honest, decent, and, I may say, a God-fearing man."

We weren't listening. All of us, including my mother, were intensely alive to the novelty presented by this newcomer. Black faces, if they were seen at all in Vermont in those days, passed through quickly, on the other side of the tracks; Negroes could not even afford a room in the White Horse. My sister Margaret, I know, longed to fight for the rights of the Negro, and would waste no time in taking Mr. Aaron Johnson under her wing. My sister Jane, fascinated as she was by Stowe's *Uncle Tom's Cabin*, would gawk at him if he walked into the room.

My thoughts focused on the piquant image of a black cock stretching my white ass. I had heard, in schoolyards and bars, of the legendary advantages of the colored races, and hoped they were not exaggerated.

"I'll be off right now, father," I said, more eager to get to the office than ever before. "Leave him entirely to me."

Was it my imagination, or was that a look of distress, disappointment, disgust that flitted across my father's face? What did he know? How much did he guess?

"Good-bye, girls," I said, running out of the room.

As I raced down the hall, struggling into my jacket, I heard Margaret's familiar cry: "It's not fair! Why wasn't I born a boy!"

My ass was twitching and my dick half-hard as I walked along the road to the spa. I had envisaged it all: Aaron Johnson, young and athletic, his ill-fitting clothes revealing the magnificent animal beneath, meek and respectful as I walked into the office, gratefully accepting my offer of friendship and guidance, shocked at first when I put my hand into his pants but then unable to resist the tidal wave of feelings as they surged through him... Lying back as I rode his massive cock to glory, as I'd ride our black stallion... Following me slavishly but at a respectful distance, waiting for me to notice him again, ready to fuck me whenever I gave the command.

As I walked through the gates of the Hydropathic Establishment, I was nearly knocked down by a fine white horse cantering down the path, obliging me to step quickly aside. Some wealthy customer, I thought, looking at the stylish cut of his clothes, the bright whiteness of his riding gloves. I swallowed the curse that was on my lips, remembering my father's injunction to treat the customers at all times like little gods.

The horse stamped to a standstill, the rider jumped to the ground and turned to face me. Underneath the black riding hat, above the white collar, was a face of the most beautiful brown I had ever seen.

"Pardon me, sir," he said, touching his brim. "My horse is a little too eager."

My eyes were goggling out of my head, until I remembered that this was an employee, and I his employer's son.

"I'll thank you to take more care in the future, Mr. Johnson."

"I am expected, then," he said in a voice less friendly than before.

"You are. Stable your horse and report to the accounts office." Oh, how prim and prissy my voice sounded! He rode off without another word, and I did not see him again until Mr. Windridge led him into the accounts office a half hour later.

"And this is our little home away from home," Windridge said, his nasal voice more ingratiating than ever. "This is where the real business of the day is done, I like to think." I tried to look busy, scratching in a ledger with a pen that seemed intent on blotting everything, the paper, the desk, my fingers and cuffs.

"And this," Windridge continued with considerably less enthusiasm, "is Mr. John Edgerton, the proprietor's son."

I half-hoped that Johnson would cower respectfully before me, regretting his earlier insolence, giving me the opportunity to be magnanimous in my forgiveness. Oh, the fantasies that played around my mind! They shame me now.

"We've met," he said, extending a hand. "Aaron Johnson. Pleased to meet you."

I got to my feet and held out a dirty hand, which he grasped. Ink, still wet, stuck our fingers together for a second.

"I'm sorry," I said. It should have been him apologizing, not me, I thought.

"Don't matter, Jack," he said—was that a wink? "It won't show on my hands."

I sat down, completely abashed, and listened as Johnson asked Windridge question after question about profit and loss, adjustments, discounts, offsets, and a thousand other things that I did not understand even after a year in the accounts office. It was quite clear that this was a man with a future, a man with ambition and drive and all those other qualities I so obviously lacked.

Windridge's answers were long, droning, circumlocutory. I started to drift off into a daydream, largely inspired by the back of Johnson's neck, the only part of his skin that I could really see. Occasionally his large, square hands with their pale palms and neatly trimmed fingernails would flash through the air, but apart from that, and the dense, closely cropped hair on his head, there wasn't much to look at. But it was enough, and I was already imagining how good it would be to eat his big, round ass.

"And you will be working under young Mr. Edgerton, at least to start with." Windridge's voice for once commanded my attention, and I sat up. Johnson was to be my subordinate?

"How will you like that, sir?" Johnson said, turning in his chair to fix me with a penetrating stare. "Think you can handle me?"

"I imagine so, Mr. Johnson," I said, suddenly pretending to be busy with a complicated calculation. "Forty, forty-three, at eighteen percent, over a period of seven months..."

"Well," Windridge said, "I'll leave you in young Mr. Edgerton's capable hands. I have business to attend to in the director's office."

It was then that I thought my hastily formed plans would come to fruition; I imagined a furtive game of show-and-tell, a quick suck under the desk, a rendezvous made for later, when I would bend Johnson to my will.

"So," I said as soon as Windridge was out the door, "you're going to be working under me. That sounds like an interesting position." I had used lines like these, and even cornier, to good effect with other Hydropathic employees.

Johnson, however, became suddenly businesslike. "Certainly. I want to learn as much about your father's business as I can."

"Why don't I show you around?"

"Mr. Windridge has already done that."

"Did he show you the stables?" He could fuck me over the saddle rack, I thought, with the smell of horses and straw rising around us.

"I have seen the stables. They're very fine."

"How about the hot pool? It's under maintenance at the moment, but if I ask them they'll fill it for us."

"I'd be more interested in the books, Mr. Edgerton."

"Please. It's Jack."

"How old are you, Jack?"

"Twenty-one. How old are you, Aaron?"

"Thirty-one. But not too old to learn. Perhaps you'd like to explain this complicated calculation you're undertaking. What was it? Forty-three at eighteen percent over a period of seven months. Oh—" He looked at my notebook, perhaps expecting to see calculations, perhaps not. What he saw was my usual doodles, fortunately a little less blatantly phallic than usual. "You like flowers and birds, do you, Jack? And what's this? A railroad train, perhaps."

"They're just notes."

"And I'm sure they mean a great deal to you. Now, if you would just hand over the ledgers, I'll make a start."

I had a smart riposte on my lips, and was ready to make it, but one look at Johnson's serious face, his furrowed brow, killed the words in my mouth. I handed over the book.

"That's a good fellow. Work for work time, play for playtime. Let's get cracking, shall we?"

Oh, he would pay for that, my fine Mr. Johnson, my supposed subordinate. I planned out the witty things I would say, the clever strategies for undermining his confidence, all with the purpose of bending him to my carnal purposes. I wanted to put him in his place—and that place was up my ass.

But somehow it didn't work out like that. In private,

when we were alone in the office or when I engineered an "accidental" meeting in the remoter corners of the building, Johnson was polite, professional, and distant. In company—when Windridge or my father was in the office, or when paying social calls at the house—Johnson was much friendlier, treating me as a pal, a buddy, the butt of his jokes (how my father enjoyed his remarks about my professional expertise!), and leavening his mockery with just enough flirtatious humor to keep me from protesting. It was the exact reverse of the situation I wanted. I would have preferred him to be formal in company, but friendly in private—very friendly, and very private. If Johnson had set out deliberately to keep me at arm's length, he could not have done a better job.

His visits to the house, at first duty calls, soon became a regular Sunday occurrence, and after he'd been in Bishopstown for a couple of months he was as much a part of the family as I was. My sisters made no secret of the fact that they were both in love with him, and he was able to talk to them on exactly the right level. With Margaret, he discussed politics and the Rights of the Negro. He entertained Jane with stories of his Virginia childhood, whereby we learned that he was the son of a slave woman and a white plantation owner; there was little doubt from whom he inherited his complexion! His mother had died, and his father, stricken with conscience, raised the boy as part of his own family—or as much a part as his wicked legitimate sons would allow. They put him down constantly, landed him in trouble, told lies about him, and did all they could to persuade their father to disinherit him. Aaron kept his head down, did well at school, and finally left home at the age of 18 to make his way in the world. Since then he had plowed a lonely furrow, without home or family, welcomed by neither his black brothers nor his white peers. By the end of one of these recitations, my mother and sisters had tears in their eyes, my father was pacing up and down huffing and puffing about social injustice, and I was fuming about how this charming cuckoo was ousting me from the position of favored son.

"So why did you leave your last job?" I asked one Sunday afternoon, as the table was cleared. "You seem never to stay anywhere very long. Are you going to leave us in the lurch as well?"

My father frowned, and my mother tutted, but Johnson just smiled. "Oh no, I'm in no hurry to leave Vermont," he said. "Believe me, Jack, compared to the South, this is an earthly paradise. Where else would a man like me find a welcome at the family table, the respect of his brothers and sisters"—here he gestured toward my family, who positively squirmed with delight—"and the love of comrades?"

His eyebrow was cocked, his head to one side. I could have cursed him out loud.

"But surely more good can be done in the South, by setting an example to these secessionists we hear so much about?"

"Ah, yes, there's no doubt that that's where my duty lies, Jack." Johnson looked serious now.

"Then why are you here? Why hide yourself in the North? What are you running away from?"

"That's enough, John," my father said. "It's none of our business."

"Have you ever been to the South, Jack?"

"No, of course not, but—"

"Do you know what a lynch mob is?"

My sisters gasped in excitement.

"Of course I do."

"I left Virginia hotly pursued by one. So far, Vermont seems a lot less dangerous. Give me a chance to catch my breath and maybe we'll go back and face them together, Jack. What do you say?"

I said nothing. My father laughed. "Show your mettle, Jack! Make us proud!" He marched around the table whistling "Yankee Doodle Dandy." "Oh, no fear, not our Jack! Always with his nose stuck in a book, or running around town with his fine college friends!" This was the convenient fiction that had been established in the family to explain my nocturnal ramblings. "But if it comes to war with the South, what will you do? Eh?"

"Please, let's not talk of war at the table!" my mother said.

"Do you think it will come, Johnson?" my father said.

"Of course. As sure as rain and snow."

"And will we be safe here?"

"We'll be safe nowhere, sir."

"Oh dear," my mother said, suddenly busy with a duster. "Let's not frighten the girls! Come on, Margaret, Jane. You can help me in the…er…in the parlor."

"I'm not frightened," Margaret said. "If it comes to war, I'm ready to fight for what's right."

"I believe you would, Miss Edgerton," Johnson said, "but God forbid we should ever see ladies reduced to the bestial condition of men. Jack, let's take a walk and leave your family in peace." He stood up, folded his napkin, and led me out of the dining room with a heavy arm around my shoulders.

We walked through the hall, out of the house, and onto the road at a striding pace, not saying a word. It was only when we had reached the stream, some 100 yards from the house, that he slowed down. The arm remained around my shoulders.

"You don't like me very much, do you Jack?"

I was unused to direct questions like that; in our circle, things were expressed in much more roundabout ways.

"Of course I like you."

"Then why do you torment me?"

"I don't."

"Let's cut the crap."

I had never been spoken to like that before, even by my conquests at the White Horse, who were a rough-mannered lot.

"How dare you?"

"Ever since I arrived, you've been buzzing around me like a horsefly. If you weren't my employer's son I'd have swatted you down so hard your ass would have made a hole in the ground. Now tell me, Jack, what's your problem?"

"I don't have a problem. If anyone has a problem, it's you." I tried to sound authoritarian, but it came out as pompous.

"You're full of shit."

"Oh!" This was too much, and I was about to say something that I would very much have regretted. Fortunately, Johnson didn't let me get a word in edgewise.

"You're a spoiled little mother's boy, you ain't never done an honest day's work in your life, and, God damn it, I want you to be my friend not my enemy. Why does that make you so damn mad?"

"It doesn't. I just—"

"You do everything you can to get me in wrong with Mr. Windridge. You make your smart little comments and I bite my tongue, every time. You make out that I'm some kind of criminal, or worse. You needle me, Jack, at every turn. What have I done to you? Don't you like this big black face?"

He stuck his face very close to mine and grinned in a parody of the Nigger Minstrels who came to town on fair day.

"Don't be ridiculous."

"So why can't we just be friends and drop all this bullshit?"

The time had come for me to answer that question, both to Johnson and to myself. I knew the truth, of course; I was angry with him because he hadn't fucked me, and I was acting like a child deprived of a coveted toy. I was angry because I thought of him as my natural subordinate, yet it was clear he was my superior in every respect. I did not like this reversal of what I had always thought of as the natural order. God, what a shameful admission! I could barely acknowledge it even to myself. Instead, I dressed the truth up in fancy costume.

"I want to be your friend, Aaron. I would like nothing more. But you have kept yourself at a distance. You have spurned my offers of companionship. Is it any wonder that I react with wounded pride?"

He looked me in the eye, his face still close enough for me to smell the coffee on his breath, and frowned. "Pride, is it?"

"Yes." Oh, the shame.

"Not something else?"

"Like what?"

"Wounded vanity, perhaps? Or disappointment? Frustration?"

"I don't know what you mean," I said, furious that he'd read me so plainly.

He walked to the water's edge and stared into the trees.

"You and I are not so different, Jack."

I stood beside him, searching the darkness of the opposite bank as if it held the answer to some great riddle. "Are we not?"

"We are both proud."

"Perhaps."

"Vain."

"Perhaps."

"Pigheaded and stubborn."

"Granted."

"I was very much like you at your age."

"I doubt that," I said, thinking of the delights of my ample leisure hours.

"But I learned…restraint."

This reminded me of the sort of lecture Mick would

sometimes give me about "safe conduct in public" and other subjects dear to his heart.

"Damn restraint."

"Very well. Damn restraint." He turned and faced me. "Let's do whatever we want to do. Let's forget the consequences. Let's not think about our families, our friends, our future, our safety. It would be so easy, wouldn't it, Jack?"

"What would?" Things were moving too fast; I was not in control.

"To kiss you."

Silence between us. The light was fading, the birds were no longer singing, even the stream seemed to have slowed its usual rush to a meek trickle. Nature was holding its breath.

"So do it," I said at length, closing my eyes and parting my lips. "Do it now."

And he did. With one hand on the back of my head, the other over my heart, he kissed me full on the mouth, his lips pressing into mine, his tongue finding mine, locking together, struggling, slipping, caressing. My knees went weak, and my cock sprang to life. I could feel from the pressure at his hips that his had done the same.

When I opened my eyes, the world was still the same, the stream still flowed, but something inside me had changed. It was like that time in the White Horse when I first discovered cock. What had I discovered now?

"What happens next, Jack?"

"We go somewhere."

"And we...lie together."

"Yes."

"I want to." For the first time, he sounded uncertain. "I've thought of nothing else since the first day I arrived, when I nearly ran you down with my horse. I've dreamed of you, your naked body, your skin against mine. Of all the things we could do together. I've watched you in the office, your tongue sticking out between your lips as you scratch

42

away at the ledgers. I've seen you daydreaming, wishing I could be there with you in your dreams…"

"You can. We can be together."

He kissed me again, briefly this time, a mere peck on the lips. "We can never be together, Jack. You know that as well as I do."

"Why not? I want you more than I've ever wanted anyone."

"And what you want, you get, huh?"

"Why not? What's to stop me?"

"The world, Jack. The times we live in. God in Heaven himself. I don't know. How could we ever be together?"

"I know a place in the woods…"

"Where we could go now and I could fuck your white ass."

"Yes. Please."

He thought for a while, and I could see that the idea was not repulsive to him. "And then, for an encore, I could ride into town, throw a rope over a tree, hang myself, maybe tar and feather myself, maybe cut my cock off. And what would happen to you, do you think? Well, you'd have to leave town, of course. You'd drift around. Maybe you'd end up in Boston or New York, in rented rooms, watching your life run down the drain, wondering if it was worth all that pain and trouble for just one fuck with the black man."

"Don't be ridiculous. Nobody needs to know."

He laughed out loud. "Nobody needs to know? You think things like that can happen without people finding out? Wake up, Jack. Wake up and face reality."

"Nobody knows what I get up to," I said, thinking myself very fine and clever.

"You mean what you get up to with Mick?"

That took the wind out my sails.

"And the other fellows at the White Horse? You're mighty popular down in that part of town, Jack. I've heard that there's very little you won't do. And what a fine, generous young man you are."

"You don't know—"

"I know plenty. People do, Jack. I imagine even your father knows more than he'd like to."

"But what's that got to do with us? You wouldn't tell. I wouldn't talk."

"You think we live in a world where every man is his own master, Jack. Where nobody minds anyone else's business, and everyone can live and let live. But I tell you, we've already done more than is safe. If I didn't believe that your family is indoors right now, that the light is failing, and that nobody has trespassed on your grounds, I would never have come within three feet of you. I would never speak to you in this way. I would never have kissed you."

"But we can be alone together, far from everyone."

"Like you were with Mick in the woods? Up at the ponds?"

Had Mick talked? "Who told you about that?"

"You were seen, Jack. People have eyes."

"But who..."

"Nobody's done anything—so far. They hate what you do, they would kill you if you weren't the son of the wealthiest man in town, and Mick would be run out of the state if he weren't under your protection. And he knows how to look after himself. He doesn't tell you about that, does he? About the fights and the abuse and the threats that he gets. You think all those men in the downtown bars are just there for your pleasure, Jack? They'd cut your throat if they thought they could get away with it."

I was shaking now.

"But that's nothing, nothing at all, compared to the hell that would be let loose if they found out that a black man had been sticking his big nigger dick up your ass. Ooooh, my soul! Dey chase dat boy all de way to de nigger-hangin' tree! Dey burn yo' house down! Dey take yo' sistah and yo' muddah and dey throw dem in de rivah!"

"You don't know what you're talking about."

"I've said too much." Suddenly he was Mr. Aaron Johnson again, formal, distant, polite. "Please forgive me, Jack. I hope I have not alarmed you. Now there are business matters that I must discuss with your father. Good evening."

He turned on his heel and walked back to the house.

I sat on the riverbank and stared into the gathering darkness, imagining the twinkle of 100 pairs of prying eyes staring right back at me.

III

SUDDENLY, THE WORLD CHANGED. WHEREVER I WENT, FROM
the office to the town square to the bar of the White Horse,
the talk was of war. In March, President Lincoln declared
that secession was legally void. In April, confederates fired
on Federal troops at Fort Sumter in South Carolina. The
world was on the march, communities were divided, and
our lives would never be the same again.

Even in Bishopstown, prosperous New England backwater far from the battle lines to the south, there were ran-
kling divisions springing up in unlikely quarters, splitting
our town in two and making the streets unsafe to walk at
night. Old resentments flared up like fires long smothered
but never extinguished. Mr. Windridge declared himself hot
for the rights of slave owners, and started to frequent hotel bars where like-minded anti-abolitionists flaunted their
views without fear of attack. In the town square, there
were rallies in favor of Mr. Lincoln, in favor of abolition,
in favor of joining the army right there and then to go
and fight for the Union. I watched them from a distance,

listened to the speeches, and feared for my future.

Mick, my longtime lover and mentor, disappeared one day from the bar of the White Horse, without a word of where he was going; I suspect he'd returned to some long-forgotten homestead with the vague impulse to defend the family who had rejected him. Only when he was gone did I truly value him, as the ache in my empty ass, and the hunger in my guts for his vigorous loving, attested. I still had other playmates around town, but as the excitement grew around the war, their tolerance for my high-handed, selfish pleasure-seeking diminished. Soon, even the junior employees, the stable hands and groundskeeper at the spa, were giving me their cocks with barely concealed contempt. More and more money was leaving my pockets and entering theirs. At the age of 21, I was paying for it, like a man twice, three times my age.

My father asked me outright what I intended to do.

"I won't fight, if that's what you mean."

"Why not?"

"I don't believe in war as a solution to a purely political problem." I was spouting the kind of talk I'd heard in college; how inadequate it sounded now.

"And if the Rebels move north? If they attack?"

"I hardly think they'll move on Vermont."

"Why not, Jack?" Aaron Johnson asked, witnessing this conversation one afternoon in the office. "It's a wealthy part of the Union. The South is poor, they feel threatened, they'll fight to preserve what's theirs, and they'll take whatever they need."

"What then, son? Will you believe in war then? When they're riding through town looting and burning?"

"This is ridiculous," I said. "We have state troops."

"So did Fort Sumter," Johnson said, leaving the room.

My father stayed, pacing up and down the office.

"We live in troubled times, Jack," he said at last. I always knew that when my father uttered such platitudes he was building up to some major announcement.

"Yes, sir."

"Change is coming."

"I guess so."

"You guess so? You better do more than guess so, Jack." There was anger in his voice, and for a moment his eye flashed at me. Then he continued his pacing. I pretended to read some papers, and waited.

"This way of life, Jack…"

"Yes, Father?" Was he about to accuse me of something?

"It must end."

"I don't believe things have gotten so bad…"

"I mean this life that you're living. Your aimless, godless wanderings. Don't think I don't see you, sitting here day after day like a prisoner, counting the hours until you can leave and join your…friends."

"Father, I—"

"I hoped that my son would make me proud. That he would make his way in the world, make something of himself. Or at least be a helpmate in the business. You're twenty-one, Jack. When are you going to begin your life?"

"I have a life, Father."

"I know what sort of life you have. Throwing your money around those bars downtown, wasting your youth and your education with people from God knows where and getting up to God knows what."

God knew what, indeed, and I began to believe that, as Aaron had warned me, others knew too. Including my father.

"I see I must become more serious, Father."

"More serious!" He shouted the words, almost screamed. The door opened an inch, and Mr. Windridge's nose appeared, then hastily withdrew. I did not hear his footsteps, and imagined his delight in eavesdropping.

"You must change your life, Jack. You must...change... your life." He glared at me, and I glanced shiftily back, ashamed of myself, for all my bravado and bluster. When I went over the scene later in my mind, I thought of all the clever things I should have said. I should have told my father that I was not ashamed of my friends, that I would save him the trouble and expense of my keep, that I would make my way in the world, proud and independent. Instead I sat there blushing, almost weeping, as he stormed out of the room. Windridge entered immediately, pretending that he had heard and seen nothing.

"Are those figures ready, Mr. Edgerton?"

I almost knocked him down.

I found Johnson out by the boiler house, overseeing a couple of engineers who were patching up a leaky pipe.

"So, not content with running the office, you're now the director of works as well, are you?"

"Ah, Mr. Edgerton. We're attempting to save the business several hundred dollars a year by increasing the efficiency of the plant."

I looked into the boiler house, where two apes in heavy cotton coveralls were attacking the boiler with wrenches and saws. One of them, a heavy-browed, dark-haired brute of, I think, Italian extraction, had shot his load in my face one wild night at the White Horse. The other was a young, fair-skinned, freckle-faced Irish lad whose job seemed to be to hold things.

"Good morning, gentlemen," I said. "I see you have some very large tools. I hope you know what to do with them."

They looked up, puzzled, as if awaiting orders.

"Walk with me, Jack," Johnson said, taking my elbow. "Keep at it, Benny."

"Sure, boss," came a thick, hoarse voice from the boiler house.

"Boss?" I squeaked, as Johnson hustled me across the yard to the stables. "So now you're the boss! Is that what this is all about? You turn up here like a genie out of a bottle and suddenly you're taking over—"

He pushed me through a door and I landed on my back in a pile of straw. Thankfully, it was clean; the stables were mucked out in the morning.

"Now shut that pretty pink mouth of yours, Master Jack, and listen to me. I heard what your Daddy said to you. I know you got all riled up. Your pal Mick left town, right? And you're as fretful as a kitten up a tree. You start shaking your little white ass around the engineers, and you know they'll give you a taste and make no fuss because you line their pockets. Well, it's time you learned that you don't treat people like that."

"Jealous, Johnson?" I said, lying back in the straw and stretching my arms behind my head. "You want my pretty pink mouth and my little white ass for yourself?"

"I should whip you for saying that."

"Go ahead. Take that thick leather belt and tan my hide for me." I turned over and wiggled my tail at him, wondering how far this game would go.

Crack! His belt found its mark, and it stung like hell. I was so shocked I could not even cry out. Crack! It came down again.

"Johnson, stop!"

Crack! A third strike, and even through the thick wool of my pants I could feel the bite of the leather.

I looked over my shoulder to see him breathing hard, his mighty chest working inside his shirt. I was in pain, but I was excited too. His pants, unsupported by the thick leather strap that was doubled up in his left hand, were sliding down his hips.

"Do your worst, Johnson. Fuck me if you want."

With a growl, he jumped on me, grinding his groin into

my ass, pressing the rock-hard swelling against my burning cheeks. His mouth was on my neck, my ears, kissing, licking, and biting. He was like an animal in rut. I twisted my head to take his kisses on my mouth, pressed my hips back and up to meet his thrusts. The horses, separated from us only by a low wooden bar, stamped and snorted.

"I'll fuck you, Jack. I'll fuck you from here to kingdom come." His hand reached down inside my pants, found my hole, and started brutally fingering it. "You've wanted it ever since you first saw me, haven't you? Waggling that ass at me like a barroom whore…"

These words, so coarse in black and white, were murmured in my ear like the tenderest endearments. I felt my guts melt, and I was ready to take whatever he could give me.

But suddenly, the thrusting stopped, the string of obscenities was hushed, and his body lay limp and heavy on top of me.

"It would be so easy, Jack. So easy."

He stood up, brushed the straw from his clothes, held out a hand, and helped me to my feet.

"Why not? I want you so much." I wanted him to see, to understand. I rubbed my crotch to draw attention to the swelling there.

"You make me mad, Jack. A madman."

"So, be mad. Fuck me."

"Jack… I can't…" He ran out of the stable, and was across the yard and back indoors before I could say another word.

I was furious, frustrated, filthy, covered in straw, sweating like a horse, and hard. I could not go back into the office; I could not, as Johnson apparently could, turn my feelings on and off like a faucet. I brushed off the worst of the dirt and, without really thinking about what I was doing, strolled back toward the boiler house where Italian Benny and his freckle-faced assistant were still banging away.

"Need a hand?" I felt reckless.

"I think we got it covered," Benny said, his face and hands smeared with oil.

"I can hold your tools for you."

"Oh, yeah?"

The younger one looked puzzled; why was the boss's son offering these pointless services?

"Yeah. And I'll do more than hold them. I'll work 'em." The danger of the situation was affecting me like a drug; my cock was as hard as the wrench in Benny's hand.

"You'll work 'em, huh?" Benny said, dropping a hand to his crotch, idly cupping it. I knew from our previous acquaintance that he had a big, uncut, veiny cock in a deep black bush of soft hair.

"Yeah." I licked my lips. "And I'll finish the job for you."

"You know what we got here, Pete," he said to his young companion, who was scratching his head just behind the ear, looking confused. "We got a queer boy that wants a taste of cock."

"All right!" Pete said, the truth dawning on his simple, freckled face. "He wants to suck my prick?"

"Yeah. We gonna let him?"

"Maybe. Cheaper than buying us a woman."

"Oh, yeah," Benny said, laughing, "he's cheap, all right. Get down on your knees, Jackie Boy, and let's see what Pete's got for you."

I did as I was told, kneeling in the oily mud that surrounded the boiler.

"C'mon, Pete. Show him that thing."

Pete grinned and unbuttoned his fly, hauling out a fat white prick that was several shades paler than the skin on his sunburned face and hands. It looked like a long hunk of uncooked dough that had been left to rise.

"What do you think of that, Jackie?"

"It's big."

"You want to kiss it for him?"

"Yes."

"You want to suck it, boy? Want him to fuck your mouth?"

"Yes."

"Yes what?"

"Yes, sir."

So this was Benny's game; a little bit of table-turning. It suited my mood perfectly.

"Ask him nicely, then. Let's see some of them fancy manners."

"Please, sir, may I suck your cock?"

Pete laughed. "Listen to him! Fuckin' fairy."

"You gonna let him put his lips around that thing, Pete?"

"Yeah. Let him suck it." He waggled his cock at me; I moved my face closer so it slapped me on the forehead and nose. Benny grabbed me by the hair—little wonder that it was falling out, with the amount of tugging it had taken in the last couple of years—and pulled my head back. My mouth made contact with Pete's half-hard cock, which he took great delight in rubbing and bouncing off my face.

"You better feed the faggot," Benny said, pulling my mouth open. I liked this pretense that they were forcing me to do something against my will; I'd already learned that this particular performance enabled some men to give me a far harder fucking than a gentler, more agreeable approach would.

The head slipped between my lips, and I immediately closed my mouth around it, sucking Pete way inside me so that he touched the back of my throat.

"Jesus!" he whispered. "He's really eating it! Look at that!"

"Yeah, he's done it before," Benny said. "Let's see what he can do with two." Out of the corner of my eye I saw a familiar thick, dark, veiny shape emerging from the front of his pants. Soon Benny's cock was contending with Pete for possession of my mouth. I knew I couldn't suck both of them fully at the same time—I'd tried that before at the White Horse and been frustrated at my limitations—but I knew that I could give pleasure to both, so I allowed Pete's cock to slip out until only the head was in my mouth. That way, I could stretch my lips around two heads rather than just one. I held on to each shaft and worked them so that they rubbed and pressed together in my mouth.

"Fucking cock-hungry bitch," Benny said, laughing as he saw my mouth stretched into a clown's grimace. "Now you're going to get it up the other end."

Unwilling as I was to relinquish the dual delight in my mouth, the thought of taking these two monsters up my ass was too good to turn down.

"Hold him, Pete."

Pete pulled me to my feet and held my arms behind me, while Benny tore at my clothes. He sensed rightly that I wouldn't complain, however rough their treatment, and took the opportunity to wreak a bit of revenge on the ruling class. He tore off my shirt and threw it in the mud, pulling my pants down, heedless of the pain that they caused me as they dug into my legs. Thus hobbled, with my pants around my ankles and my boots still on, I felt Pete's hard cock pressing into my bare ass. My own dick, hard as hell, swung in front of me.

Benny ignored it, although I knew from our previous encounter that he wasn't averse to a taste of cock when there was no one else to witness it. "Okay, pretty boy, you're going to get fucked. Pete and me are going to fuck you so hard you'll be screaming for your mama. But you make one single noise and we know how to shut you up." I didn't think he meant he'd stick his cock in my mouth again. There were plenty of tools lying around the boiler house that could have silenced me quickly and effectively.

"Yes, sir."

Benny stepped out of his coveralls; underneath he wore only a rough cotton shirt. The loose garment slipped over his boots. His legs were thick, the muscles knotted, the hair black and dense on his thighs. He pulled the shirt over his head; naked, apart from his work boots, he looked like a painting of the Minotaur in my book of Greek legends, minus the bull's head (although there was something bovine in his countenance), plus a big hard dick. He lay down on a dry piece of stone flooring, spread his legs, and held his cock perpendicular.

"You better sit on it, boy."

I needed no second bidding, but I knew that if I was to survive the kind of rough treatment Benny and Pete had in store for me I'd need something to make the ride a little smoother, otherwise I'd be yelling the house down, no matter how hard I tried to keep quiet. I saw a grease gun lying among their tools, and picked it up.

"That's it, Jackie. Make yourself nice and slippery for me. Hey, Pete, give him a hand."

Pete, still grinning from ear to ear—he seemed to regard this kind of adventure as everyday fun and games—took the grease gun, inserted the nozzle in my ass and pumped a couple of hefty globs inside me. He then smeared them around with a thick, work-toughened finger.

"He ready?"

"He'll do."

"So sit on it."

I could tell by the stiffness of Benny's cock that he was enjoying this as much as I was, for all his hostile bluster. The moment his exposed head made contact with my greasy ass ring, I saw a look on his face—an expression of longing, or delight—that betrayed his lust for male contact. It was time for me to take back some of the control of the situation. Opening my ass muscles, I allowed him to glide into me at a rate of two inches a second, so that very soon I was sitting right down on his thighs. His prick filled me, set me on fire—and I clamped my ring around the base as hard as I could.

"Wooh! Fuck, boy, what you doing?"

"Shut up and fuck me."

And he did. He bucked his hips, tossing me up in the air, landing me back down, burying himself inside me. My own cock, still as hard as could be, slapped against my belly and oozed over his.

"I never knew it could be done," Pete said, mopping his brow on a rag. "He took that big old thing right up his ass. Fuck, don't it hurt, Jack?"

"No, man," I said, "it's the best...uh!...feeling...uh!...in the world."

"Oh, shut him up for me, Pete. I'm sick of hearing his voice."

Pete planted a foot on either side of Benny's waist and brought my head down on his cock.

"Now we got you nice and full," he said.

We might have stayed like that quite happily, but Benny had other ideas. I suspect that the pleasure of rubbing his dick against Pete's in my mouth had given him a taste for cock that he could only satisfy with difficulty.

"Join me up here, Pete. Come on. There's plenty of room, ain't there, Jack?"

In answer I relinquished Pete's cock from my mouth and leaned forward till I was almost resting on Benny's chest.

"There you go," Benny said. "Reckon you can find a way in?" Benny lifted his hips off the ground, and me with them; Pete was quick to slide his knees underneath and aim his dick against the target. It was not the most comfortable position, nor particularly effective, but it did allow both their dicks to fill my ass, at least for a few thrusts.

"Damn it, Jack, we keep falling out of you," Benny said, after the third or fourth mishap.

"So, do something about it."

We disengaged.

"Down on your knees in the mud."

This way they could take turns fucking me from behind, and I noticed that Benny took every opportunity to guide Pete's prick into me. They were becoming less guarded in their handling of me, of each other.

Benny came first, slamming into me with great hammering thrusts, spewing his load deep into my guts. Then he pulled out and Pete took his place—fucking me more gently at first, but building in pace and vigor as his orgasm approached. When I sensed that he'd reached the point of no return, I was astonished to feel a hand slipping around my waist and seeking out my own cock. He grasped it and stroked it, and rested his hot forehead against my sweating back as he came, shuddering and sighing as he did so.

"You really like that?" he said, squeezing my still hard cock. "I mean, you really like it?"

"Sure he does. He's like a woman."

"He ain't like no woman I ever went with," Pete said, still holding on to my cock.

"You never been with another fellow before, Pete?" Benny said, picking up my torn shirt from the floor and cleaning himself up with it. It was soon covered in mud, sweat, oil, and sperm.

"Never. Never knew of such things."

"Well now you know. You see, Jack here, he likes it so much it don't even hurt him when you stick it up his ass."

I was still kneeling as Pete pulled out of me. My ass felt raw and bruised, and I was desperate to come. I staggered to my feet, my legs cramping and spasming beneath me, and almost fell. Pete grabbed my arm.

"That was good," Pete said. "A good fuck."

"Yes..." I said.

"You going to...you know? Play with it?"

"Want to watch, Pete?" This was Benny, sneering again now that it was over.

"Sure, why not?"

"You ain't turning queer on me are you?"

However interesting this conversation was becoming, I was intent only on getting off, getting out, and getting cleaned up before anybody saw the state I was in. I leaned into Pete's arms and started to jack off. He held me tight; his arms were strong.

"Look at that, man," Pete said. "He's gonna shoot."

Benny was staring at us, frowning, undecided. I noticed his dick, still enlarged, was stirring again.

"Oh, what the hell," he said, and joined us, one arm around Pete's shoulders, the other caressing my leg. When I came, much of it went over Benny's hairy forearm and wrist.

I slipped through the back entrance to the baths, bundled up my clothes behind a cupboard where I could retrieve them later, and headed straight for the showers. Fortunately for me, there were no customers around, and I managed to wash myself clean of mud, oil, and sperm without attracting too much attention. I persuaded one of the attendants to lend me a clean shirt (some far-fetched story about a pen leaking in my pocket) and then, with a little careful dabbing with a wet cloth, removed the worst of the filth from my pants and jacket. They wouldn't pass close inspection, but at least I didn't look to all the world as if I'd just been double-fucked on the boiler house floor.

Aaron Johnson was waiting for me in the office, going through some figures with Mr. Windridge. He looked up at me with pain in his eyes—perhaps he'd guessed where I had gone after our last conversation, and what I had done. I tossed my head, avoided his gaze, and composed myself to do a pretense of work.

Eventually, my attention was drawn by the tenor of their conversation.

"Mr. Edgerton has been very generous," Windridge was saying, "and has agreed to hold your post open for you."

"So I understand, but—"

"In which case, Mr. Johnson, I can hardly give you more than a month's salary in hand."

"In which case, Mr. Windridge, that will have to be sufficient for my needs."

"I will draw a check for that amount."

"I would prefer cash."

"Of that I have no doubt."

Johnson walked out of the room, leaving the door open; I could tell that he was fighting an inclination to slam it.

"Is Mr. Johnson leaving us?" I inquired.

"Yes. And so soon after he arrived."

"That will be a great loss."

"To me, Mr. Edgerton? Or to you?"

"To the establishment, I meant."

"Ah," Windridge said, pressing the tips of his pale, bony fingers together. "Undoubtedly he will be greatly missed."

"And why is he leaving all of a sudden?"

"He feels he must look after his family."

"His family? But—" I remembered, just in time, that Johnson had recounted his personal history to our intimate circle, and it was not for public consumption. "Well, that's very admirable," I concluded.

"Indeed," Windridge said, his voice laden with insinuation. "But what a sudden announcement! Why, only this morning he was speaking of his plans for the winter, his economies in the heating department. He was very busy down at the boiler house, I believe."

"I saw something of the kind." Why was Windridge smiling? How much did he know?

"And then, not half an hour ago, he asks your father if

he can take an indefinite leave of absence. Just like that. I wonder if he'd had some bad news," Windridge said, rolling his eyes.

"Perhaps," I said. "I will go and ask him."

"You won't find him here. He's gone back to his rooms to pack up."

"Then I shall find him there. Good afternoon, Mr. Windridge."

He didn't even bother to maintain a facade of politeness, but laughed openly at me as I walked out the door, my cheeks flaming. Had it come to this? Mocked by my father's employees, fucked and doubtless despised by the engineers, the laughingstock of all, a fool, a freak whom even his own father disowned. Perhaps the time had come for me, too, to leave town, and I had a sudden vision of Aaron and me on the road together, heading west, perhaps, living in log cabins, comrades and lovers with no one to judge us but God and nature.

Oh! This idea was seductive. By the time I was out the gates I was whistling a merry walking song, imagining the pack on my back, the clank of a coffee pot and the thud of a water bottle, the sting of cold spring water as we bathed together after a night under the stars, the heat of his kisses as we sprawled in sunlit meadows...

"Where do you think you're going?"

My father's voice.

"I'm going to remonstrate with Mr. Johnson. He has some crazy idea of leaving us."

"You will do no such thing. You may be my son, but you are also my employee. You will return to your post and try, at least, to justify the money I give you."

"But Father, surely you don't want Mr. Johnson to leave us?"

"Whatever Mr. Johnson's reasons, I'm sure they are honorable and right."

"That's ridiculous—"

"Get back in there before I horsewhip you!"

At five o'clock, as soon as the spa was closing, I dropped my pen, grabbed my jacket (the mud was dry and flaking off), and ran out the door. Johnson's lodgings were in the center of town, a 15-minute walk away; I made it in five. I arrived, out of breath and uncomfortably hot, and hammered at the door.

The landlady opened up. "Young Mr. Edgerton!"

I sometimes forgot that, as the son of one of Bishops-town's leading citizens, I was well known to complete strangers. Perhaps Aaron was right; perhaps my every move was watched and noted. Perhaps I was in danger.

"Ah, good evening, Missus…"

"You'll be looking for your friend."

I accepted without surprise the fact that she knew who I was, what I wanted, and the relationship in which I stood to her lodger.

"Johnson. Is he here?"

"Bless you, Master Edgerton, he's been gone two hours. His poor mother, sick on her bed of pain she is, and he rushes to her side like the dutiful son he is. What a comfort to a mother to have a son like that."

"Yes…" Considering that Johnson had told us, at some length, of the distressing aftermath of his mother's death some years ago, I thought this haste to be at her sickbed had come a little late.

"When you hear something like that, from a nice fellow like Mr. Johnson, you can really believe what the abolition-ists say, that they've got souls just the same as us, praise the Lord."

"Indeed." I stepped inside the house. "So he's left."

"Like I told you, sir." She stood aside.

"Has he left anything behind?"

"A trunk, sir, that I'll store in the cellar."

"Nothing besides?"

"Well, sir, he did say something about the eventuality of you calling."

The wheedling tone of her voice told me what to do. I withdrew my wallet and counted off a substantial sum. "I see."

She rummaged in her pinafore and drew out a letter.

"I'll take that. Good day." I practically threw the money at her and ran downtown to the White Horse. There, at least, I could read my letter in peace.

The front door was boarded shut. One of the boards was crudely daubed with the words CLOSED UNTIL FURTHER NOTICE in white paint. The shutters were locked, the signs advertising imported wines, Kentucky sour mash, and clean rooms hastily concealed by burlap sacks.

The world was changing faster than I liked.

I continued out of town, to where the Connecticut River divided us from New Hampshire, spanned by what towns-people still called the "new" bridge. The last time I'd crossed it had been with Mick, on one of our adventures in the hills and forests...

He too was gone now.

I stood midway across the bridge and opened Aaron's letter.

Dear Jack, it began. I thanked God it was not going to be one of his formal, "Mr. Edgerton" announcements. I read on.

> You will know by now that I think it best for me to leave Bishopstown. Perhaps I will return one day, when times are better. At present, it is neither wise nor safe to remain. The situation between you and me makes it impossible for me to continue in your father's employment. I have covered my retreat

like a coward with lies and deception; I have neither the time, nor the moral strength, to prepare a more suitable exit.

Jack, you must repair the wreck that you—that I—have made of your life. I know that your appetites are strong. Mine were too at your age, and remain so, but I have made myself their master. For the sake of your family and your future, I beg you to do likewise. The risks you take are too great.

I have told you all that I wish to tell you, face to face, and will not compromise you by reiterating it in writing. Trust nobody, say nothing, and pray for better times.

Do not look for me.

Your friend,

Aaron Johnson

I held the letter out over the wide rushing river, my eyes blind with tears. The wind caught it, tore it from my grasp, and blew it away to God knows where.

IV

I LEFT HOME A MONTH AFTER AARON.

I wish I could say that I packed a bag the very night Aaron left, setting off in hot pursuit of the man I loved, and who I believed loved me. I packed the bag, all right, with books that I thought I could not do without, with paper and a supply of writing materials, with clothes and food and a few personal items that I could not bring myself to leave behind. There was too much, of course, so I unpacked it all and started again. Still I could not carry it. By the fourth attempt, I had worn myself out, and I gave up, hoping that the morning would bring fresh courage.

It did not.

The morning brought only breakfast with the family, dark looks from my father, nervous chitchat from my mother, and, afterward, a rain of questions from my sisters. Where had Mr. Johnson gone? Why was Father in such a temper? Had I done something to annoy him? Why was Mother crying in the night, why were her eyes red and her face pale this morning? Why were they, as "mere girls," shielded from the

Great Matters of the Day? (This came from Margaret, whose every pronouncement seemed to have capital letters.)

I avoided their questions with shrugs and evasions, happy for the time being that they should believe (as I knew they would) that this was serious war business, that they were being excluded from matters fit only for men. The fact was, I was as much in the dark as they—more so, probably, seeing as even Jane took the trouble to read newspapers and keep herself informed about events. I preferred to remain in ignorance, pursuing my own interests. But, as I was fast discovering, I was about to be ejected from my fool's paradise. Everywhere I turned, another door was closing. Aaron was gone, Mick was gone, the White Horse was closed, my reputation at the spa was (I realized) little more than a joke, my own father was compromised by my behavior, and had it not been for the restraining influence of my mother he would have thrown me out. Far away, war was raging—and how soon would it be on our own doorstep?

One thing was clear to me; I could not, with any decency, stay in Bishopstown, living off my parents and jeopardizing the family business. After breakfast I wrote in haste to my school friend James, upstate in Montpelier, begging him to give me sanctuary; he, like me, was back in the family circle after completing his studies, but was gainfully employed at a large local bank, shaping up to be a pillar of the community, putting behind him the follies of youth. We had been friends, and more than friends, at school, indulging in a little romantic play, although nothing, I now realized, to the real thing as I had discovered it in the bars of Bishopstown. James was now preparing to marry a local girl, his second cousin, I believe, an advantageous marriage that would please everyone. But we had sworn eternal friendship and support, and I knew he was far too honorable to turn me away, however little he might like giving shelter to a black sheep such as me.

Within a week, I was packing a bag in earnest, having

received from James the welcoming reply that I had hoped for. He had even read between the lines (I had mentioned something about "still looking for employment suitable to my talents") and suggested that there was a post for me at the bank, if I would not consider it beneath me. I considered it very much beneath me, of course, but I was grateful for the opportunity to leave Bishopstown with something approaching dignity. I had a job to go to, a (temporary) home, and, as I told my parents, it was time to cut the apron strings and see if I could stand on my own two feet. I mixed my metaphors quite cheerfully, so glad was I to be escaping from an environment that had become insupportable.

James's parents and mine exchanged letters, and everyone appeared to be very glad at this change of circumstances. His father told my father that he had always thought me "a fine young man," and his mother told my mother that James's sisters were "delighted at the thought of another brother to torment." We all pretended that all was for the best, that I would probably fall in love with one of the girls and come home a responsible married man with a fine set of blond whiskers and a baby in my arms.

I set off for Montpelier early one Saturday morning, the plan being that I would arrive by evening, settle in on Sunday, and start work on Monday.

I never arrived.

I took a coach north out of Bishopstown, my trunk strapped to the roof, sharing with a family from New York who, they informed me at great length, were on their way to relatives in Canada because "we don't want to get our throats cut by runaway slaves." We stopped at Rutland and put up in a spacious, comfortable inn, the sort of place where the sheets were clean, the food good and plentiful, and the company agreeable. I ate well, a steak and fried potatoes, washed down with beer.

"Good honest Yankee beer," a voice behind me in the dining room said. I paid no attention and continued eating.

"Yep, a man needs a glass of ale after being on the road all day."

This time, I looked around, as nobody else in the room seemed to be in the mood for conversation. My traveling companions had already gone up to their room to settle the children, and my fellow diners were silent.

One figure stood out like a candle in the darkness. Leaning against the bar was a spruce young man in military attire—although I recognized it as neither the gray of the Confederacy nor the blue of the Union. His jacket was red, with gold braid edging. His pants were dark, either black or blue, and as tight as a second skin. He wore boots, the sort of boots that imparted a swagger even to the most unathletic build. But here, they completed an already impressive ensemble. He looked as if he owned the place. His brown hair, a little longer than was the fashion, was swept up and over his brow, glistening with some kind of pomade. He had a handsome face, what my mother would have called "a little too handsome," with twinkling eyes and the suggestion of a smile. His shirt, which was white and ruffled, was unfastened to halfway down his chest. He was looking directly at me.

"Thirsty on the road, isn't it, my friend?"

My instinct was to turn away from such uninvited familiarity, or to mutter something like "Are we acquainted, sir?" But now I was a traveler, an independent young man seeking his fortune, and it ill became me to turn down the hand of friendship, however specious it might prove to be.

"Thirsty indeed."

"May I join you?" the stranger asked.

"Gladly."

He snapped his fingers and gestured to my table; the serving girl followed with a tankard of beer. He turned a chair around and sat astride it, spreading his legs and resting his arms on the back.

"Good health, prosperity, and happiness," he said, holding up his tankard. Foam ran down the side; he swiftly licked it up with a pink, darting tongue.

"Good health to you too." We drank, and he wiped his mouth with the back of his hand. He couldn't have been much more than my age, but with his military air, his tanned face, and his swaggering manner he seemed very much my senior.

"Do you travel alone?"

This was the kind of question I had been raised never to answer, but in the event I blurted out, "Yes. I'm going to Montpelier."

"Montpelier! Christ, that's a dull place. All bankers and bankers' wives. What's a youngblood like yourself doing in Montpelier?" He dragged out the "e"—Mont-peeeeeelyer— to make it sound like the dullest spot on the planet.

"I'm going to see a friend."

"A friend? A sweetheart, you mean." I blushed, remembering some of my more tender moments with James in days long past.

"No, I assure you—"

"Ah, you don't have to assure me of anything, young fellow. Drink!" He drank deep. "Hey! Over here! There are thirsty men! More beer!"

"I don't think—"

"Good lad. Don't think. Drink. Here." He held up his tankard and waited for me to do the same. "Down it goes."

We tossed our drinks off together. I felt elated, and slightly sick. An earthenware jug of beer appeared on the table between us.

"And what will you do with yourself when you get to Montpelier?"

"I'm working—"

"Ah, don't tell me they got you in one of those damn banks."

"Well, yes."

"Which one?"

"The Vermont State Agricultural Bank," I said.

"On Woodstock Avenue."

"You know it?"

"I've had dealings there."

"What a coincidence."

"Not so great a coincidence. I was the paymaster for my regiment not long back. I've had dealings with most of the banks in the state."

"How interesting."

"So you've not started work there just yet?"

"No."

"Then you don't know the manager. A Mister Swales. Terrible old bastard, if I'm frank with you. Don't envy you."

"I have not yet met him."

"Don't listen to me. I've no patience with men in stiff collars and ties. I prefer the outdoors, the road, the camps, the fellowship of comrades. It's a grand life."

"You're in the army, I take it."

"Lieutenant Bennett H. Young, sir, at your service."

"John Edgerton."

"Good to meet you, John Edgerton."

"My friends call me Jack."

"Of course they do. Well, Jack, here's to you."

We drank again.

"What regiment are you with?" I asked, thinking it was polite to make conversation, and in truth charmed by his twinkling eyes, his easy manner. I wished I was like him, the sort of confident young buck always ready with the right word.

"We're a sort of advance party, Jack, drawn from several regiments."

69

"But are you Union?"

"You could say so." He lowered his voice. "We're working for the government."

"The government in Washington? Or the government in Richmond?"

"Ah, if only it were that simple, Jack. We work for the real government. There's things that you don't know about. There's powers behind the powers. You don't read about that in your Boston newspapers."

"No." I was thrilled; it was exactly the sort of thing I'd heard my sister Margaret droning on about for months. Was I about to be inducted into some kind of secret order, some band of conspirators who knew the truth about things like war and money and power?

"I've said too much. I apologize for my intrusion."

"Not at all, lieutenant."

"My friends call me Bennett."

"Bennett. I appreciate the company." It was my turn to lower my voice. "To tell you the truth, my fellow travelers are a little less than inspiring."

He turned his chair around and leaned toward me.

"The big fat mama?"

"And her snot-nosed brats."

"The poor old fellow looks as if he ain't had it in months."

"Who'd want it, with her?"

"Oh, Christ, Jackie, I'd rather—" He made a fist over his lap and moved it up and down.

I spluttered into my beer. "Hah! I'd much rather do that!" I realized, even as I said it, that I sounded a little too enthusiastic.

"Well, who wouldn't? Nothing a woman can do for me that I can't do for myself. Or for a buddy."

Had I been sober, I might have seen the danger signs at this point, and realized that Lieutenant Young was playing me like a fish on a line. But instead, buoyed up on my second tankard of beer—this was stronger ale than the watered-down bilge they served at the White Horse—I assumed that I was embarking on a wonderful adventure with the new friend of my heart.

"For a buddy?" I said, with what I thought was a seductive expression on my face.

"Sure, why not? We look out for each other in my company. All the guys will…lend a hand."

"Just a hand?"

"What else, Jackie?"

"Are you staying here tonight, Bennett?"

"Maybe. Depends."

"Depends on what?"

"If your bed's big enough."

"I guess it is."

"Then I guess I am."

I gulped down the rest of my beer; the tankard was immediately filled.

"I should go and rescue my trunk," I said. "Don't go away."

I pushed my chair back, but Young restrained me with a hand on my shoulder.

"What's your hurry? Your trunk's in good hands. Stay and drink with a lonely soldier."

"Where's the rest of the company?"

"At camp."

"Where's camp?"

"You ask a lot of questions, Jack. How do I know you ain't a spy?"

"Me? That's a good one."

"Yeah, looking at that face I guess I can trust you." He held my chin between thumb and forefinger. He smiled. "Yeah. I reckon you won't give me too much trouble."

"Depends what kind of trouble you're looking for."

At that, Young laughed out loud, and, in retrospect, I can see why. At the time, I thought it was because I had made such a witty, suggestive remark.

"So, why don't you show me up to your room, Mr. Edgerton?" He stood and bowed in a parody of formal New England manners.

"With pleasure, Lieutenant Young."

"I'm right behind you, Mr. Edgerton."

I took my key from the porter, and made an inquiry about my trunk. "It's all under control, sir," he said, with a glance toward Young.

"Told you, Jack! Come on, race you!"

He bounded up the stairs two at a time, his boots raising a hell of a racket that must have sounded throughout the inn. I imagined the family from New York kneeling to say their final prayers, convinced that those runaway slaves had come to cut their throats. In Young's company, I felt reckless.

When we reached the top landing, he turned and faced me, panting. I could see his brown, slightly hairy chest working away where his white shirt gaped open.

He whooped. "Didn't think I'd find a friend like you on the road, Jack!" He threw an arm around my shoulder and ruffled my hair. I must have flinched; anyone could have stepped out of their room and seen us. "Hey, shy boy! I like 'em shy. You're cute, Jack. I could fuck you right here and now on the landing."

"Bennett!"

"Oh, I forgot. College boy, I guess. Modest and virginal."

"Not exactly."

"Wild and willing, huh? Like a firecracker."

I fumbled with the key in the lock; Young was fumbling with my ass.

"C'mon, Jack. I can't wait to get you naked."

I was in just as much of a hurry as Young, and we fell

rather than walked into my room, tearing at each other's clothes, stumbling blindly as we kissed and caressed. Young kicked the door shut with his booted foot as we sank to the floor. I had never known such an eager lover; even Mick, my mentor, had been more restrained than this. Young, however, had his hands down my pants and his tongue down my throat, kissing me as if his life depended on it. He soon had me exposed, my pants around my knees and my shirt up to my chest, the whole expanse of my torso and groin bare to his eager assault. He chewed my nipples and played with my cock like an expert. Soon I had that familiar feeling of mounting heat, a fire that swept away all consciousness.

Young held me in his arms and whispered in my ear. "I need to fuck you now, Jack. I want to be inside you. All night."

That was just what I wanted to hear, as he had no doubt guessed. I scrambled onto the bed and watched as Young divested himself of that strange assortment of military garments: the scarlet and gold jacket, the fancy shirt, the tight black pants, and the riding boots. He stood before me naked, apart from a pair of white wool socks, from which his tanned, hairy, muscular calves rose in stark contrast. His cock was long and slender, curving upward; his balls hung low. I struggled out of my own clothes as quickly as I could.

I reached out and grasped him.

"Take it, Jack. I've waited so long to find a friend like you."

"Me too," I said, and I meant it. He, I soon found, did not.

I drew him to me, delighting in the heat and hardness of his cock, and he lay on top of me. Our two pricks jumped when they touched, slipping and rubbing against each other, both wet and sticky.

When he entered me, lubricated only with spit, my head spun and colors burst before my eyes. But I knew by now how to manage sensations that would have had a novice screaming out in pain, and by breathing deeply and regularly and relaxing my ass muscles I soon had him right inside me, and any discomfort was translated into waves of pleasure.

When I'm getting fucked, I lose myself entirely in the experience. My soul, my consciousness, leaves my head and travels downward. As Young began pumping me, my whole world was concentrated on the point where my ass lips stretched around his long, probing dick. I heard nothing but his breath in my ear, the creaking of the bed. I suppose I was conscious on some level of other sounds—cries in the courtyard, the rattle of wheels, the slamming of doors—all the usual noises of daily life—but they did not register. There could have been a thunderstorm, a revolution, a battle, and I would have been none the wiser.

Young was as good as his word, and fucked me all night, or at least till first light. The first time he came was soon after he entered me; that was a hard, fast fuck, and we brought ourselves off together. My load went over my hairy belly; his went deep inside me.

We recovered quickly. By the time Young had washed his prick in the ewer of cold water on the dressing table, he was already starting to get hard again, and wasted no time in sticking it in my mouth. "I wanted to see those lips around my dick as soon as I saw you, Jack," he said, stroking my hair as I guzzled his rod.

Then it was his turn to put his mouth to use, and he ate my ass, licking and nibbling it before sticking a good inch of his tongue up me.

"Best pussy I've ever tasted," he said. I basked in his admiration, and squirmed under the assault of his tongue. I was ready to be fucked again.

This time he took me from behind, slamming into me even harder than before; my head was pressed painfully up against the fancy metal bedstead, my neck twisted at a crazy angle, but I didn't care; the discomfort heightened the pleasure. When we had finished this time, I had deep grooves impressed into my forehead and cheek; he kissed them and ran his finger along them as we lay together in the now quiet night.

We may have dozed for a while. I came to with the sensation of fingers probing my sore ass; Young was ready for round three. This time he was gentler, more tender, talking to me as he lay on his side, entering me slowly. "Don't go to Montpelier, Jack," he said, between kisses on my neck. "Come with me. We could have a grand life. I need you."

"Oh, Bennett," I said, sighing like a schoolgirl. "I'll never leave you."

And with that, I pushed my ass back into him and surrendered once more to his expert fucking.

When I came this time, it was like swooning; sleep claimed me, and I fell into the depths of unconsciousness.

The room was flooded with light, and Young was standing at the window, shaving, when I awoke.

"What time is it?" I mumbled, my voice thick and slurred.

"Good morning, Sleeping Beauty!" He leaned over the bed and kissed me, smearing my face with lather. "Ready for your breakfast?" He was wearing only a towel wrapped around his waist; he parted it, and showed me the cock I had been riding all night.

"The coach," I said. "It must leave soon."

"Come on, Jackie," he said, the blade of his razor scraping across his bristly chin, "give it a little suck."

I couldn't resist, and half clambered out of bed so that I could reach my "breakfast." It soon began hardening in my mouth. Young kept shaving, stretching his body so that he could see the small pocket mirror that he'd hung on the window catch. He moved back, step by little step, so that I was obliged to crawl from the bed and across the floor to keep ahold of his prick. Soon he was fucking my mouth and shaving simultaneously.

I forgot all about the coach for a moment, and concentrated on sucking. I looked up, expecting to see Young with his eyes closed, his head thrown back in heedless delight, as I'd seen so many men. Instead he was looking down at me with a steady, ironic gaze, and I was suddenly aware of the naked razor that hung in his hand a few inches from my left ear. He could have cut my throat right then and there. What did I really know about this man into whose hands I had put my life?

I stopped sucking; some instinct told me that I was in trouble.

I sat back on my heels. "What time is it, Bennett?"

"Don't know." He squinted out the window, wiping his face on his towel. "About eleven?"

"Eleven!" I leaped to my feet and leaned out the window, stark naked as I was. "But the coach leaves at nine."

"Left at nine. Didn't you hear it? Boy, you were sleeping deeply."

"You mean it's gone? It's gone and you didn't tell me?"

"I did tell you, Jack. I shook you and told you it was leaving. You mumbled something about wanting to sleep, and then I guess we both dropped off."

"But my trunk!"

"You and your trunk!"

"It's got everything I own in it."

"I'm sure it will be perfectly safe."

"That's what you keep saying." Certain things were beginning to form disturbing, vague patterns in my mind. I was not sure what the picture was just yet, but something was struggling through the mists of sleep and sexual satiation.

"Now, where were we?" Young's cock was still fully hard, inviting my attention.

"When you met me last night—" I said.

"It was love at first sight. Come on, Jack. I need you."

"You knew where I was going, I suppose."

"You told me. Montpelier."

"The bank. My trunk. My papers."

"You've got a suspicious mind, Jackie-boy."

"I suppose by now someone's well on their way to Montpelier in my place. Is that the name of the game? Someone's using my letters of introduction to the manager of the bank, getting inside, and then what? Robbing a Union bank to pay for a Rebel army?"

"Well that's a fancy imagination you've got there. If you must know the truth, Jack, and I see that nothing else will do, your trunk is currently resting in the landlord's cellar, where my men entrusted it last night."

"Your men? Entrusted it? What the hell is going on?"

Young sat down on the bed and patted the crumpled sheet beside him. I sat, our legs touching. His cock, slightly deflated, rested on his thigh.

"I couldn't let you go, Jack."

"What are you talking about? Have I been kidnapped?"

"You could say that, I suppose. I prefer 'recruited.' "

"How dare you?"

"Easily. I'm a daring fellow, Jack."

"And what do you plan to do with me?"

"We'll go north, into Canada, where the company is camped. Fifty of us, Jack, Rebels and Unionists, grays and blues, blacks and whites, we don't care, we live in comradeship and peace. We trouble no man."

"What are you, Young? A bandit? A highwayman?"

"I've taken nothing from you that you didn't give willingly, Jack."

"But why?"

"I told you. I need a friend."

"I'm sure you're not short of friends."

"It's true, we are all good pals in the camp. You'll meet

many men up there, Jack, who will be proud and happy to call you their friend. But I need someone to be by my side at all times. To take care of me and love me."

"And you thought all that, did you, as you saw me eating my supper in the bar last night?" I made the words sound as ridiculous, as unbelievable, as I found them.

Young put an arm around my shoulder and looked me straight in the eye. "I did."

He drew me to him and kissed me on the mouth, softly, without aggression. His face, which had ripped me raw with its stubble in the night, was smooth and soft now. His body was warm and hairy. And his cock—that ever ready cock—was pointing to the ceiling again.

With a feeling of giddiness, of half-delightful vertigo, I abandoned myself to his embrace.

By midafternoon, we were on the road: Bennett Young, myself, and a company of three other soldiers of fortune, as I assumed them—us—to be. They were all arrayed in odds and ends of military uniform, scavenged, I guessed, from camps and stores around the country. They respected Bennett as a leader, they welcomed me as a comrade, and, just as had been promised, they had my trunk, still tied with cords as I had left it on the roof of the carriage.

We camped that night in the woods south of Barre. Two tents did for us all—one for Bennett and me, one for the other three. They were a handsome enough group. One of them appeared, by his complexion, to be Spanish, Italian, or Mexican, and answered to the name of Bruce. A gold hoop in his right earlobe proclaimed that this was no ordinary soldier. The other two, Doty and Gregg, could have been brothers, sharing the same pale skin, blond hair, and brown eyes, although Young assured me that they were not. "They're as close as brothers, though, Jack, like I told you. They'll stick by one another now, till death."

"Poor Bruce, then. Three's a crowd."

"Perhaps you'd prefer him to bed down with us, then? He's eager to taste your ass, Jack."

"Another night."

"Good boy. I want you all to myself. Like I told you, I love you."

And so, as if in a dream, we traveled northward, avoiding towns except when we needed provisions, when I was dispatched to the local store with a list. We camped in fields and forests, we bathed in streams, we shared our rations and our bodies.

By the time we crossed the border into Canada, I had forgotten my new life in Montpelier, my family and friends, the warnings of Mick and Aaron.

I was content, and blind.

Part Two:

Go Down, Aaron

V

DEAR JACK,

I want to tell you that I am alive, that I am well, that I have not forgotten you, and that I am writing this letter to relieve the feelings of a heart too full. I hope that you are safe at home, that you remember the words of a friend who never wished you anything but happiness, and who will always cherish the time he had with you. I know, and you know, that I can never send this letter, but writing it and keeping it by me through the dark days ahead is some comfort.

I have settled in the place to which I swore I would never return, Richmond, the Rebel capital, a place where I have few friends and many enemies. The town looks superficially the same, but is totally different. The faces wear a new expression: one of fear, and hope, and hatred, rather than the uniform expression of haughty pride that they once wore. I have met no one I know. What is one more shiftless, rootless black man in a town full of freaks and oddities of every color? War has brought the circus to town, every day of every week. Up is down, wrong is right, day is night, and in such an environment I can live in relative safety and seclusion while I decide how best to shape my future. I know that my father is dead, that I have been defrauded of the inheritance that he promised me by the connivance of my so-called brothers, those jealous thieves who resented my presence in the house from childhood. Should I pursue them, punish them, and secure what is rightfully mine? Or should I, as the Good Book teaches me, turn the other cheek?

We shall see what Fate washes my way. Once again, my life is a blank slate. I thought, when I moved to Vermont, that I would turn a new page, accepted by your family and townsfolk, able at last to make something of my education. That dream is over. It has faded, just as the cuts and bruises that I took with me from Bishopstown have faded. I did not leave town without a warm send-off by Windridge's gang. Or did you not know? He made some unpleasant friends at his anti-abolitonist rallies, the scum of the North who wanted nothing more than to ape the nigger-hanging ways of their Southern brethren, and who saw my friendship with your family, and particularly my friendship with you, as all the pretext they needed for stringing me up from the nearest tree. I escaped, and took great pleasure in busting a few noses as I did so. I stole Windridge's horse, and left its owner writhing in the dust as I galloped to freedom. They were too fat, and too slow, to catch me.

Happy to have escaped with my life, it did not take me long to realize that my dreams were shattered and my heart broken. Why did I ever meet you, Jack? Why did we allow ourselves those dangerous intimacies? You and I are from different worlds, and we should never have come so close. I believed at first that we could be friends, that we could tame our baser passions and prove to the world that men like us—for I do believe, Jack, there are thousands of us, who crave the love and companionship of our own kind—could live noble and blameless lives. But we know how that dream ended, in the filth of a stable.

I could think of nothing else as I rode out of town, the road blurring in front of my eyes. I could see only your face, your lips, your taunting smile as you lay there in the straw daring me to take what I wanted but I knew I must never have. I thought of the other men to whom you had given it—so casually, so cheaply!—in the bars of Bishopstown, in the woods, on the floor of the boiler house that same afternoon. I saw you, Jack, and I watched for as long as I could before the urge to kill someone drove me away.

My horse slowed to a canter, to a walk, and stopped altogether, cropping the grass at the edge of a field.

I dismounted, and was violently sick.

I puked until there was nothing left to bring up. I had been kicked in the stomach, of course, that was the reason—and yet I felt as if I was voiding all the love that I felt for you, Jack, all the sweetness that had turned to bitter bile. I was empty. I remounted my horse, my guts in pain, and rode slowly into the night.

Ill-equipped as I was for life on the road, I had no alternative but to avoid towns and large settlements and to put some distance between myself and Bishopstown. I slept that first night in the woods, under my coat; luckily for me the night was dry and I was unmolested by animals. I woke up aching and sore in my limbs, but rested and ready to face whatever fortune might throw at me.

Fortune played her first trick: the horse had worked loose from its tether in the night and gone, presumably to find its way back to Bishopstown. I cursed my carelessness, and the stupidity of the horse: it deserved a better master than Windridge. I was alone, and on foot.

The first question was which way to head. North, toward the Canadian border? South, into Massachusetts and Connecticut? West, into New York State? And then where? To stay in the Yankee states, or to return to the South?

Whichever way I turned, the path seemed strewn with dangers. As a lone black man, on whichever side of the political line, I ran the risk of being arrested, declared "contraband of war," and set to work on the railroads, a fate I will avoid at all costs. But New England, far from being the haven of tolerance and opportunity I had fondly imagined, had dangers of a subtler sort. I thought, by and large, my best chance lay in the South, to return to Virginia, claim whatever remained of my inheritance, and then to continue my travels as far west as possible, to California, maybe, or even into Mexico. Away from all these fine gentlemen and their not-so-fine friends, from ladies who smile at you in church but whisper behind your back in the street.

And away from you. Poor Jack—poor, childish, brave, fond Jack, too spoiled to know what life could do to an ill-matched pair like us! We were nothing but a danger to each other. I thank God that I never took the final irrevocable step that would have bound us together, however much I may have longed to do it.

Putting on my shirt, I munched on a piece of stale bread that I had managed, despite my haste, to shove into my bag, and I quenched my thirst with water from the stream. The first priority was to equip myself with the necessities of life—a horse, if possible, warm clothes, a weapon, blankets, food. I had a little money, all that I had saved, rolled up and stuffed into the toe of my boot. It was enough to feed me for a few days, to make a few necessary purchases, but it would not furnish me with a mount or the means to protect myself. Those things I would have to earn or steal.

The other side of the mountain, there was a village where I knew there were farms; and where there were farms, there was work, and outbuildings, and horses, and all manner of useful things for a man in need. My inclination is to be honest, but I've seen enough of how the world treats an honest man to consider the alternatives.

The sun was up, and the farms would be busy, and I thought this the best time to present myself as a hired hand—and also, if I was lucky, get a little breakfast into the bargain. The first establishment that I found was a run-down farm, just a house and a barn with a few ill-tended vegetable patches, a cow in desperate need of milking and a handful of scrawny chickens pecking for worms in the yard. But there was smoke rising from the chimney, and a good smell of coffee, so I braved the yapping of the mangy yellow dog that snapped at my heels, and presented myself at the door.

I knocked, although the door was open, and shouted a hello. There was banging within, and an upper window was flung open. "Get away from here!" came a high, frantic, female voice. "There's nothing for you! My husband will come out and shoot you!" I could tell she was on the verge of tears, and I had no desire to frighten her further—not least because she was waving a shotgun out the window. I bowed, and tried to look harmless.

"I'm just looking for work, ma'am," I said.

She was surprised, as white folk always are, at my accent, which does not accord with my appearance. The gun stopped waving, and she realized that she was not about to be raped and murdered.

"There's no work here! Go away!"

"I could milk the cow for you, ma'am, or weed that pumpkin patch, or chop you some wood."

"No... Thank you. My...husband takes care of all that."

I could see that she was weighing in her mind the usefulness of a fresh pair of hands around the place, against the dangers of letting an unknown black man onto her property.

"Perhaps I could talk to him?"

The gun started waving again, and she passed a hand across her brow, pulling back loose strands of brown hair.

I reckoned she was 30 years old, but she looked tired and careworn, as everyone does these days. I knew there was no husband in the house, no man at all, possibly just her, and she knew that I knew. It was better for us both if we maintained that convenient fiction.

"He's...he's just ridden down to the...er...lower field to see the men... And he'll be back any minute for his breakfast."

"Perhaps in the meantime I could start by milking the cow? She looks mighty uncomfortable."

"Don't you come into the house, you hear me? And stay where I can see you!"

She banged the window shut. I walked over to the cow, found a clean-looking pail in the shed, and started milking her right where she stood. She bellowed loudly as the first few squirts came out, but soon she was calm and the milk flowed, thick and copious, into the pail. If nothing else, my efforts would be rewarded with a cup full of that.

The woman stood on her porch, watching me with her arms folded. It would have been so easy to knock her on the head, steal her gun, ransack the house for money, and run. Plenty of men would have done it. I think she expected me to do it, and knew herself to be at a great disadvantage. War has made women like her vulnerable. I suspected that her husband was away fighting, that she was left, like so many, on her own, to scratch a living from the soil, unsupported by family or friends. I could not bring myself to add to her woes.

"When you've done that, you can chop some firewood for me."

"Yes, ma'am."

"And then perhaps I can bring you some breakfast."

"Thank you, ma'am."

An hour later, almost faint with hunger, I sat on the edge of the porch with a mug of coffee, a hunk of cornbread, and a pork chop, still sizzling from the pan. There were apples and milk waiting for me indoors. I ate ravenously, tearing the meat with my fingers; she had not given me a knife. She watched me nervously, still scared, but delighted, as all women are, to see her food appreciated.

"Well, thank you, ma'am, that was a good breakfast. Now I must be on my way."

"Where you headed?"

"South." I gestured vaguely in that direction.

"Not planning to stick around? I could...we could use a hired hand. You could sleep in the barn, it's warm and dry, and we'd feed you and...well, I can't pay you but...we'd look after you. What do you say?"

I was astonished, and sorry to let her down. "I'm afraid I can't stay around here," I said. "And it wouldn't be good for you either. There's too many who take exception to the color of my skin."

"The Lord says it don't matter."

"People have a way of ignoring what the Lord says, ma'am. That's why we're fighting a war against our brothers."

Her hands hung down by her side, and her face crumpled. And then, in a gesture she had made a dozen times before, she pushed back her hair, straightened herself up, and swallowed her grief. "Well," she said, "we live in wicked times, that's for sure. And when my husband gets back from the—" She looked crestfallen, as if she'd given away too much.

"From the lower field, ma'am?" I said.

"Yes, from the lower field," she said, smiling for the first time. "Well, then we'll get this place going again, and we'll be fine with our neighbors, and you'll come back and we'll show you our gratitude for your kindness. But till then, there's nothing I can give you. Unless you want my dog. Can't eat him, he don't give milk or lay eggs, and he ain't much use as a guard."

"Thanks, but I prefer to travel alone."

"You could stay for a night, maybe?"

I saw the loneliness and fear that made up her day-to-day life. I might have stayed there, licked the farm into shape, kept her safe—but how long before I was chased out of town again? And this time they wouldn't hesitate to kill me. A black man shacked up with a white woman? It was their favorite nightmare.

"Thanks, but I better be moving along."

"Wait," she said, and ran into the house. When she came down, she had a rolled blanket under her arm. "Here's a few things I don't need no more. You can keep them or sell them, whatever…"

The roll was bulky. I could see from the expression on her face that it was best not to look inside it just now. Instead I expressed my thanks, and walked on, with many glances back to that brave, lonely woman as she stood, watching and waving, at her kitchen door.

Regaining the relative shelter of the woods, I unrolled the blanket and took stock of its contents. Two clean white shirts, a pair of pants, a pair of thick woolen socks, and even, to my astonishment, a large hunting knife. I took it from its sheath and felt the edge; it was as sharp as a razor.

And so I found at my first stop several of the necessities of life, but I was still lacking a few essentials. I knew I had to move quickly; word of my presence in such a small community would soon get around, and I was reluctant to travel much further on foot. A horse was at the top of my shopping list.

Keeping to the woods, I skirted two more farms where the yards were busy, the comings and goings too regular. I had not consciously decided that I was going to steal a horse; the plan seemed, instead, to have formed itself in my head without my wishing it.

Finally, I came upon a house at the far end of the village; like the first, it had that unkempt, wartime look that spoke of absent men and struggling women. There was a stable building, and the unmistakable scent of horse shit.

Dropping down behind the house to avoid being seen from the windows, I ran quietly to the stable and looked in. There were three horses in there, all sound-looking animals. And there was something else: a stable boy. He was crouching at the furthest of the three stalls, picking at the horse's hoof with a small knife. He was half naked; his shirt was hanging over a saddle rack, presumably to protect it from the muck that inevitably comes with horse husbandry. For a moment, I could study him unobserved. He was a strong lad, perhaps 19 or 20 years of age, with curly brown hair that could do with a trim, a snub nose, and freckles across his face and neck, extending over his broad upper back. There was a patch of hair on his chest and a little on his stomach, standing out in stark relief from the milky whiteness of his skin. As he delved away with his knife, the muscles bunched and extended under that skin; his lower arms were sunburned to a brick red. It was obvious that he was well fed, and could look after himself in a fight. But he was, I reckoned, shorter than me by a good six inches, and if it came to a simple trial of strength, I could overpower him in a second.

I had no desire to harm him, however, not least because I was enjoying looking at him so much. Where you, Jack, are smooth and slender, with blond hair and a skin that tans gold, this lad was stocky and sturdy—a worker, rather than a student of life. And he was good at his work; with a final, deft twist of his knife, he shot a jagged stone the size of a walnut out of the horse's hoof, and stood up, patting the beast on its big brown behind.

I thought it better to announce my presence, not least because he had a knife in his hand, so I coughed gently. He didn't jump. Instead he just looked toward the door, shielding his eyes against the light, which was behind me and put me into silhouette.

"Ben, is that you?"

"No, it's not Ben," I said, taking a step forward. When he saw me more clearly, his hands went to his sides and he adopted a defensive posture. The muscles in his chest bunched up, with two pink buds on top of them that looked good enough to eat.

"What do you want? Who are you?"

"I just wondered if you were interested in maybe selling me one of your horses."

"Selling? You were planning on stealing one, more like." He relaxed a little, and rubbed a hand across his torso, where a trickle of sweat ran from neck to navel. His hand left a dirty track behind it.

"And could you stop me if I did?" I asked, smiling.

"Maybe."

"And maybe not." We stood facing each other, and I became aware of the scent of his sweat above the smell of the horses—a rich scent, like wood smoke. I was already half-hard from watching him at work, and that smell finished the job. I saw him glance down toward my swollen crotch, and his body relaxed.

"We don't have to fight," he said. "You can take one of the horses, as far as I'm concerned. They're not mine, and I don't care what happens to them. But if you do take one, you can do me a favor and take me as well."

"You want to ride with me?"

"I want to get out of here."

"Why would I want to saddle myself with a boy like you?" I said, liking the idea very much indeed.

"You want the horse?"

"Yes, I want the horse. But do I want you?"

He looked down again and smiled. "Looks like you do from where I'm standing." He laughed and licked his lips.

"So—do I have a ride?"

"I've never ridden a black stallion before," he said, his

hand straying back to his chest and finding one of his nipples, which he unconsciously played with till it was stiff.

"You better have a good seat if you're going to ride this," I said, squeezing my cock.

In answer, he turned around and dropped his pants. "How does this look? Good enough for you?" He bent forward slightly, and parted his ass cheeks with his hands. Through the dark hair, I could see his pink hole. My head swam, and all the frustration of the last months blinded me. God knows, Jack, I was aware of the dangers. But now, all my fears had been realized: I was an outcast, struggling to stay alive. And, you see, I needed that horse.

I leaped forward, fell to my knees, and dived in. My tongue found his asshole and started licking. He gave one loud "God damn!" and then surrendered to the experience. His ass tasted of sweat, but it was clean and sweet as I lapped at it. My cock was like an iron bar inside my pants, and it was desperate for release. Unwilling to relinquish his ass, I started struggling with my belt and buttons, and ended up losing my balance and rolling over in the straw of the stable floor.

"Shit!"

I looked up and saw the boy gazing down at me. His pants were around his ankles, and his cock, which was small and thick, stuck up at a jaunty angle from his furry belly.

"Need a hand?"

He didn't wait for a reply, but knelt beside me and continued to open my trousers. I put my hands behind my head and let him get on with the job. When my dick was finally free, it sprang out of my pants as if it was on a spring.

His eyes goggled, and his mouth fell open. "Gee... I've never seen one that big before... I don't know if I can... Well..." He started toying with it, stroking the underside with his fingertips, tracing up to the tip, where my foreskin was starting to pull back. Finally he grasped it, and moved his hand up and down. With each stroke, more of the head was exposed. He appeared to be transfixed. I reached around with one hand and found his cock. He was still rock hard, so I guessed that any misgivings he had about my size were not enough to scare him off. We stayed that way, playing with each other, for a while, as the sun illuminated the dusty straw and the horses occasionally snuffled and stamped in their stalls.

"What's your name, boy?" I said.

"Edward."

"Well, Eddie, you want this up your ass?"

"Yeah..."

"Then you'd better get it nice and wet."

I wanted to see his cute little face looking up at me while my dick plowed into his mouth.

He lay down beside me, his head near my stomach, so I could play with his curly hair while he made a few tentative licks and kisses on my cock. It had been a long time since I was touched there, and I could have wept with relief. Finally he opened his mouth wide and took the head. I rubbed the back of his neck and encouraged him gently downward. When he'd got the measure of me, and was working his lips up and down my shaft with increasing pace, I moved my hand over his shoulders and down his back until I could play with his ass. I kneaded the white, elastic flesh of each cheek, and then, by poking and prodding, I found his hole. Wetting my finger with spit, I pushed it into him to the first knuckle, then the second. He didn't stop sucking, but started moaning. He was ready.

He rolled off me and, lying beside me, kicked off his boots and pants. Now he was completely naked, while I was fully clothed, with my pants open and my shirt pushed up. The contrast—his nakedness and my clothes, his white skin and my black—made me even more eager to fuck him.

I thought I would have to break him in gently, but this

94

jockey knew exactly what to do. Springing up, he placed a knee on either side of my hips and, holding my prick, guided it to the target. He ass was wet and open, my dick was lubricated with his saliva and the juice that was flowing out of the tip. All I had to do was brace my hips slightly upward, and I entered him. He bit his lip and closed his eyes, still holding on to me. Then, relinquishing his grip, he started to lower himself. He took it slowly, and I didn't thrust, unwilling to hurt him—but, when he reached the thickest central part of my shaft, he stopped.

"It hurts," he said.

"Take your time, Eddie."

His thigh muscles were tensed; I stroked them, and they felt like steel. His cock had gone soft and was nestling in his bush like an acorn. With one finger, I stroked the hairy passage between his ass and his balls, then the tight skin of his ball sack. His cock stirred back to life, and as it grew he moved himself gently around my cock, getting used to the feel of it inside him. Then, as his dick began to swell and climb, his ass suddenly relaxed and he sat all the way down.

"Are you inside me?"

"Every inch, boy."

"Oh, fuck."

In response, I gently thrust. His cock danced further upward until it was rigid against his bush. He reached around and felt the lips of his ass stretched around me, and squeezed my balls. He started to move, meeting my thrusts, and gradually the motion became faster, bigger, harder. My dick was getting even bigger inside him, and his ass took everything I could give him. He settled into a rhythm and, supporting himself with one hand braced against my leg, started to jerk himself off.

I put my hands behind my head again, tensed my stomach muscles, and shoved my dick as far inside him as I could. He responded by thrusting his ass up and down like a pump;

all I had to do was stay still and let him do the work. Finally, he screwed his eyes up and started squirting all over the muscles of my stomach. His ass clamped around me as he came, and we remained locked together as he emptied himself of every drop.

To my surprise, he neither went soft nor made any attempt to dismount. He leaned forward and kissed me full on the mouth, then, pulling me up and forward, rolled over onto his back. Somehow, I kept my cock inside him. He pointed his legs at the roof and said, "Fuck me. Hard."

And so I did. I nailed him to that stable floor. Sweat was pouring off me, dripping from my forehead and the end of my nose onto his face. We kissed, eating each other's mouths, bruising our lips. His spunk was now smeared from my stomach onto his body; we were glued together. The scent of sweat and sperm and horse shit filled my nostrils. I braced myself on my arms, lifted myself a little so I could look into his eyes, and fucked him harder than I had fucked anyone before. He pushed his prick forward, so I could see that he was still stiff. His face, neck, and chest were flushed a bright pink, the same color as the head of his dick. When I started to come inside him, he moaned and squirmed, but stayed staring straight into my eyes.

We lay like that for a while, until our breathing had slowed and the position became too uncomfortable to sustain. I pulled out of him and immediately plugged the hole with two fingers. With one arm around his shoulders, lifting him so he was resting partly on my lap, I kept fucking him that way until he brought himself to another climax.

We cleaned up with straw, dressed ourselves, and then, without much discussion, saddled the horses and rode quietly away from the stables. When we had covered a couple of miles and reached open country far from any habitation, we slowed to a walk and he told me his story.

He had been orphaned at the age of six, when his mother died in childbirth. His father, who had traveled west to seek out a new home, had been killed in an outbreak of cholera just after Eddie was born. He and his infant sister were looked after by a succession of relatives, none of whom really wanted them, until the girl was sent into service in Boston and Eddie, at the age of 15, was left to fend for himself. He'd worked his way around the local farms, finally finding the position as stable boy, groom, and man-of-all-work where I found him. His employers, a tight-fisted couple whom he described as wretched Puritans, had fled the area at the first news of Confederate incursions out of Virginia, imagining that they would have their throats cut by Rebel soldiers within days. He had not heard from them in weeks, and kept the farm going as best he could. When I found him, he had been on the verge of selling the horses and joining the army.

We sold the third horse, a sorry-looking gray mare that looked far from roadworthy, to a traveler we met on the road. He got the horse; we got razors, soap, blankets, matches, and a couple of water bottles. I know who got the better bargain.

Thus equipped, we turned south, and rode all day until we pitched camp just above Shelburne Falls. We lit a fire, made beds in an abandoned hut, and settled in for the evening. Eddie prepared our dinner, and we slept together, rolled in blankets, as warm as two bears in a cave. As he breathed gently in my arms, I allowed myself to believe that I had found the friend I had so long searched for, and that the open road, the woods and mountains, would give us the freedom to live and love in peace.

VI

Six days out from the farm, Eddie and I passed through New York State, working our way into Pennsylvania, avoiding towns wherever possible, except to buy or steal food. The advantages of having a white companion were soon apparent to me; Eddie was welcomed in every community, bought food at a fair price, and was frequently offered accommodation. Provided I stayed in the background, or in darkness, we were comfortable and well fed. In addition, I fucked him every day and in every way, in houses, huts, and forests, on his back, on his front, on his side, in beds, over tables, and, on one occasion, in a hammock, which we brought down with an almighty rip and crash. I had never fucked one man in so many ways for such a long time, and I was grateful for the experience. I began to dream of a future for me and Eddie, much as I had dreamed of a future with you, Jack—but, of course, no such future is possible. Well, I was reckless for once, I took pleasure where I could, and that was enough.

The trouble began when we reached Allentown. We

followed our usual routine, camping out the first night on the outskirts of town—there were plenty of abandoned barns and farm buildings to give us shelter—and then obtaining provisions for the journey. Eddie washed himself, put on a clean shirt, and rode into town, while I gutted and cooked a couple of rabbits that I'd trapped the night before. The cleaned skins were packed away ready for trade, the meat was cooking on green sticks over the fire, and the carcass was boiling up in our little cooking pot with a few wild herbs. When Eddie returned, hopefully with bread and fruit, we'd have a fine meal. I'd learned to love our self-sufficient life on the road, and imagined the road stretching on forever.

Eddie returned with his bag full of provisions, and his eyes full of trouble. When I asked him about the town, and about our prospects for work and housing, he was evasive and sullen. Normally he was full of news about the people he had met and the things he had seen; he loved our traveling life as much as I did, and relished each new encounter. But today he ate in silence, staring at the trees, the ground, his feet—at anything but me. I washed the pots and plates in the stream, wrapped the leftover meat in some fresh leaves secured with wooden picks, and packed up the camp. Eddie watched me, scowling.

"What's the matter, kid?" I said. "Got a sore ass?" He loved this kind of taunting, and it usually escalated into a quick, hot fuck on the bare ground.

"No."

Not today, obviously.

"So what's up? Cat got your tongue?"

"Nothing."

"Nothing means something. Come on, you better tell me what's on your mind. You've been like a bear with a sore head since you got back from town."

"Just thinking."

"Someone's said something to you, right?"

"Maybe."

"Someone seen us riding in?"

"Maybe."

I had been waiting for this moment, dreading it, ever since we set out together. I sat beside him on a fallen log and went to put my arm around his shoulders. He froze. Something was wrong. Usually my touch was enough to have him fawning on me like a puppy dog. I rubbed the back of his neck, as I'd done so many times before when he was sucking my cock, and felt him relax slightly.

"We can't go on together like this, Aaron."

"Why not?"

"It's too dangerous."

"Says who?"

He lost his temper, like a child. "Everyone knows it's dangerous! Traveling on the road, in the middle of a war, we've got no protection, we don't even know where we're going..."

"Someone's threatened you."

"Don't be ridiculous," he huffed, convincing me that I was right, "nobody frightens me. I'm just trying to talk some sense into you."

"Who's got to you, Eddie?"

"I told you, nobody."

"What did they say? That you ain't got not business riding around with a nigger?" I said the words in an approximation of a Yankee accent. "That you should stick with your own kind and they don't take kindly to seeing no mixin' of the bloods?" I was gripping his neck hard now, my fingers pressing white patches into the sunburned skin.

"Get off me! Don't touch me!" He leaped to his feet and ran three paces away. Something was badly wrong.

"Hey, calm down! What's happened? You've got to tell me."

"I can't..." His eyes were wet, his voice trembling.

"What happened, Eddie? You'd better tell me right now. Are we in danger?"

He would not look at me. "No. Nothing..."

I grabbed him by the shoulder and spun him around. "You tell me what's going on or I swear I will—"

There was a cracking noise nearby—slight, but enough to tell me that we were not alone. I froze. Silence. Then, again, a crack and a rustle from the trees. My ears are attuned to danger. One man, two men, possibly more. I grabbed Eddie by the throat—that pretty throat down which I had shot my load so many times—and stared into his eyes.

"You've sold me."

"I haven't... They made me..."

I pushed him from me with such force that he sprawled on the ground, and I started to run—but suddenly there was a whoop and a crash, and four men burst into the clearing, each of them carrying a gun.

"We got him, boys!" one of them said, a tall, ugly bastard with hair like dirty string.

They moved in swiftly, two in front, two behind, like the jaws of a trap. I had just time to whip my hunting knife from its sheath and hold it to Eddie's throat. One stroke, and he would be dead. I didn't figure that it would matter much to men like that—bounty hunters, I guessed, who would get a price for my head, delivered (still attached to a working body) to the local sheriff and sold into slavery and certain death on the railroads. This kind of contraband dealing was rife in the South; I had no idea it had infected the North as well.

"Take one more step and I'll kill him," I said, in the calmest voice I could muster. I had no desire to kill Eddie; if he'd betrayed me, I knew that it must have been under the severest duress.

"Please don't, Aaron," Eddie whispered. "Please don't kill me."

"I won't," I said softly in his ear, then shouted, "I mean it! I'll slit his throat!"

The men stopped in their tracks, waiting for a clear lead. Eddie whimpered and moaned, the blood rushed in my ears, and from a nearby tree a robin trilled a carefree song. It was a ridiculous situation that could end only in someone's death, it seemed.

"Let him go," the stringy-haired one, obviously a leader of sorts, said, "and we'll let you run."

"Like hell," I said. "I know your tricks."

"So cut his throat," he said, "and then we'll shoot your legs off and leave you to die with him. Wouldn't that be pretty?"

The men laughed.

"You promise you'll let me go?"

"What do you want? Should I swear on a Bible?" They all laughed.

There was no alternative; whatever happened next, whether they kept their promise or not, I had one chance at least of living. And if I could save Eddie's life too, it wasn't such a bad bargain. I removed the knife from his throat—a tiny bead of blood appeared, as if he'd cut himself shaving—and pushed him away from me. He picked himself up and ran outside the circle of men. They paid him no heed. Nor did they move.

"Now let me go."

"Why would we want to do a thing like that?"

I was going to say "because you said you would," but that sounded laughable even to me. The choice was clear—either fight (and, with four guns pointed at my head, that didn't seem wise) or submit.

I held out my hands and looked at Eddie. His head hung down.

I was quickly bound at the wrists and led on a long rope back to town, two men ahead of me, two behind me with guns. Eddie disappeared, and I cursed him as he fled. The gang didn't seem interested in him anyway, not even for what I'd been enjoying. They were even more barbarous than I thought.

In town, I was delivered to the sheriff's office, thrown into a cell, and given a piece of dry bread and a beaker of water. The men left, presumably to collect their reward. I was told nothing, but I knew enough about these situations to guess that I would be kept alive (just) in captivity until my new "owners" from the railroad company came to collect me. They would work me as hard as they could, for very little outlay in the way of food, until I died.

This I could not have, so I set about planning my escape. The cell itself was impregnable, with a solid wall at the back and bars on three sides. The cells on either side were, for the moment, empty. There was a drunk in the last cell of the four, sleeping off his liquor. The jailer was an old man with a disgusting habit of chewing tobacco and spitting a long stream of brown liquid into a large brass pot in the corner. He had obviously not washed for some time, and the combined smells of stale tobacco juice, greasy hair, and stale alcohol were making me feel sick.

However, at present this old bird represented my only chance of escape, and I was willing to try anything.

"Excuse me, sir."

"What do you want, nigger?"

I had the immediate impression that my captor was not an abolitionist.

"I wondered if you could tell me if there's a minister in town."

"A minister? Why? You planning on dying?" He thought this was mighty funny, cackling for a while and then putting a stop to it with another long, juicy spit.

"No. But I'd like to clear my conscience."

"You ain't going nowhere yet awhile. You won't need a minister."

There had to be some way of getting another, more sympathetic individual into the jail. I sat silent for a while, then tried again.

"Getting late, isn't it?"

"What you say, boy?"

"Getting late. You must be tired."

"Darn it, don't you ever shut up?" I had spoken twice in two hours.

"Do they keep you here all night?" I have always found that an appeal to a man's selfish inclination to grumble works wonders.

"They would if they could, boy, damn their eyes, and if that damn fool Jed Brown don't get here soon I'll just lock you in and damn the consequences." I knew this was not allowed by law; there had to be an attendant at all times, as a few too many prisoners had roasted to death in fires.

"Well, where is that Jed Brown, in God's name?" I asked, trying to sound sympathetic.

The answer came in the form of shouting and banging from outside. The doors burst open and there was Jed Brown—at least, I assumed it was him—leading two bruised and bloodied white men, both of them chained at the wrist.

"Two more outliers, Zachary!" he said. The men were detached one from the other and thrown into cells on either side of me. The doors clanged shut and Zachary, the old tobacco chewer, rattled his keys in the lock.

"You got 'em, sheriff!" he said, all sycophantic now. There was no more "damn fool Jed Brown."

"Yep, I got 'em. Up by Monroe's farm, sleeping in a barn."

"Deserter scum!" Zachary said, spitting again but this time missing his receptacle and making a sticky patch on the grimy wood floor.

104

"Get out of here, old man, and take that filthy mess with you!"

"Goodnight, Jed. Sleep tight!"

Zachary scuttled off to his lair, while Jed Brown strode around the jail taking off his gun belt, hanging his coat on a peg, checking the log book. He was a big man, way over six feet tall, broad in the shoulders and thick at the waist, his legs as strong as tree trunks. His thick, curly hair had turned the color of gunmetal, and in his fine set of whiskers there was more white than black. I guessed he was ten years my senior, maybe more.

He made a few notes in the log, scratched his head with the pen, and looked over at the cells.

"Well bless my soul, what have we here? A nigger in the woodpile, huh?" He laughed, a deep, booming laugh which somewhat mitigated the tone of his remark. I stood up, but made no reply.

"Where'd they find you, boy? With your hand in the chicken coop, stealing eggs?"

"No, sir," I said, "I was taken prisoner in the woods."

My educated accent took him by surprise, and he stepped up to take a closer look.

"What's your name?"

"Aaron Johnson, sir."

"And what's the charge?"

"What's written in the book?"

"Vagrancy."

"That's the usual charge, isn't it, when arresting a black man?"

He scratched his beard, and it made a crackling noise as he did so. "You steal something?"

"No, sir."

"Kill anyone?"

"No, sir. I didn't get the chance."

"Ah. So you were trying to."

105

"I'd kill bounty hunters who sell free men into slavery, yes."

He turned and went back to the desk, put his feet up, and appeared to fall asleep. I turned my attention to my fellow prisoners—poor, half-starved creatures, bloodied around their mouths, their faces bruised and grazed, who were huddling on the floor, whimpering. I could not see much; there was a single lamp on the sheriff's desk, and it cast a fitful light over the cells, enough to show their injuries but little more. From odd bits of torn, filthy material, I could guess that they were dressed in the remnants of Union uniforms.

One of them was nearer to me, lying against the bars that divided us, and I could easily reach out and touch him. He flinched at the contact, and looked up at me with hooded eyes. I gestured toward my beaker of water, and offered it to him. He looked around, saw that we were unobserved, and tried to grab it through the bars. There was not room for the whole vessel to pass through, but, if we both knelt, I could tip the brim of the beaker to his lips. He drank greedily, the water spilling down his throat. When I could feel that half the contents had gone, I pulled it away, and his lips kissed the empty air, hoping for more.

I would have repeated the performance with my other neighbor, but, as it turned out, our captor was not asleep.

"If they want a drink they only have to ask."

His feet in their heavy boots dropped noisily to the floor. I said nothing, waiting to see how things developed. He walked over to a brass pot in the corner of the room.

"Any of you boys need to take a piss?"

We all said that we did.

"Well, wait your turn." He arranged himself in front of the pot, his back to the cells, and I could only imagine, in the dim light, that he was hauling his cock out of his pants. The noise left little doubt as to what he was doing; it rang the metal vessel like a wet bell.

When he had finished, he shook himself off, stuffed himself away, and picked up the pot. He placed it on the floor in front of the first cell.

"Hope you ain't pee-shy," he said to the soldier inside.

The poor bruised boy got painfully to his feet like an old man, bracing himself with his hands on his knees. His fingers were dirty and swollen, but he managed to unbutton himself and pull out a fair-sized prick. Even in the dim light, I could see that it was markedly cleaner than the rest of him. Holding it with one hand and supporting himself against the bars with the other, he maneuvered himself to a position where he might reasonably hope to reach the pot.

The first few drops hit the floor, but soon a steady stream was arcing into the pot. It didn't flow as fast as the sheriff's, but there was no lack of volume; the flow seemed to last forever. Judging by the acrid smell that tickled my nostrils, the soldier hadn't pissed in a while. The tone changed as the pot filled up, a queer ringing sound climbing the scale. I judged that, with two loads inside it, the pot was at least half full.

When the first soldier had finished pissing, the sheriff pushed the pot with his boot over to the other side of me, and the performance was repeated. My left-hand neighbor was in better shape than his comrade, and stood with less difficulty. The sheriff watched the performance like a hawk.

Turning to me, he said, "Now your turn, boy. We've saved the best till last." His voice was low, and he licked his lips.

Unwilling to disappoint him, and needing to empty my bladder, I whipped out my dick—which was half hard—and pointed it through the bars, waiting for the pot to line up. The sheriff positioned it a good yard away.

"Think you can hit that?"

"Yeah."

By alternately relaxing and clenching my muscles, I built up a good head of steam, so to speak, and sent the first volley right over the pot onto the floor around the sheriff's boots.

"Whoa, boy! Steady, there."

The stream settled, and, with a little aiming, I managed to hit the very center of the pot, to my immense satisfaction. The changing tone told me that it was nearly full.

"Looks like I got to go again myself," the sheriff said—an obvious excuse for getting his big dick out. It was almost fully hard, and would be difficult to piss through. Nevertheless, just as my stream started to wane, he managed a couple of creditable squirts. The pot was full to the very brim. Neither of us put our dicks away.

"Now, ain't that pretty," he said, stepping toward the bars. "I ain't never seen that before. A black one and a white one. And I do believe it's almost as big as mine."

He stepped up to the bars, took both weapons in his hand, and measured them, tip to tail. His was larger, for the moment, but mine was catching up. The heat of his cock, the softness of the skin, and the firmness of his grasp were priming me nicely. I held on to the bars and pushed my hips forward, letting him set the pace. I still didn't know if he was friend or foe, and feared that he might wish me harm after he'd had his fun. But this was the best opportunity I'd yet found for making my escape.

Soon we were matching inch for inch as he gently rubbed and stroked us both.

"Hmmm," he said. "Looks like we got ourselves an interesting situation here. What do you say, boys?" The two soldiers were watching, rubbing themselves through their trousers, uncertain of how to proceed. The old drunk at the end snored on regardless.

"What do you say to a little cockfight?" Brown addressed me this time.

"I'm game."

He let go of our pricks, which bounced and swayed

through the bars, both of them fully hard. Grabbing his by the base, he waved it in the air, striking at mine; when they made contact, they bounced off each other like rubber billy clubs, making a dull slapping sound. The two soldiers watched and laughed, occasionally passing comment on a particularly successful thrust. This continued for a while, but I was getting sore from hitting the iron bars as often as hitting his cock.

"We could have a lot more fun if you was to open the door," I said.

"Yeah," the sheriff said, "I reckon we could. But then you might just run away, and leave me and the boys all by our lonesomes."

"Now why would I do a thing like that, when there's a big old dick just waiting for me to take care of it?"

"Because you know and I know that you want to get your ass as far from this jailhouse as possible before the railroad men arrive."

"Can you blame me?"

"Nope. But I can't let you go, neither. So what we going to do, boys?"

"Hey, come on, sheriff," the fitter, cockier of the two said, "why don't you get in there with him?"

"Aww, you want to watch the show?" the sheriff said, fetching his keys off the hook by the door. As he walked, his dick swung, hard and heavy, a sticky drop hanging from the end of it. As he came back, he licked his lips. "Well, I'd hate to disappoint you. Now you just stand back, boy, while I let myself in." I half thought of running at him headfirst, winding him with a blow to the stomach and making a break for freedom—but the chances were too slim, and I had no desire to sabotage my potential advantage. So I leaned against the back wall, jerking myself to stay at maximum hardness. He removed the gun from his holster, placed it on the desk, and unlocked the door. Once he was in the cell, he locked the door behind him, attached the keys to his belt, and faced me.

"Boys, you could do something to help me out here," he said, addressing the soldiers on either side. "Take your clothes off and let me see you naked."

That was when I realized that my chances for escape were pretty good; any man so entirely addicted to sex as the sheriff was bound to make mistakes. The soldiers complied, and stood barefoot and bare-ass on the filthy floor. They were both semihard, perhaps out of curiosity as much as anything.

"So, you going to suck me, Aaron Johnson?"

I had every intention of doing so, and in answer I dropped to my knees and opened my mouth. The sheriff walked toward me with that bandy-legged loping stride characteristic of men who spend a long time on horseback. His dick brushed my lips, and I met it with my tongue. He inhaled sharply, and put his hands on his hips. I ran my tongue around the head of his cock, tasting it, caressing it, determined to convert Jed Brown from a stern, play-by-the-book law enforcement officer to a drooling halfwit who would sell his own mother for a moment of pleasure. I don't suppose he went too short of sex in his job—there were always men behind those bars, and it's well known that captivity makes queers of us all—but I was planning on taking him places he'd never dreamed of going. I opened my mouth, engulfed his cock, and slid my lips right down to the thick, warm bush. Looking up, I could see that his eyes were closed, his head thrown back, exposing his hairy throat. He was mine.

After sucking on his cock for a while, I stuck a hand inside his pants and fished out his balls. They hung heavy, suspended from his cock by thick cords, the wrinkled sack covered in hair. I weighed them in my hand for a while, then went to work on them with my tongue, licking all around and then, one by one, popping his nuts into my mouth. I don't think anyone had ever done this to Jed Brown before, as he announced, in a startled voice, "Jesus! My balls!"

My neighbors, naked and filthy, were humping the bars like dogs in heat, sticking their cocks through. Now, it pains me to see a hard cock unattended, but I was more interested in focusing my efforts on the sheriff, rather than jerking off a couple of horny deserters. Fortunately for those boys, though, Jed Brown was a greedy son of a bitch, and I decided that this was a game that any number could play.

"Let's see how that pretty face looks with a big black prick sticking into it," he said to the soldier on my right. "Come on, Johnson. Feed him."

I stood up and walked over to the bars, where the young soldier was pressing himself. His body was pale and almost hairless. I took hold of his cock, which was fully hard, and pulled him downward. He knelt, looking up at me with a mixture of fear and longing in his eyes. He knew what was required of him, and his mouth fell open. His lips were red and wet, and his tongue, which trembled over his lower teeth, inviting.

"Fuck his mouth, Johnson," Jed Brown said, leaning against the back wall. "I want to see how much of a stud you are." He watched, idly playing with his cock, as I fed my dick through the bars. It wasn't the best head I've had, but he was nice looking, and horny, and the entire ridiculous situation was stimulating in the extreme.

"Yeah, that looks good, don't it?" Brown said to the other prisoner.

"Sure."

"You like to get your dick sucked, soldier?"

"I guess."

"You let those whores down in Allentown suck your dick?"

"No, sir."

"How about your sweetheart back home? She do it for you, boy?"

"No sir, we never did much more than kissing."

"God damn, boy, ain't you never had your dick sucked?"

"No, sir."

"We got ourselves a little virgin here, Johnson," Brown said. "Don't that seem a shame? He's going to spend the rest of his life locked up for deserting, and then he'll get his dumb ass shot, and he ain't never had a friendly pair of lips around that pretty dick of his."

He was working himself up to something, that much was obvious.

"Yeah," I said, too wrapped up in my own business to pay much attention, "it's a shame." My boy was learning fast, and was starting to suck on my dick as if he really meant it, moving his lips up and down in rhythm with the gentle thrusting of my hips against the bars. He was a natural, and I wondered if his ass was as quick to learn as his mouth. I caressed his head through the bars, feeling the cuts and bumps of his recent fighting. I was almost ready to come.

From the other side of the cell, I heard a jangle and a sigh, and looked around to see Jed Brown on his knees swallowing the soldier's hard cock. The boy looked stunned, as most men are when they first feel a hot, wet mouth on their shaft; I remember it well myself. Brown was working on him like a starving man who has just been served a steak. The keys, hanging from a loop on his belt, were banging between his boots and the floor.

A plan began to form in my mind.

I pulled my prick from my soldier's mouth and motioned him to his feet. To my delight, he was still hard, and the veins were standing out on his cock as if he was about to come. I slipped a hand through the bars and around the back of his neck, pulling his face toward me. First of all I kissed him—I couldn't resist tasting my own juice on that sweet tongue of his—and then whispered, as low as I could,

"Keep quiet. We're getting out of here."

I moved over to where the sheriff was greedily feeding through the bars, and stuck my wet cock right in his face. His beard grazed me as he turned his head to start licking; I could tell that he was completely cock-crazed, and would be easy to defeat. With my hands in his dark-gray hair, I maneuvered his head so that I could fuck his mouth hard—but, crucially, I also positioned him with the back of his head against the bars. I fixed the soldier, who had so recently had his cock where mine was now, with a penetrating stare. He was no fool, and he realized at once that I had a plan.

Brown was sucking happily on my dick, and I kept moaning obscenities to keep him happy. "Suck that fat black cock, yeah"—that sort of thing. In truth, I was close to shooting; he was a very good cocksucker.

The soldier silently, stealthily picked up his pants from his cell floor and withdrew the belt. Thank God—he had read my mind, and realized that we must take advantage of Brown while we had a chance. Then he knelt behind the sheriff and started playing with his cock through the bars. He may have been a virgin, that boy, but he had a good understanding of the masculine mind. As long as Brown was happy, he wasn't going to be thinking too hard.

With his other hand, the soldier passed one end of the belt through the bars to me; I held it just out of sight by my thigh. Saliva was running down the sheriff's chin, and his hips were bucking; he was close to the edge. He started sucking me with so much vigor that I knew that I too must come soon. Would I be able to keep my head while he gave me his?

"Work that cock," I said, both to Brown and to the soldier, who was looking up at me for guidance. "Make him come."

Brown was moaning now in a deep bass voice; I could actually feel the vibration of his vocal chords on my dickhead.

The soldier kept jerking him, and suddenly the sheriff was coming, great white jets of spunk shooting from his prick. Now was the time to act.

I slipped the belt around his neck and passed the end back to the soldier, who now had a loose loop around the sheriff's neck. Just as I began to shoot my own load into Brown's mouth, I shouted "Pull! Now!"

The soldier did as he was asked, and Brown's neck jerked back against the bars. My dick slipped out of his mouth, and I shot my load all over his face. His hands grasped the belt, scrabbling for a hold, and his legs kicked out violently in front of him—but the boy was strong, and he kept pulling. Brown's cock was still hard, still dribbling spunk.

I sat down hard on his legs and grappled with his arms. He was strong as an ox and could easily have beaten me in a fair fight—but the belt around his neck was starting to sap his strength. Pinning both his wrists with one hand, I slipped the keys off his belt and sprang to my feet.

He was still kicking, weaker now, as I fed the key through the bars and unlocked my cell, letting myself out and, of course, locking the door behind me. I quickly released the other boy, who took the keys from me. I picked up Brown's gun, which he'd left on his desk; it would have been far too dangerous for him to take it into a cell with a desperate prisoner.

"Let him go now."

The soldier released the belt from Brown's neck, and the sheriff rolled onto his side, gasping for breath, my sperm rolling down his cheeks.

"Sorry to leave you here like this, Jed Brown," I said, releasing the second soldier, "but me and the boys have a pressing engagement with liberty. Now you just keep quiet."

I kept the gun trained on him while the soldiers dressed; I had no wish for him to raise the alarm. Eventually, Brown raised himself on one hand.

"You win, Johnson. This time. I'll be looking for you."

"I bet you will. You want another taste of this." I squeezed my package.

"Goddam nigger cocksucker..."

"Where are your manners, sir?"

"I'll fucking get you, black bastard."

I couldn't resist it; I picked up the brass pot, brimming over with four men's piss and a good deal of Old Zach's tobacco juice, and hurled it against the bars. It emptied itself all over the recumbent sheriff.

"Explain that when they let you out, lawman."

As we left the prison, I took one last look at the soaking, stinking, cursing sheriff as he wiped the piss from his eyes and his dripping beard.

The old drunk in the next cell had slept through the whole thing.

VII

THE TWO YOUNG DESERTERS AND I SLIPPED OUT OF Allentown by moonlight, unchallenged, and headed straight for the woods. After a week of sleeping out, three in a hut or a cave or under the stars, I had those two soldiers trained up to my liking. The younger of the two, whose name was Billy, soon became an accomplished cocksucker, and would happily have spent 24 hours a day with one or both of our dicks down his throat. And after a cautious start, and with plenty of goose fat which we got from an obliging farmer's wife, he learned how to take it up his ass as well. His older comrade, a brown-haired, athletic lad named Charlie, talked a lot about girls and pussy, and couldn't wait to get to a big town where he could "try all this out with a woman," but for the time being he was more than happy with what Billy would do for him. I loved to watch the two of them fucking, or to share Billy, flipping him this way and that as Charlie and I abused him in either end.

How far I had fallen from my own high standards! Now I was a runaway, a vagabond, heedless of danger, contemptuous of safety, an animal who fed when he was hungry and fucked when he was horny. You would not recognize me as the old, high-minded Aaron Johnson, Jack.

After a few days, I thought the time had come to teach Charlie that real men could take it as well as give it, as he was becoming a little too cocksure and confident that Billy would take care of him without him having to do anything. So I set about leading by example. We were washing in a stream one morning, high up in the hills above a small town; nobody could come up the path from the town without our seeing them. In those rare moments of security, we always took the opportunity to wash our clothes and bedding, clean our weapons (I had my hunting knife and Sherriff Brown's gun), and take care of our own hygiene. Inevitably, our nakedness, the fresh air, and the cool water soon had us all stiff, and as Charlie and I lay back on the grassy bank of the stream, Billy moved his mouth from one stiff prick to the other.

I put my arm around Charlie's broad, tanned shoulders, as Billy sucked away down below.

"It's good for friends to share moments like this," I said.

"Yeah," he said, relaxing his body into mine, "it sure is."

"Look at Billy working away on that big cock of yours."

"Mmmm..."

"Looks like he's enjoying himself."

"Yeah. Suck it, Billy."

"I wouldn't mind a taste myself."

"You? But you—"

"Sure, why not?" I said, as Billy moved from Charlie to me. "Tastes good, don't it, Billy?"

"Yeah, tastes good." Then he went down on me.

"Maybe I'll find out for myself." I ran a hand down Charlie's flat, firm stomach, where the wet hair stuck to his skin, and started rubbing the base of his groin.

117

"But you ain't a cocksucker, Aaron," he said.

"What makes you say that? You saw me suck that lawman's dick."

"Yeah, but that was just so's we could get out of jail."

"True, true..." I took hold of his cock and started playing with it. "But maybe I liked it too."

"Oh yeah? You want to suck me, is that it?"

"Sure."

"Well, be my guest."

I leaned over—and Billy, to his credit, never let my dick slip from his mouth—and started kissing the end of Charlie's prick. "Mmmm, that's sweet," I said, tasting his nectar. "I'm going to eat you." I opened my mouth and swallowed him to the hilt, holding him at the back of my throat until I needed to break for breath. Then I moved my lips up to the crown and down, up and down, establishing the familiar rhythm that would soon, I knew, have the boy squirming and shooting his load down my throat. But not yet. I had other plans for Charlie.

I moved from his cock to his balls, tasting them, feeling them tighten, and then started working my way down. The firm, hairy passage between his balls and his ass tasted just as good as his cock, sweet and clean from the stream, and he relaxed as I licked and kissed it, spreading his legs as wide as he could. I moved around for better access, obliging Billy (to my regret) to relinquish my cock; he sat, fingering his own hole, and watched.

I think Charlie knew what was coming, but that couldn't prepare him for the first touch of my tongue on his asshole. His body twitched, and he clenched his buttocks.

"What are you doing, man?"

"Eating your ass."

"I know...but I mean, what do you think... I'm not..."

"How does it feel?"

"I don't know. It feels weird."

"In a good way or a bad way?"

"Just weird."

That was as near as he would come to giving me permission to continue, so I gently pried his buttocks apart and went back to work on his hole, gently licking it, kneading the muscular globes of flesh on either side. As he relaxed and his breathing became heavier, I pushed more insistently with my tongue, letting him feel just how much pleasure he could get from a part of his body that, hitherto, had only been used for its most mundane function. It was working; his dick, when I squeezed it, felt like rock under the silky skin.

Charlie's legs relaxed and floated skyward, as I burrowed my tongue further into his hole until the tip was actually inside him. This was new territory for the young soldier—and he was ready to explore.

"You like that?"

"I don't know," Charlie said, in a voice which clearly meant "yes."

"Your cock seems to like it."

He looked down to where his dick was oozing a puddle of precum onto his hairy belly. "Yeah, it does. Ain't that something?"

"That's a fine big cock you've got there, Charlie." I figured that a little flattery would allow his masculine ego to make the great sacrifice I was about to demand.

He made his cock jump, and laughed. "Seems to be getting bigger," he said.

"No wonder Billy likes it up his ass so much. Look at the way he's playing with his hole now." Billy had two fingers up his crack, contorting his torso to fuck himself as hard as he could. Poor kid; I've have to take care of him soon.

"He's fucking crazy," Charlie said.

"He doesn't look crazy to me," I said, rubbing my fingers around Charlie's wet asshole. "Looks like he's enjoying himself."

"Yeah, well…"

"Does it feel good, Billy?"

"Yeah."

"You like a cock up there, don't you, Bill?"

"You bet."

I was pushing into Charlie's hole harder now, and his ass lips were opening up to my fingers a little.

"Wouldn't you like to feel what it's like, Charlie?"

"I don't know…"

I slipped one finger inside him; his ass ring bit down on it.

"Hey! What the fuck do you think you're— Ohhhh…"

The connection had been made—that first moment when a young man realizes that his ass is a source of pleasure almost as great as his cock. By the time I'd finished with him, I wanted Charlie to regret the wasted years.

"I'm going to fuck you, Charlie-boy."

"No," he moaned, moving his ass around my invading finger.

"And you're going to fucking love it."

"Oh God…"

Picking up his heavy prick, I gently masturbated him while pushing further into his hole, feeling the soft, yielding walls beyond the tight, elastic ring of muscle. Then I found what I was after, the firm bump of his prostate gland, and I gently pressed. Charlie's eyes shot wide open, and every muscle in his body tensed.

"What the fuck!"

"See? You're going to feel so good, Charlie."

"I don't know… Don't you hurt me."

I went back to eating his ass, and this time he was on fire. He pushed into my face, and I was merciless, digging my tongue in as far as I could, eating him like a ripe peach. When I guessed he was ready—and it didn't take long—I hitched his ankles over my shoulders and lined up with the target.

"Okay, man. You better fuck me and get it over with."

He was so businesslike and serious-looking, with an expression of such concentration on his face, that I had to kiss him. Just as he was about to complain, I breached his ring with my cockhead. His groan of pain was muffled inside our joined mouths.

I love breaking in a new colt for riding, and I know how to take my time. Charlie was resistant at first, but determined to prove that he could take it; all I had to do was wait for the pain to turn to pleasure. His cock had softened slightly, so I caressed it back to full stiffness. That done, he was ready to be fucked.

I started gently, getting him used to the idea, and once his pelvic thrusts were meeting mine I picked up my pace. Charlie was a strong young man, and his taut body was more than a match for my weight bearing down on him. We fucked like crazy, and with each stroke I felt him opening to me. I could tell from his noisy appreciation that each stroke was revealing a new world of sensation of which he'd never dreamed.

I wanted Charlie to come while I was still fucking him, so I took him by the wrist and placed his hand on his cock. He got the message, just as surely as he did back in the jail cell, and started pumping himself. It didn't take long before he was coming, and, as I gave him a few more sledgehammer strokes, he shot a load that went way over his head and onto the grass behind him. The last shots covered his neck, chest, and belly.

I slowed the pace of my fucking, but did not stop entirely; he had to be completely, utterly possessed, and I wanted him to feel the exquisite torture as his hypersensitive ass received its final pummeling. He groaned and wrapped his legs around my back, pulling me into him. My job was done.

I pulled out, tugged on myself three, four times, and then, taking careful aim, added my load to his before collapsing on top of him.

Our breathing slowed gradually, and we might have fallen asleep, but for Billy.

"Hey, what about me?"

Charlie and I bounded to our feet and leaped on him. Charlie, with a new understanding of these things, stuck two rigid fingers up Billy's ass and, to my delight, started sucking his cock. I squatted over Billy's face, allowing him to suck my balls and my limp prick, and within a few moments he was adding his own contribution to the mess on Charlie's upper body.

Charlie and Billy proved to be better, and more loyal, companions of the road than any I had previously encountered. But the road was becoming a dangerous place, and the further south we traveled the greater our need to find a safe haven. We were heading toward Richmond, Virginia, the Rebel capital—an odd choice of destination, perhaps, but a city which I know well, and which has become the refuge for all the flotsam and jetsam of the current hostilities. Nobody would come looking for a couple of Union deserters down there, and if my instincts were correct, there would be plenty of opportunities for a man without too many scruples to make a decent living for himself. Besides which, it would put me in a good position to survey the financial chicanery of my so-called family, and to extract from them the money that is mine by rights.

As we got closer to Richmond, the roads got busier, and by the time we were within 50 miles of the city they were positively crowded. And so we were able to travel by day, more or less unmolested among the flood of displaced persons fleeing the advancing Union regiments. I was not the only one to have decided, rightly or wrongly, that the eye of the storm is the safest place to be. Whole families were moving from the rural areas to the relative safety of the city: farm laborers, deserters, old men, children, and even a few of my black brothers and sisters, all were on the move. In this great wave of humanity, one can travel the roads unchallenged; there is safety in numbers. Perhaps the Union troops were unwilling to attack parties of civilians, although we heard horror stories from upstate about surprise attacks, kidnap, murder, and rape.

We concentrated on attracting as little attention as possible, although Charlie was unable to resist attaching himself to a family with three fine young daughters. The parents, and certainly the girls, were delighted to have secured such a strong-shouldered young protector, and they believed Charlie's claim that he was a student returning from the Northeast to his home in the South. He embroidered (unnecessarily, I think) by telling them that Billy was his brother, and that I was their "hired man." This caused us some laughter when we left the road for a while to bathe, and I forced myself into Charlie's lying mouth. He sucked and swallowed with enthusiasm, but I am afraid he is only a "companion of the road," increasingly keen to practice his newfound skills on a young person more to his natural taste. Billy, on the other hand, will travel on the same road as me—and, perhaps, further than me—for the rest of his life.

The routes into Richmond appeared to be open and undefended, despite the fact that, not so very long ago, there were Union troops besieging the city. We gained the city center unchallenged, and set about finding lodgings and food.

Our first shelter was a single room at the back of a bar, where Charlie had ingratiated himself with the owner, a typical Virginian whose only interest, it seemed, was how to extract as much money from his customers as possible. Charlie was more than a match for him, with his easy charm and talent for lies, and persuaded him that he was a man of property with a case full of cash with which he was more than ready to part. It was a good thing we had dressed ourselves in stolen clothes before hitting town; if the landlord had seen us, dirty and travel-weary, just a few hours ago, he would never have served us a drink, let alone rented us his precious, massively overpriced accommodation. Eyebrows were raised when I walked into the bar, but I busied myself with our scant "luggage" and tried to look convincingly servile. "The boy can take your bags in now," the landlord said, as Charlie, acting high-rolling as if to the manner born, downed shots of rye with his new drinking buddies. He waved his permission to me, and I picked up our few possessions, nearly all of them stolen along the way. He would pay for his arrogance later, I swore, with a particularly brutal fucking.

Billy, meanwhile, was out in town scouting for likely employment. His first port of call was the theater, or the Richmond Alhambra, as it was rather grandly known, where he inquired of the proprietor if there were any openings for stage hands, cleaners, and the like. A protracted interview followed, in which Billy's oral and anal skills were put to the test, and he left with jobs for all three of us, and a warning—more of a threat—from the manager that if his wife heard a word of this Billy and his friends would be leaving town without their balls.

"Dirty old bastard," Billy said, as we lay down to rest at night. "He was just as interested in cock as I am, just doesn't have the guts to admit it. Oh well, he's a good fuck, and he'll lodge us and pay us as well, especially when he gets a look at these two beauties." He stopped talking and set to licking the hard pricks—mine and Charlie's—that he held in his greedy hands.

The Alhambra is situated in one of Richmond's less respectable neighborhoods, a network of three or four streets where every other house is a bar, or a brothel, or divided into lodgings for the most transient of visitors. There were whores in great numbers clustering around the doorways and porches of the most successful houses, which rejoice in such poetic names as Les Champs Elysées and the Chinese Palace. They whistled and called out as we walked down the street this morning, and I could see Charlie preening like a peacock, although his strut was somewhat impeded by a sore ass. He complained, when we woke this morning, that I had used him too roughly—but his performance last night belied his rueful morning mood. He rode my prick like a man in a frenzy, calling out the most obscene endearments, and even took Billy's cock in his mouth at the same time. He remained rock hard throughout his punishment, and shot one of the biggest loads I have ever seen. A sore ass, and a sore disposition, often follow when a young man goes further into the realms of male sex than he had intended. Charlie feels himself in danger of going completely queer, and is desperate to find a female balance. Well, he won't have far to look—if he can afford it.

Mr. Harold Chester, or "Captain" Chester, as he likes to call himself (I don't believe he's any more of a captain than I am, despite his pseudomilitary uniform), is an impressive man of about 45 with the finest moustache I have ever seen, a luxuriant nut-brown thing that curls over his mouth, sweeps down in two elegant curves, and sits perkily up at the ends, thanks no doubt to a good deal of daily tending. He is a handsome, shifty-looking fellow, deeply tanned, his hair a little too brown to look natural, tall, and strongly built. It does not surprise me that Billy was down on his knees within five minutes of being in the Captain's office; he's just the sort of father figure that appeals to boys like Billy.

Captain Chester introduced himself to us at the stage door, gave us all warm handshakes, and took us straight to the dressing rooms. As it was only ten in the morning, they were empty—but the odor of sweat, tobacco smoke, powder, and alcohol lingered from the night before. Costumes and underwear hung from rails and over the backs of chairs—and, from the gaudy, scanty nature of those garments, I had little doubt that Captain Chester's theater was not dedicated to the serious dramatic arts. Charlie's eyes were out on stalks—the scent was having an aphrodisiac effect on the poor, pussy-starved boy—and even Billy was examining the gowns with an appreciative eye, although perhaps for somewhat different reasons.

"Now, which one of you boys is the best at cleaning up?" asked the Captain, winking at Billy, who smirked winningly. "You reckon you can get this place cleaned up and fit for human habitation before the girls come in after lunch?"

"Where do you keep your broom?" Billy asked, already rolling up his sleeves.

"Now, young man," Chester said, turning to Charlie, "you look like a presentable young fellow."

Charlie puffed out his chest like a good soldier; he seemed to have forgotten that he's actually a deserter. "Yes, sir!"

"But can you be trusted, that's the question?"

"Yes sir, I can be trusted."

"With money?"

"Sure."

Now, I would sooner entrust my money to a habitual thief than hand it over to a pussy-chaser like Charlie, but I kept my own counsel.

"Well, it just so happens that I have a vacancy in the box office, after my last employee...found an alternative position," the Captain said, ruefully rubbing his chin. (I suspect some young fellow made off with the week's takings.) "But you'll have to fill in all the paperwork, hand me the takings when we close up each night, and it had better all be there, every damn penny of it, or I will—" He coughed, composed himself. "You think you can handle that?"

"Yes, sir," Charlie answered. "I learned bookkeeping back home in...er...Pittsburgh." Charlie could always think of a plausible lie. I knew right away that I'd be helping him cook the books before the night was out.

126

"And that leaves you, my fine friend," the Captain said, walking around me, measuring me up like a piece of live-stock. "Does he speak?"

"Sure he speaks," Billy said, already rolling up stockings and hanging discarded dresses.

"What's your name, sir?"

"My name," I said, "is Aaron Johnson."

"Whoa! That's a fine voice! You ain't from around here, I guess."

"On the contrary, I grew up not twenty miles from here."

"Well, here's my advice, Aaron Johnson," the Captain said, laying a hand on my shoulder. "Keep your mouth shut and your eyes open. People around here like to think they know what's what. An educated Negro, that's something they just won't understand. What they want is this." He squeezed my shoulder and ran his hand down my arm. "A bit of muscle. Think you can provide that, Aaron Johnson?"

"Sure, if that's what's needed."

"I need someone to exercise a little control over the drunken bums that spend their money in my theater," he said. "Someone who inspires, shall we say, respect."

"A doorman?"

"That's the idea. I guess you can handle yourself."

Charlie and Billy both spluttered, trying to suppress laughter.

"I guess I can."

"Good, then you're hired, all three of you. Got myself a cleaner, a desk clerk, and a doorman. That's the best bargain I done all week."

"And the pay?" I asked.

"You get your lodging and one meal a day, and I'll give you...let me see...a couple of bucks a week. That's enough to get drunk on."

"Hey, that's—"

I interrupted Charlie, "That's just fine, Captain Chester."

"Good," he said, shaking my hand—having realized, I suspect, that I was the ringleader of our ill-matched gang. "We have a deal. And Billy? When you've finished in here, come to my office. I got a few jobs that need attending to back there."

And so we find ourselves employed in the world of entertainment—which, to my astonishment, not only survives but thrives in Richmond. Never has the appetite for distraction been greater, according to Captain Chester, who walked me around the premises and shared a smoke with me on the theater roof, which commands a good view of the city. It was late yesterday afternoon, and the Alhambra was about to open its doors for business.

"Each and every one of them has a secret," Chester said, waving a large hand across the horizon, a trail of fragrant smoke in its wake. "The highfalutin folk in the big houses, the clerks and the scribes and the honest shopkeepers, the soldiers and the sheriff, the drifters and bums in the streets. They have their public face, and their private face. And who's to say who's the good guys and who's the bad guys?"

I was surprised to find the Captain in such a philosophical frame of mind, especially with me—the hired muscle—and I wondered what he was leading up to. I suspected that Billy had said something to him while attending to those various "jobs" in the Captain's office earlier in the day.

"I've learned one thing on my travels," I said, to break the silence as much as anything, "and that's to trust no man but myself, to take my pleasure where I find it, and to endure injustice with as much fortitude as I can muster."

"That sounds mighty fine, Mister Johnson," the Captain said, leaning over the low wall that capped the Alhambra's facade, "and a good philosophy of life in this uncertain world of ours. Young Billy told me you were a wise man."

"Did he, indeed?"

"Good lad, young Billy."

"Very good."

"Obliging."

"Extremely."

The Captain stared out over the town, and silence fell again.

"Pleasure..." he eventually said, after smoking another half-inch of his cigar.

"Ah, yes."

"The quest for pleasure leads us to interesting places."

I began to hope that the abstract conversation would soon resolve itself into something more positively carnal, but I supposed that Captain Chester, like many married men, took his time to work around to what he really wanted.

"It leads a paying public into your theater," I said.

"It sure does, and they pay well, as you'll find out."

"I hope so. And shouldn't I be down there on the door?"

"Not yet, Johnson. The fun never starts much before ten. That's when I'll be needing your strong arm."

"And what should I do with the rest of my time?"

"Man like you, never short of opportunities."

"That's as may be."

The Captain turned his back to the town, and faced me, leaning against the rampart. Surely he didn't expect me to get down on my knees for him?

"Thing is, Johnson," he said, "that young Billy's given me a few ideas."

"Oh yeah? Showed you a trick or two, has he?"

"He certainly has. I mean, he done things that no woman ever— Well, I expect you know what I mean."

"You mean he sucked your cock?"

The Captain looked around—which made me smile, as we could not possibly be overheard, or indeed overlooked, ours being much the tallest building in the neighborhood.

"He sure did. And not just, like, mumbling on it, like some of those lads. I mean, he really seemed to—"

"Enjoy it?"

"Yeah."

"He's a fine cocksucker, my Billy."

"You mean he's—"

"Sucked me? Many times. And I've fucked his ass too. Which he loves."

"I bet he does, the little—"

"Don't worry, Captain," I said. "You're not stealing anything that's mine. Billy's a greedy boy. He'll eat you and he'll eat me and he'll still want more."

"Never knew a man could be so...hungry for it."

"Perhaps you've never tasted it yourself."

"Well..."

"It's good," I said.

"Really?"

I had finally figured out where this was leading, and I knew that within a minute the Captain would be down on his knees tasting his first (or he'd say it was his first) cock. Perhaps just his first of the day.

"Oh yeah, man. You ain't lived till you've sucked a big, hard, juicy dick."

"Mmm-hmm..."

"Tasted it in your mouth, and felt it shooting off in your throat."

"Is that so?"

"Say," I said, as if the idea had only just occurred to me, "you can taste mine if you like. Nobody would know."

"Well..."

"And besides, who's going to believe me if I say that Captain Chester is a cocksucker?"

"Good point."

I went and stood beside him, shoulder to shoulder, and took the cigar from his hand, stamping it out on the gravelly rooftop. He stood motionless, waiting for a clear lead from me—so I unbuttoned my pants and hauled out my cock, which was already half hard from our talk.

"It's so big," he said, under his breath.

"You can take it. Go ahead."

He squatted at my feet, unwilling, I suppose, to sully his trousers on the dusty theater roof—and his thigh muscles bulged impressively in the thin dark cloth. He took my prick in a firm grasp, feeling its girth and length, and moved his mouth toward it. I leaned back, my elbows on the wall, and pushed my hips forward.

The first thing I felt was the Captain's splendid brown moustache tickling my cockhead. I looked down and saw a drop of sticky juice smeared across his whiskers. He winked, opened wide, and went down.

For all his acting, this was not the Captain's first blow job—either that, or he was a natural. For the next 20 minutes, he fed on my cock, now fast, now slow, now sucking, now licking, now running his hands all over it. Finally he kept up a steady assault with his hands, and I hit the top. I had just time to warn him that I was about to come—and he opened his mouth and engulfed me. I shot a big load into the back of his throat.

Afterward, he wiped his moustache with a clean white handkerchief, brushed down his trousers, and fished a couple of bills out of his wallet.

"Now, that's money well earned," he said. "But don't expect more where that came from. I'd be ruined within a month."

"Hey, Captain," I said, stuffing my half-hard cock back into my pants, "you can have it for free anytime you want."

"You ain't never going to get rich that way, Johnson. And there's money in that dick. Lots of money."

And so I settle down to my new life in Richmond, a whore by day, servicing the gentlefolk of Richmond, or any who can afford it. By night I keep the riffraff out of the Alhambra, and accept drinks and dates from those who are interested in buying a little of my time.

As I hit my straw mattress at six o'clock this morning, I realized that I had found just the right hiding place in which to wait out the war. And, as I drifted off to sleep, I found myself thinking of you, Jack, far away in Vermont, in a world that now seems impossibly remote, a fond, foolish dream. And so I picked up pen and paper and wrote you this letter that will never be posted. The old Aaron, as you see, is dead and gone. In his place is a creature of the war. How could I ever have thought that a man like me, for all my education and refined tastes, my politics, my belief in justice, my hopes for a better world, could make his way and lead a life that was both just and honorable? Goodbye, dream. Goodbye Jack, God bless you. And good night.

Your friend,
Aaron

PART THREE:

North and South

VIII

BENNETT YOUNG'S CAMP WAS CALLED HARMONY, AND FOR the first few weeks it seemed an apt name. It was positioned in a broad river valley south of Montreal, about five miles from the nearest town, with fresh water running nearby; well-drained soil that not only supported the huts and tents we slept in, but also sustained some small crops of fruit and vegetables, provided grass for the horses, and space for a few chickens and goats. It was sheltered from the wind, sunny in the mornings, and cool in the evenings. Nobody could approach it without being seen—there was a constant lookout at the head of the valley to warn of visitors—in short, it was the perfect location for a band of brothers to live out a modern version of Eden.

Young's merry band consisted of some 20 men, sometimes more, from all parts of the country. Some were Southerners, with broad, drawling accents and pleasure-loving temperaments. Others were from my part of the country, although none was from my class. They seemed, like Young, to be associated with the army, for they all sported some version of a uniform, and the camp was run along military lines. A bugle sounded at 6 A.M., although the tunes it played had more to do with the popular stage than with West Point. Before breakfast, there was drill on the "parade ground," as Young rather fancifully called the area of flattened earth beyond the encampment. There was a quartermaster, a big jovial New Yorker called Hutchinson who somehow dished out excellent, plentiful meals three times a day. There was beef, pork, and chicken, fine fresh eggs, milk and butter, coffee, tea, and sugar; it never occurred to me to wonder how a bunch of "special" soldiers managed to acquire such good rations when their brothers in arms in both Union and Confederate camps were, the newspapers said, starving on bread and water. Meals were eaten around the campfire in the evenings, as we told stories and sang songs and passed the bottle until everyone was tired and fuzzy and ready for bed.

We slept three or four to a hut, or two to a tent, depending on our billet. Young kept me to himself in the largest of the log cabins at first, letting it be known that I was his and his alone, and I was not displeased with the arrangement, as he was an untiring lover whose appetite for carnal indulgence matched mine. I quickly realized that not only did the men accept their leader's predilections, they also shared them. Special friendships came and went, some endured. There was one pair, Caleb Wallace and George Scott, big hulking bears both of them, who were, Young informed me, like an "old married couple," having joined their fortunes back in the '50s and remained together, through thick and thin, ever since. I wondered just how "married" they really were, when I saw Caleb staring at me through the campfire flames one night, licking his lips—and more than once I saw younger members of the gang accompanying them to their hut at the close of the day. I dreamed of taking those two huge grizzlies up my ass—one day. For the time being, it was kept very busy with Young's tongue, fingers, and dick.

There was something to suit every taste at Harmony—and, seeing as my tastes seemed to run to just about every type, so long as it was masculine and not entirely hideous, I was delighted by the spectrum of shapes and shades offered there. Alamanda Bruce was a handsome brown-skinned man, tall and lithe with the kind of muscles that you could count individually through his skin, his right ear pierced with a gold hoop. Thomas Collins, on the other hand, was a stocky little Irishman with thick red hair and freckles on his hands. Jim Doty and Samuel Gregg were the two lanky blonds from Kentucky, friends from childhood, happiest when they were racing along the river, climbing trees or hunting for wild turkey like overgrown kids. Turner Teavis, or "Squire," as he was known, was the oldest of the group, a gray-haired man in his 40s who wouldn't have looked out of place behind a desk in a bank or a pulpit in a church.

Whatever the difference in their backgrounds, all shared one thing, an almost fanatical devotion to Bennett Young. They called him "Boss," they fetched and carried for him, and I am quite sure that they had all, in their various ways, satisfied his appetites. Young took their adoration as a matter of course, and spoke of them as a general might speak of his armies. He sent them off on missions, mostly, it seemed, concerned with the getting of food. He spent hours in conference with his trusted subordinates, planning "operations"—discussions to which I was not party. When he was not working, or fucking me, he would write in a large, leather-bound notebook which he kept closed with a padlock. "My memoirs," he said, whenever I questioned him about them. "You'll read them one day."

Details of "operations" were kept from me, and to tell the truth I was none too curious. I believed Young's vague stories about "special assignments" from some mysterious power that was controlling the conflict, and I asked no questions. I was happy in my new life, fucking all night, sleeping for most of the afternoon, waking only for meals and exercise. Occasionally I was sent into town to buy provisions from the store, or to conduct business at the bank, accompanied by Squire Teavis or Caleb and George, who would ride with me and wait, with the horses, just outside town, as a kind of guard. "You got the kind of face and voice that people in these parts trust," Squire Teavis said, when I asked why he didn't simply conduct the business himself. "They hear a Southern accent up here, they think the worst. We don't need to draw attention to ourselves."

Young himself never left the camp—or, if he did, it was at night, when I was sleeping. He certainly went nowhere near the town.

Our honeymoon lasted for a couple of months, before Young announced one night that he and a small group of men would be going on a reconnaissance mission down into Vermont. I would not be joining him, he said, despite my protests.

"I need you here, safe and sound, to wait for me," he said. "It might be dangerous where we're going."

My questions were all in vain, and the next morning Young departed with Thomas Collins and Alamanda Bruce, each equipped with a large leather satchel stuffed with food and clothing.

That night, there was a festival atmosphere around the campfire. The men, for all that they revered Lieutenant Young, obviously enjoyed his absences as well, and intended to abandon discipline and drill and give themselves over to drink. I was alone in the hut, daydreaming about my various adventures and dimly wondering what had become of Aaron, of Mick, of my family, when the door opened and a grizzly head stuck in.

"Hey, boy," Caleb Wallace said, grinning through his thick beard. "You in the mood for a party tonight?"

"Sure," I said. "What's the occasion?"

"You'll see."

I dozed off, wondering what Young was up to in Vermont, and dreamed of the happy sunlit summers of my childhood. My sisters were in my dream, but Young was there too, and, inexplicably, Aaron. The girls disappeared, and I was stranded out in the middle of a large expanse of water, watching Aaron and Young fighting on the far shore...

I was woken by the sound of shooting, and, assuming that the camp was under attack, I grabbed a gun (I had no idea how to use it) and peered cautiously out the window. Red firelight flickered around the camp, figures flitted between buildings—was this the end of Jack Edgerton? I tried to muster the courage to go out fighting, to make a good end protecting my comrades, but my hand froze on the door, and I felt sick. I sat down on the bed and swallowed the rising bile.

A banging on the door made me jump—literally, I stood up and leaped about six inches in the air.

"What you locked in there for? You takin' a shit?" It was Jim Doty's Kentucky drawl. Perhaps I was not about to die after all.

"Er...yes."

"Well, hurry up! We can't start without you."

Start what, I wondered, putting the gun back in its rack with a shaking hand.

"Oh," came Doty's voice again, "and be sure to wash yourself."

It seemed an odd injunction, especially as I was a good deal more finicky about personal hygiene than some of my fellows. I had bathed in the river earlier in the day, and I knew that I was, as my mother would have put it, "nice."

Straightening my sleep-rumpled clothes, and trying to still my nerves, I took a deep breath and opened the door. How fear alters our perceptions! Whereas before I had assumed that the firelight and flitting figures betokened some kind of attack, now it was quite clear that there was nothing more dangerous than a party in the offing. It was not a party as we knew them in Vermont; there were no ladies in muslin dresses, no cloths spread on the ground, no bottles of lemonade cooling in the stream. There was one big bonfire crackling away on the parade ground, and groups of men in twos and three with bottles. From the cookhouse, as we rather grandly called the tin and wood structure where Hutchinson prepared his culinary miracles, came the smell of bacon and potatoes.

Doty saw me descending the steps of the cabin, and whooped loudly. "Here he comes, boys, the guest of honor!" He was answered from around the camp by a series of yells and whistles, and soon I was escorted by some five or six men toward the bonfire.

"Hey, young feller," Caleb Wallace said, dressed only in pants and braces, his huge hairy barrel of a chest gleaming in the firelight, "come sit by me."

I did as I was bidden, and a bottle of beer was thrust into my hand. Caleb put his arm around me; it was heavy, and hairy, and warm.

"The Boss said we're to look after you while he's gone, so me and the boys thought we'd throw a little party in your honor."

George Scott, Caleb's equally hairy, equally ursine "husband," stood by the fire massaging his crotch. "We've waited for this for a long time," he said.

I had a pretty clear idea what "this" was, but I played dumb, uncertain whether the party was sanctioned by Young or not.

"Bennett said I was to wait for him," I said, my voice sounding squeaky compared to the booming tones of Scott and Wallace.

"Ain't fair, the Boss having you all to himself." This was

140

the voice of Squire Teavis, whose regular conservative appearance had been completely abandoned as he toweled himself down after a recent dip in the river. "We share everything in this company. Food, clothing, liquor."

"And pussy." Doty again, standing now with his arm around Sam Gregg, their unkempt blond hair mingling.

"Take a drink, Jack," Caleb said, pushing the bottle toward my mouth.

"Is there anything to eat?"

"Yeah, plenty," he chuckled. "You hungry?"

"He's always hungry," Scott said, still massaging the growing lump in his pants. "I've watched him and the Boss together."

This was news to me, although I was hardly surprised; when Young and I were together, the whole camp knew about it, so loud were we. The walls of Young's cabin were full of knotholes—perhaps made, or assisted, by the men.

By now the fire was encircled by all the men in the camp, at least 20 of them, most of them drunk and in a state of undress. I may be greedy, but this was more than even I thought I could take.

"Git up, Jack," Caleb said, taking the bottle from me. "We want to see you dance."

"Dance?" I could execute a reasonably proficient waltz, thanks to my upbringing in the salons of Bishopstown, but I didn't think that was what they had in mind.

"Yeah, like one of them Yankee whores in Boston and New York City," Gregg said, swigging from a bottle of whiskey.

Fortunately, I'd seen one or two such performances in the White Horse, where, occasionally, one of the local ladies would come in to entertain the more conventional-minded patrons. I knew the basic routine—bump, grind, wiggle, and pout—and thought I could pull off a reasonable imitation.

I jumped to my feet, my boldness returning, and grabbed

141

the bottle from Gregg. "I'd better have a little inspiration, then," I said, taking a long swig. The whiskey ran down my throat, set my stomach on fire, and burned away the last few inhibitions. I was ready to perform.

"What would you gentlemen like to see?" I asked, thinking I sounded very seductive but probably just slurring.

"Your ass!" chorused the reply.

I started to dance, clumsily at first, tripping over my feet, but gaining in confidence and giving my audience a few of the moves that I'd seen down at the White Horse—vastly improved, I thought. I ground my hips in a figure-eight pattern. I squatted down on my haunches, as if lowering myself onto a big juicy prick, I bent over until my nose was almost touching the ground and wiggled my behind. The men responded with obscene encouragement; one or two of them, including Scott, had hauled their dicks out and were openly masturbating. Doty and Gregg whipped harmonicas out of their pockets and gave us a selection of battle songs popular with both Johnny Reb and Billy Yank. Hands drummed on thighs, on logs.

A slow-hand clap and cries of "Get 'em off!" indicated that the audience was ready for some flesh, and I was more than ready to show it. The heat from the fire, the whiskey, and my own gyrations had got me sweating.

I started off with my necktie, which I removed with a great deal of business and, I thought, a certain amount of artistry. This was obviously not what the men wanted. Caleb stepped up beside me, started grinding his hips in time with mine, and then, grabbing the front of my shirt with both hands, ripped it clean off my body. His efforts were rewarded with the loudest whoop of the night. Doty and Gregg increased the pace of their playing, the clapping accelerated, and more items of clothing were deposited on the ground.

I realized that I had better get stripping if I didn't want

my entire wardrobe to be shredded, so I unbuckled my belt with the minimum of fuss and started lowering my pants. This is what they wanted to see; the hollering subsided, breaths were held, and the music hushed to an anticipatory hum. I turned and turned, inching down my waistband, until my ass was exposed to the burning eyes of the men and the heat of the fire.

This was the signal for all hell to let loose, and any ideas I had of enchanting them with my performance were quickly abandoned. Scott, who had been manipulating his huge club of a cock throughout, grabbed me by the hair and pushed me down to my knees. He slapped me rhythmically around the face with his hard member and then started rubbing it against my lips.

"Suck it!" roared the men. I had every intention of doing so, and opened my mouth. Scott wasted no time in getting inside me, thrusting to the back of my throat. My eyes opened wide in surprise, but fortunately the whiskey had relaxed me, and I didn't gag too much. He pulled out—the head glistened in the firelight—and then shoved it back in again.

There were hands at my backside; I looked around and saw Squire Teavis kneeling behind me, stark naked. There was little I could do, even if I wanted to; my ankles were still bound by my pants and boots. He spat in his hand and rubbed the saliva around my hole. If anyone had to be first, I wasn't too displeased that it would be him, with his handsome lined face and his steel-gray hair. His finger entered me, and I responded to the pressure by pushing my ass back against it.

A line was forming at both ends—about ten at my mouth, and ten at my ass. It was going to be a long night. Scott was fucking my mouth now with some vigor, and I could feel from the tightness in his balls that he wouldn't be long coming. Teavis pulled his finger out and replaced it with his cock, which glided up me and was soon buried to the hilt. It was not the first time I had been used in such a way, and I quickly fell into a rhythm and started to enjoy myself. Two men—I could not see who—busied themselves with my boots and, when they were off, removed one leg from my pants, so that I could spread my ass even wider. Teavis never broke his stride for a moment.

Scott grabbed the back of my head with both hands, vigorously fucked my throat four or five times (it was all I could do not to choke), and then pulled out and came copiously in my upturned face. I saw the first huge glob come flying out of his piss slit, then closed my eyes and felt his sperm raining down on my face like lava from a volcano. It dripped down my cheeks and chin and splattered on the ground. What was left he smeared around with his still hard cock.

He was replaced—pushed out of the way, in fact—by Doty, who still had his harmonica in his mouth as he presented his hard cock at my face. Scott had been thick, dark, and veiny; Doty, on the other hand, was long and thin and smooth. His pubic hair, which I could see in the vee of his open pants, was pale and sparse. He took his time, holding his prick back so that I could lick his balls, feeling my lips with his fingers, running the sticky head of his dick around my already wet face. It gave me a chance to catch my breath, for which I was grateful. Besides which, I was concentrating on tightening my ass around Teavis's dick, which was pumping in and out of me like crazy. I reached around and felt his balls; yes, he too was ready to drop a load.

I pressed back into him, clamped my ass ring around him, and let him thrust into me. At the same moment, Doty slid his slender cock into my mouth—and the sight of that must have sent Teavis over the edge, as he hollered and grunted and rammed himself as far into me as he could go. Doty breathed hard and started fucking my mouth; the harmonica, which he held between his lips, made a strange wheezing music of its own.

Two down, only another 18 to go.

It would be tedious to explain exactly how I serviced the entire camp, and to tell you the truth, after the first three or four had fucked me, I no longer knew nor cared who was up next. I had become a thing to be used, and I loved it.

This went on for an hour and a half, by which time my ass was sore and my jaw felt as if it was going to break. I had been turned over, stood up, sat down, held in the air, and pushed into the earth. My entire body was covered in semen—none of it my own, as I had scrupulously avoided touching my cock, knowing that if I allowed myself to come, as I desperately wanted to, the ride would be much less comfortable. My army of lovers knew this, I think, and made no attempt to bring me off.

Inevitably, no sooner had the last one shot his load than the first was ready to begin again, but this time around they would not be satisfied by the simple pleasures of sucking and fucking. They had all been drinking heavily by now, and needed stimulation of a different nature if they were to continue—as they clearly intended to. I needed a rest, and I wanted my supper, although the several loads of semen that I had swallowed had taken some of the edge off my hunger. But they had not finished with me yet.

"I need a piss," Scott said, staggering around with a whiskey bottle in his hand. He headed off toward the trees, but Caleb had other ideas.

"Don't waste it, man," he said. "The boy needs hosing down."

I did, it's true—by now I was far from "nice"—but bathing in piss wasn't my idea of hygiene. Still, Scott seemed to like the idea, and changed the course of his staggering. He stood over me, playing with his half-hard cock. I lay back on the ground, supporting myself with my elbows, waiting for the first splash. It took a while to come—but, after much vocal encouragement from his peers, he unleashed a torrent of urine on my stomach and chest. It splashed up to my neck and chin, it ran down my sides and puddled in the grooves of my stomach. He finished off by directing the jet straight at my cock, and the force of it nearly made me come. Only by closing my eyes and clearing my mind did I fend off the encroaching orgasm.

"Piss on his ass, boys!" Scott grunted as he padded off to the river. I was picked up by four pairs of hands and deposited in a kneeling position. A booted foot kicked my knees apart, and I fell forward so I was leaning on my forearms. My buttocks were held apart, and my poor hole, raw from use, was exposed to the evening air. I heard someone behind me spit on the ground, and then a stream of piss hit my right buttock. There was some protest from the men holding my ass open, and the pisser—I have no idea who it was—redirected his stream straight to the bull's-eye. The drumming sensation, the wetness and heat, were too much. I reached back, grabbed my cock, and started to come. I spewed my load over the soaking ground, and fell forward into it, not caring how dirty I got. The last few drops of piss were sprayed over my back.

Young and his companions returned three days later—three days in which I had been fucked repeatedly by every man in the camp—and I expected him to kick up a ruckus when he found out. Instead, as I spilled out my sorry story (I wasn't sorry a bit, I'd enjoyed every minute of it), trying to sound contrite and avert his wrath, he just laughed, winked, and tweaked my nipple through my shirt. "So, you been playing around with the boys, huh? Good. That's good."

I guessed the romance was over. I tried to question him on the subject, to get some notion of his feelings for me, whatever they were, but he was not interested in such discussions. "There's work to be done, Jack," he said. "Now you run along and see if any of my boys need sucking off. I need to write my journal." He tapped the thick leather binding of the mysterious book, which had accompanied him on his journey, and motioned me out of the hut. I found Alamanda Bruce and Thomas Collins finishing off their dinner at the back of the cookhouse, and without waiting to be invited I unbuttoned their flies and started sucking them alternately. They put their bowls aside, wiped their mouths, and simply let me get on with it. When they finished—dark-skinned Bruce came first, deep in my throat, while red-haired Collins preferred me to jerk him off over his pale hairy stomach—they ruffled my hair, said "Thanks, Jack," and disappeared about their business.

I was beginning to wonder if Young had picked me up merely to be a sucking-and-fucking machine for the men of Harmony, and I thought, on the whole, that while I had enjoyed a delightful few weeks, it was time to move on and make something of my life. Much more of that kind of usage and I was going to start fraying at the edges.

I was pacing the outskirts of the camp, kicking at clods of earth and whacking the grass with a stick, when I heard Young's voice calling my name. I jumped and ran—I may have resented him, but I still adored him, and I hoped that he was now ready to give me some of the loving I'd missed while he was on the road.

Young was putting the journal back in its usual hiding place under the bed when I bounded into the room. "Hi, Bennett," I said.

"Sit down, Jack." He patted the bed beside him. "You've got dried spunk around your mouth. Wipe it off." He handed me a clean handkerchief. Whatever he had in mind, I guessed it wasn't one of our usual enjoyments.

I sat, Young stood.

"Jack," he began, his hands clasped behind his back, "have you ever asked yourself why you're here?"

"Here in Harmony, or here on earth?"

"At the camp, with me. With us."

147

"I assumed," I said, casting my eyes to the floor, "that it was because you wanted me to be here."

"Yes, but what for?"

"I thought that was obvious."

I had the horrible feeling that I was about to be thrown out of the camp, and, more important, out of Young's affections. Was his desertion of me—for so I saw it—and his willingness to hand me over to the rest of the gang just a pretext for getting rid of a plaything of which he had tired?

"You're a great fuck, Jack, none better. I'd happily spend the rest of my life with my dick up your ass. But in case you hadn't noticed, there's a war going on."

This remark stung, as Young had done more than anyone to divert me from my intended path. And, while I had never planned to join the Union Army, I had left home with the intention of taking an honest job in Montpelier and being a respectable citizen. Instead, he had turned me into a cock-guzzling camp whore.

"And what have I to do with that? You tell me nothing about your work. You send me into town to buy food and visit the bank. For all I know, you could be a desperate criminal on the run."

He looked at me with cool blue eyes, as if trying to assess how much I knew. He opened his mouth to say something, then thought better of it. After pacing up and down a little more, he sat beside me and put a hand on my knee.

"You know I told you that we work for a government that is beyond the governments in Washington and Richmond?"

"Yes."

"You know I told you that we are neither Unionists nor Confederates?"

"Yes."

"Well, Jack, the time has come when we need to test your loyalty."

148

"Loyalty to what?"

"Ah, that's just the thing. I can't tell you. I can't tell any of the men. You have to believe."

"If it's loyalty to you, Bennett, I'm happy to be tested."

"Not to me, but to what I represent. The powers," he said, glancing upward as if he meant God Almighty himself. I began to wonder if Lieutenant Young was, in fact, a raving lunatic.

"Where do these powers...reside?"

"In Montreal."

Thank God for that, I thought. If he'd said "in the Great Beyond" I would have backed out of the room and taken to my heels.

"Are they...the French?" I had a vague idea, from glancing at the newspapers, that the French were always trying to foment revolution for mysterious, atheistic ends.

"An international concern," Young said.

"Nihilists?"

"No."

"Anarchists?"

"No."

"Liberals?"

"No, Jack. A group of concerned politicians from Europe and elsewhere who wish to see an end to this ridiculous bloodshed. More than that you do not need to know. Do you want peace for your family and friends? Do you want to see your loved ones swallowed up in a senseless war that nobody can win?"

"Yes... No... Of course."

"Then have faith, Jack." He put an arm around my shoulders. "You are on the right side."

"What do you want me to do?"

"We ride south tomorrow. You and me. I will explain on the road."

And before I could ask anything more, he slipped a hand

149

inside my shirt and started to kiss my neck. I was hard in an instant—it was only a short while since I'd sucked two cocks, and I was yearning for release—and the questions that I wanted to ask died on my lips, which were soon otherwise engaged.

IX

ON THE MORNING THAT WE WERE TO LEAVE HARMONY AND ride south into Vermont, a party of some ten young men, desperate-looking ruffians, most of them, arrived in the camp, footsore and filthy from the road. Teavis and Williams hustled them off to a hut by the parade ground.

"New arrivals, Bennett?" I asked.

I was only really interested in them as potential playmates, to be honest, so Young's reaction was unexpected.

"Always asking questions, Jack, always sticking your nose in. Just keep it out of my business for once." He prodded me in the chest in a none-too-friendly manner and continued trussing up the trunk of clothes and weapons that would accompany us on our journey. He had been edgy and irritable all morning, eager to get started, and was obviously displeased that I had seen the new recruits, as I guessed them to be, arriving at the camp. But why? Weren't we all, as he had told me a hundred times, brothers in arms?

It was not the first time I had asked myself questions about Bennett Young and his company, about the nature and purpose of Camp Harmony, but now I had serious misgivings. For whom was I fighting? Who were these foreign powers to whom Young so glibly referred? Where did the rest of the company, with their mixture of accents and complexions, come from? And where were we going?

I had little time to ponder these mysteries. After a quick breakfast of bacon and bread and fresh, strong coffee, Young and I were on horseback, the trunks slung over a mule that trotted obediently behind. There was no send-off. "You'll see them all in a week or two," Young said. "Think you can live without being the center of attention for a while?" His tone was not friendly, and I thought it best to let his mood improve with a little riding before I spoke again.

The road south was beautiful, the trees in their fresh green finery, and it would have been hard not to feel some surge of joy as we rode by blue mountains and clear streams, the sun on our faces. And after a couple of hours, Young shook off his gloom and seemed ready to be friendly again.

"Well, Jack, we'll soon be back in Vermont again. Happy to be going home?"

I had a momentary pang. I had not thought of home—my mother, father, and sisters—for a long time, except in dreams. "I have no home, Bennett, if not with you."

"Aaah, you're a sentimental young fool," he said, mitigating his words with the radiance of his smile. "But we'll make ourselves a pleasant enough nest where we're going, if you're content to stay with me a little longer."

"You know I am. Where are we going?"

"A little town by the name of St. Albans. Know it?"

I had heard of it, although I had never been there; the northern reaches of Vermont were as foreign to me as California or the shores of Europe. "No."

"Good. It'll all be fresh and new, then."

"And what will we do in St. Albans?"

"We'll live like gentlemen, Jack."

"To what end?"

"Your end, if you like."

I knew Young's ways well enough by now to realize that he was trying to put me off a subject by tantalizing me with the promise of sex. I was on the point of remonstrating with him—but some little voice in the back of my head counseled caution. If there were things he did not want me to know, it was better that he thought my curiosity a weak, fleeting thing. Whatever I needed to find out, I would discover for myself; Young would tell me nothing. He thought me vain, shallow, concerned only with pleasure. He had good reason to think so. But something—my better self?—was stirring into life again after a long slumber. I made some facetious remark ("I take your point, Bennett," which made him laugh) and we rode on in silence.

It took us less than a day to reach our destination, and the light had not completely faded when we arrived at St. Albans, just 15 miles south of the Canadian border. It was a smart, prosperous-looking town, less refined than Bishopstown but modern enough with its railway terminus, its manufactories, its long, broad main street lined with stores, houses, and hotels. We announced ourselves at the Station Hotel, the grandest building in town, where Young was both expected and known.

"Ah, Lieutenant Young!" the young man behind the desk said, a bright-eyed, brown-haired boy who viewed me with barely disguised distaste. "Good to have you back."

"Good to see you, Sam. This is Mr. Edgerton, my secretary that I told you about."

"Welcome, I'm sure," Sam said, although his voice belied his words. "You're in your old room, sir."

"Good boy. Nice clean sheets?"

"Just how you like 'em, sir."

Obviously Sam had been Young's bed warmer on his last visit to St. Albans.

We unpacked in silence.

"You've been here before, then," I said, when curiosity could no longer be contained.

"You know I have. When I left you back at the camp with all your friends." He laughed and goosed me. The bed looked inviting, but I was in no mood to play.

"The boy at the desk seemed pleased to see you."

"He'll be pleased to see my cock, if that's what you mean."

"Ah."

That took the wind out of my sails. I had expected denials, remonstrations, as if I was a betrayed wife who had caught her husband in some sordid adultery with a chambermaid.

"Yes, he's a good fuck. Almost as good as you, Jack, although a little more... Delicate."

So, I was sluttier than a desk clerk in a cheap hotel in a hick town in the northern wastes of Vermont, was I? The words were desperate for release, but I swallowed them, and busied myself with my unpacking. I was becoming wary of Young, unwilling to expose myself to his anger or suspicion. I was becoming sly, underhand, dissembling. If only I had become so months earlier.

"So I am your secretary, Bennett?" I asked at length, when I felt confident that I could muster a cheery tone. "What does that entail?"

"Writing letters. Taking dic—" He paused. "—tation. Accompanying me to functions, remembering people's names, keeping my diary."

"Ah, your diary." I noticed that the locked, leather-bound volume had accompanied us to St. Albans.

"My appointment diary, Jack."

"And what sort of appointments do we have?"

"Meetings with the good burghers of St. Albans. Bank managers. Chairman and board of the chamber of commerce. Prospective clients."

154

"Are we setting up in business?"

"Indeed we are."

"What are we selling?"

"Insurance."

"Insurance?"

"Yup. An important line of work, Jack, in these uncertain times."

"And we're opening an office here in St. Albans, are we?" I thought it was highly unlikely.

"If it seems propitious, yes," Young said, combing his hair and straightening his necktie. "You can't rush into these things. Any good businessman does his research first. Gets to know his market. That's what we'll be doing. How do I look?"

The light shining through the window showed up his receding hairline, which no amount of crafty dressing or combing could altogether conceal from the malicious eye. For the first time, I saw Young as a seedy, second-rate actor, a crook.

"You look just dandy, Bennett."

"So, come here and kiss me."

I did as I was bidden. Why did I always melt at the touch of Young's lips—on any part of my anatomy? I swooned in his arms like the heroine of a cheap novel, and soon we were fucking on the big brass bed. The mattress was soft, the sheets—as the desk clerk said—were clean, at least to start with. And yet, for all the familiar, intoxicating pleasure, my mind was elsewhere, wondering what manner of man this was.

We finished, and I dozed, exhausted, on the rumpled white linen, unwilling to pursue the troubling thoughts that were chasing through my brain. Young sprang up, dressed quickly, readjusted his precious hair, and took his leave. I slept, but was worried by dreams.

That night, and for many nights to come, we dined with St. Albans's most prominent citizens. We were entertained in hotel restaurants, and we did our share of entertaining. Young never seemed short of cash, and I did not ask any questions about where it came from. He discussed business, the state of the economy, the opportunities in St. Albans for a branch of his "expanding insurance concern," and he spoke a great deal about his desire to invest heavily in the business community. All of this was greeted with shining eyes and firm handshakes by the good townspeople, not least when I was trotted out as the "secretary," always ready with a line about cost analysis, projected accounts, percentages of net and gross, and so on. My idle hours at my father's office, listening to Mr. Windridge's interminable nasal drone, had not been wasted after all, and I could bluff convincingly about things I did not truly understand. Young was delighted, and squeezed my knee under the table if I had come up with a particularly glib-sounding line. Our friends smiled and nodded at each specious pronouncement; they understood no better than me. They wanted only appearances, and those we could give them in abundance.

Young grew more affectionate as I proved myself to be a malleable helpmate. He was busy, too, and grateful to have someone "back home" (as he called the Station Hotel) who would help him to relax and take his mind off the cares of the day. I did not ask questions, I was always ready to fuck, and I didn't complain if Sam, the desk clerk, joined us. Young was an arrogant man, and having two souls in his possession delighted him. It didn't exactly disgust me either, and as for Sam, he would have sold his mother to be in my shoes as Young's secretary, I believe.

Meek and submissive I may have appeared, but inside I was a monster of suspicion and doubt. Had Young known half the things I was thinking, he would have cut my throat as I lay in bed.

One evening, as we dressed for dinner, he was spending even more time than usual on shaving his chin and dressing his hair. He selected a particularly fine necktie—a new one, I thought, and expensive, by the look of it. "Make yourself presentable, Jack," he said, tossing me a neatly folded white shirt, fresh from the laundry. "We have an important engagement."

"What's the occasion?"

"We are dining with our first major investors."

"That's wonderful," I said, wondering whether or not the hapless "investors" knew how much of their money was going to end up in Young's bottomless pockets. I had already formed some ideas of just how Young paid for his lavish way of life, and none of those ideas was particularly flattering. I did not yet know exactly what form Young's criminality took, but I accepted it as a fact of life. And I was, I knew only too well, his accomplice.

Dinner that night was a farce, at least to my eyes, but Young and I both played our parts, and our two guests— Mr. Jobling, a dry goods merchant, and Mr. Butterworth, a civil engineer—seemed genuinely excited at the idea that their dollars would be the "seed corn" (as Young put it) for what would undoubtedly be one of the great success stories of the 1860s. "Insurance," Mr. Jobling said with pride, "is the future. Insurance is how we will rebuild the Union. Insurance," he said, accepting a refill from Young, "is God's plan!"

"Amen!" Young said, his voice trembling with passion.

I had heard the term "confidence trickster" before, and had read accounts of their practices in the more lurid periodicals that my sister Jane smuggled into the house, and it now occurred to me that I was in the clutches of just such a one. Young's protean character, his ability to attune himself in an instant to the opinions of his company, equipped him well for this shady trade. Had he not won me over with a night of fucking in an inn? And had I not seen him, time and again, tailoring his politics to those of his companions? Now, it seemed, he was even ready to take up the tattered remnants of faith—although the only time I'd ever heard him mutter God's name before was in moments of sexual excitement.

Messrs. Jobling and Butterworth left the hotel well fed and watered, their stomachs fuller, their wallets emptier than when they had arrived. Young issued them share certificates, which I had written out in my finest copperplate just that morning, with many a florid turn of phrase. They believed that they were now investing in a sound business proposition. They might as well have thrown their money down the nearest well.

Young, then, was a con man, of that I was sure. Looking back, I see now that that was the least of my worries—that these little deceptions were simply a way of financing his larger plans. Had I known... Ah, well, the story would have been very different. At the time I was still half in love with Young, or at least with his body. My doubts—and they were teeming, like bees in a hive—were pacified by his lovemaking. Of all forms of blindness, willful blindness is the most pitiful.

That night, as we lay in bed after our customary sport, I stayed awake, staring into the darkness. I saw dim shapes of furniture, I heard muffled voices from other rooms—and my own thoughts were likewise ill-formed and indistinct. I knew that Young was bad news, that I was compromising myself by the association, that I should get out now before I landed in jail. But I could see no way of removing myself from a situation that, for all its drawbacks, was the only certainty in my life. I could not go to Montpelier, to my old friend James and his family, whom I had betrayed by my disappearance. I could hardly think of returning home; the shame I had brought on my parents would not make me welcome there again. And where else would I go? I had no friends, no money, no letters of introduction except those useless documents I was supposed to have delivered to the Vermont State Agricultural Bank in Montpelier. And the roads were no longer safe. The war was progressing—that much even I knew, from my ostrichlike position. Confederate forces had invaded the North, crossing the Potomac River into Maryland; if Maryland fell, what would prevent the collapse of the entire North? And where could a young man in my position possibly go for safety and friendship? Only to the cities, perhaps, to lead a quiet and restricted life...

Aaron's words came back to my memory, as sharp as a knife. *You'd drift around. Maybe you'd end up in Boston or New York, in rented rooms, watching your life run down the drain, wondering if it was worth all that pain and trouble...*

And I saw Aaron's face, his hooded eyes, his thundering brow, the angry set of his jaw as he struggled to keep himself in check. I had laughed at him then, teased him as a virtuous fool, lain on the floor and wiggled my ass at him, goading him, mocking him. I had so little respect for him—and yet, through it all, his counsel was the one thing I had still that was bright and pure. Every word he'd said to me in those last days in Bishopstown came back to me as a reproach, but also as words of hope.

Aaron. Aaron watching me across the office, smiling as I scratched away at the work I hated. Aaron hustling me out of the family dining room to ask me why I didn't like him. Aaron's warnings, Aaron's weakness, and above all, Aaron's great strength. Well, I had driven him away into God knows what danger. I needed him now—not as the big slab of black meat that I thought he was when we met, something to be consumed and enjoyed, a toy to be played with and cast aside—but as a friend and mentor. But Aaron I had lost—and in his place, snoring beside me without a care in the world, was Bennett Young, a weasel to a lion. Oh, what a falling-off was there...

Spring turned into a blazing summer as we plied our dishonorable trade in St. Albans, gathering investment in the great, glorious insurance business that, Young told his growing circle of dupes, would be launched with much fanfare in the fall. He took out a lease on a swanky office on Main Street, employed a signwriter to emblazon the words "Northern Rock Life Insurance Company" in gold letters on every window, fitted himself out with a fancy swivel chair and a leather-topped desk, all of it on credit. Potted palms in brass jardinieres, bentwood hat racks, and a couple of fine Turkish rugs completed the stage set. To the casual visitor, the Northern Rock office bespoke calm confidence, solidity, trust. To my eye, it looked like the front parlor of a pretentious whorehouse.

I spent the days sitting behind a desk, writing out investors' certificates, filling in ledgers with columns of figures that I plucked from thin air, writing and responding to correspondence. I was just as much a part of the illusion as the leather-topped desk, the potted palms. I wore a clean white shirt every day, I plastered my hair down with oil, I kept my fingernails clean and trimmed, and I addressed visitors in my best New England accent. I was meek and deferential. I made them feel good. If the Northern Rock was a whorehouse, then I was one of its most popular whores.

Young was in the office for appointments, and played the role that was required of him. The investors he had wooed and won were now treated with a certain dismissive, patronizing grandeur—and they loved it. They spoke of Young in reverential tones as "the coming man," and they thrust their daughters in his path whenever possible. Had he been that way inclined, Young could have fucked every heiress in northern Vermont—and, for all I know, he did, such was his lust for power and adoration. There may be several children now growing to school age who owe their lives to his appetite for submission. It was hard to tell, for Young was always ready to satisfy me when I wanted it—and, despite the growing contempt in which I held him, I found him as desirable as ever. Perhaps more so. I hated myself for sticking with him, for loving him in the craven way that I did, and the more I hated myself the greater the pleasure of submitting to him, of wallowing in the filth of an unsuitable, degrading attachment. And if I opened myself completely to him, lost myself in the sensation, I could almost blot out the recurring visions of Aaron that came to me with increasing frequency throughout those strange, hallucinatory months leading up to the raid.

I first learned of Young's real plans when he was out of town one night, visiting an investor—or at least that's what he told me. For all I know he could have been fucking someone's son, wife, or daughter. I did not care, and I certainly did not ask questions. I was the biddable servant, so drowsy with pleasure that I did not look beyond the charmed circle of my own satisfaction. I smiled and wriggled when he kissed me good-bye, I lisped some platitude about hurrying back, and bent my head to my dishonest task as Young stomped out of the office in his brand-new, not-yet-paid-for alligator shoes. He looked so pleased with himself, so sure of his plans, as he strutted down Main Street. He had forgotten, I suppose, that he had left his diary in the hotel. Perhaps he thought it was no longer worth hiding from me. Perhaps he thought my curiosity was dulled, or that there was no need to conceal his plans, so close were they to fruition. I waited for an hour before I slipped out of the office, turned the sign to "closed," and hotfooted it back to the Station Hotel.

Sam was at the desk, as usual. It was his habit to treat me with cold disdain if I was not with Young; when we were together, he simply ignored me. It irked and amused me in equal measure that Sam could be such a chilly fish, considering that we had shared a bed (and Young's cock) on many occasions, and had even "performed" together for Young's amusement when he was "in the mood for a show." I had fucked Sam in the mouth and the ass, in every position, over every piece of furniture that the Station Hotel provided, for Young's delectation, as he sat back with his legs hanging over the arms of a plush upholstered easy chair, toying with his cock, goading us with obscene suggestions. Sam gave a good impression of loving every minute of it when we were "onstage"—but behind the scenes he let his true feelings show.

"What do you want?" he snapped, as I approached the desk for the key.

"I need some papers from upstairs."

"I can get them for you."

It occurred to me for the first time that, perhaps, Young had warned Sam to frustrate any attempts I might make at independent action. How deeply was he in the plot?

"There's no need for that."

"I insist, Mr. Edgerton."

"Please just give me the key."

He sat behind the desk, coolly eyeing me. I could have punched him. My face was reddening in anger, and I might have given myself away with a careless word, had it not been for the arrival of a splendid matron and her mouselike daughter who sailed up to the desk and demanded Sam's attention. Thus distracted, he could not prevent me from lifting the key from its hook and bounding up the stairs.

I jammed a chair under the doorknob, dropped to my knees beside the bed, and rooted around for the small valise that contained Young's personal effects, including the diary. I knew it would be locked, and I knew the diary itself would be secured in the usual way, but I had taken the precaution of copying the keys from the office. It was the work of an instant to unlock the valise, to burrow through the wads of cash and forged identity papers—I did not stop to read them, and barely had time to wonder how many identities "Bennett Young" had—before I found the object of my quest, the leather-bound notebook, complete with brass padlock, in which Young was accustomed to write every day.

I heard footsteps in the corridor outside, and a knock at the door.

"Mr. Edgerton."

Sam had dispatched the new guests.

"Just a minute."

The doorknob turned, but he could not get in. I had to think fast.

"Could you let me in, sir?" He could not raise his voice, nor use the language I'm sure he would have preferred, for fear of other guests hearing.

I unlocked the padlock and flicked through the pages of closely written script. Spelling mistakes leaped to my eyes; Young was a prolific writer, but not well schooled. I saw my name several times in the later pages, but did not stop to read what he had said about me.

"I won't be long, Sam. I'm just...making myself comfortable." Thank God for our New England squeamishness about matters digestive; even Sam would think twice before interrupting a man at his stool.

"Why didn't you go at the office?"

"I was caught short," I said, words dancing before my eyes. "I think it was the fish we had in the restaurant last night. It's given me—"

"Please, sir," Sam said, in a hushed and frightened voice. "The guests!"

I made a revolting noise with my tongue and lips, the best approximation I could muster of a vile and liquescent torrent of shit hitting a chamber pot. Sam groaned audibly outside the door. Prissy fool, I thought, to be so easily disconcerted.

I flicked to the most recent entry and read this:

> All is ready. I meet tonight with Harper Bucking-
> ham and Foster, Lees men from Gorgia. Weap-
> ons and ammunishun $20. Tomorrow to Jenkins
> Point to meet with Teavis Bruce Collins Doty
> Gregg Wallace Scott and new rigimint and plan
> raid. Sam with Jack, safe.

I could not puzzle out the meaning of these words, but some of them—weapons, ammunition, regiment, raid—were clear enough. Sam's hand was on the doorknob again, rattling it more insistently. I buried the diary at the bottom of the valise, thrust it quickly under the bed, and pulled my pants down.

"Couldn't you wait? Jesus, there's no privacy in this god-dam hotel," I said as I let Sam into the room. "Sorry about the smell." He held a handkerchief over his nose. "What do you want, then?" It was easy to sound cross.

Sam said nothing, but darted around the room, looking for something. His eyes glanced down at the bed, then up at me, down at the bed again.

"If you think I've got Bennett Young hidden away in here for a quick fuck, you're very much mistaken." I put on my most pompous voice. "He's out visiting investors."

"I know that."

"Are you in the habit of coming uninvited into guests' rooms, Sam?"

"No."

"No what?"

"No, sir." He was squirming. I still had my pants around my ankles, and it occurred to me that I might try one of Young's tactics, and fuck the boy into silence. My dick was as big as Young's, it could go all the places his could go, and I knew how much Sam loved it, however much he disliked the person to whom it was attached.

"Shall I empty your pot for you, sir?" He looked around the room, trying to find the evidence of my malaise.

"Oh for Christ's sake, Sam, leave a fellow in peace."

"It's no trouble." He darted over to the bed, and looked underneath it. I raced around to the other side, grabbed the pot, and flung a cloth over it.

"I wouldn't dream of it."

Sam got to his feet and brushed down his trousers; he had obviously satisfied himself that the valise was still there, apparently undisturbed.

"It's no trouble."

"No, really, I— Oh, Christ." I managed, through sheer willpower, to squeeze out a fart; not much of a fart, certainly not compared to the competitive pant-rippers that I'd heard around the campfire at Harmony, but enough to convince Sam that I was about to increase the yield in the pot. He backed out of the room with his handkerchief over his face. It had not been necessary to fuck him after all. One fart and he'd flown.

I could not push my luck, though, and I knew that if I stayed any longer in the room, Sam's suspicions would be aroused. I dared not look at the diary again—but I had seen enough to know that my stay in St. Albans was about to come to an abrupt, and perhaps bloody, end. I dressed, grabbed a file of letters that happened, luckily, to be lying on the table, and locked the door behind me.

Sam was back at the desk, glowering at me.

"All done," I said, brandishing the file at him.

"The key."

"Here you go." I tossed it in a high arc; he missed it and was obliged to grovel on the floor as I walked out, whistling "John Brown's Body."

Weapons...ammunition...regiment...raid...meeting with the gang at Jenkins Point...Jack "safe" with Sam...I puzzled

165

over these fragments as I scratched aimlessly at a sheet of paper in the Northern Rock office, expecting the still air around me to explode with gunshot at any moment. Who was Bennett Young? What was Camp Harmony, and why was he raising a regiment? To whom did he answer? Who gave the commands? Was he simply a pirate, a thief, or was he something worse, a traitor and a mercenary? And what was I? What had I become?

I walked on broken glass for 24 hours, waiting for disaster to strike. But St. Albans went about its business, undisturbed. A few callers came to the office, some even deposited money that they had promised Young in return for share certificates, forged by my pen. I took the notes, I made entries in the ledger, I signed and issued certificates in my own name. What a fool I had been! A forger, an embezzler, a stooge, a sacrificial lamb, my name on everything while Young himself was invisible, a ghost...

He returned at 11 the next morning, his usual charming self, although there was something in his eyes, a strange sparkle, a slight fatigue, as if he was running a fever.

"Good morning, Jack." He ruffled my hair, kissed my head. "Did you miss me?"

"You know I did," I said.

"You been a good boy while I was away?"

For the first time, I resented him calling me a "boy"; I was nearly the same age as he. But it suited him to remind me who was boss.

"Yes. I've been good." I wondered what Sam had told him. Had Young been back to the hotel already? Had he checked on his diary? Had he noticed that it had been disturbed? I put it back as carefully as I could, but for all I knew it may have been protected by a dozen invisible security devices, hairs gummed over the pages, or something of the sort. I waited for an accusation.

"Heard you been sick."

"I had a delicate stomach."

"I heard you gassed out the whole of the Station Hotel."

My act had been convincing, then. "Please, Bennett. That's not nice."

"You're such a delicate flower." He put his expensively shod foot up on my desk. "You better now? I don't want shit on my prick when I fuck you."

"I'm better."

"Good. Then pull down the blinds and bolt the door, baby, because Bennett's balls are full of cream for you."

I did as I was bidden, and was soon sucking on his cock with a show of my usual enthusiasm. He was as hard as I had ever known him, maybe harder; perhaps the imminence of a different kind of action was inspiring him. Maybe I was just sucking better than normal. His dick tasted sweet and salty. I pulled my mouth away and a long silver string of sticky juice hung between my lips and his pisshole. I smeared it around my face, wondering if this would be my last taste of Bennett Young's love juice.

"You done those letters like I told you?" he said, caressing my ears.

"Mmmf."

"You take much money while I was gone?"

"Mmm-hmmf."

"Okay, baby. Time for you to take this up your sweet ass."

He pulled down my pants, pushed me over the leather-topped desk, and slicked my ass up with his spit. Soon the Northern Rock office reverberated with the grunting and banging of a good, vigorous fuck. I shot my load over a pile of freshly forged share certificates; Young didn't seem to care. He pulled out, darted around the other side of the desk, held my head by the hair, and squirted a huge volume of spunk into my upturned face. I held my tongue out and caught as much as I could. Even knowing what I knew about Young, and fearing much worse, I was still unwilling to relinquish a drop of him.

"Gotta go."

Normally he was gentleman enough to ensure that I came as well; now he couldn't care less. I was hard, my ass was on fire, and I needed release—but Young was putting his coat on.

"Bennett..." I tried to look seductive. "Aren't you gonna..."

"You better take care of yourself."

"You can watch." He liked watching, I knew. I lay back on the desk and starting playing with myself. There was a moment's silence, broken only by the juicy noises emanating from my cock. I sighed and closed my eyes and felt my orgasm approaching.

And then I heard Young laugh—a soft, mocking laugh.

"Hey, Jack."

I stopped stroking.

"Huh?"

I heard the jangle of a bunch of keys. I opened my eyes. Young stood there, the keys in his hand, waving them to and fro. He must have seen the fear that flitted across my expression. What did he know?

"I've got to run now, Jack. It's been fun."

He winked, turned, and closed the door behind him. And then he locked it—once, twice, the full security that we employed each night when we closed the office. I heard his boots banging down the hallway, and he was gone.

I ran to the door and tried it—knowing, of course, that I could not get out that way. The windows were locked as well, bolted shut, unopenable. I hastily dressed—my cock has shriveled pretty quickly—and thought about calling out for help. There must have been someone else in the building, someone who could find the locksmith to set me free.

I rattled the door, banged it. The rest of the building was silent.

And then, from the street, I heard gunshot.

I ran to the window just in time to see Young, mounted on horseback and leading a gang that comprised, among others, Wallace, Scott, Brown, Collins, Teavis, Doty, and Gregg. They were riding toward the bank, and shooting as they went.

X

WHAT STARTED OUT AS A LETTER TO JACK EDGERTON, wherever he may be, has become a diary, or at least a habit of writing. We live in strange times, none stranger than the times I'm having at the Alhambra Theater in Richmond, Virginia, under the paternal eye of "Captain" Harold Chester. It seems only right that I should keep some kind of record of this turbulent year of 1863, if only to read back to myself if I ever reach old age. The chances of that look, at present, fairly slender, and we have all adjusted our attitudes to suit the daily imminence of death. The cautious, pious, righteous Aaron Johnson, the ambitious clerk who counseled abstinence and respectability, seems a stranger to me now.

Richmond is in the eye of the storm, and weirdly calm, at least to outward appearances. We hear the war news, of course, and we see the stream of wounded soldiers crawling back to Virginia after the catastrophic defeat at Gettysburg. There is to some extent a siege around Richmond, although we are free to come and go as we like. But "out there," as we refer to the wider world, is dangerous, and we prefer to stay here in the relative safety of our burrows than to venture out. For Billy, Charlie, and me there are good reasons for keeping a low profile. They're both deserters—admittedly from the other side, but they have no desire to draw attention to themselves. And I, as a black man, am unlikely to find much of a welcome outside the bohemian enclave into which I have strayed. In the theater, and in the strangely theatrical world of Richmond, where all is show and parade, I am accepted, even courted. If I rode ten miles down the road, I'd be lynched or sold into slavery. So we concentrate instead on the business of day-to-day life.

"Business" is a good word for it, as everyone here has something to buy or sell, and in this particular market I find that I can command the best prices. Captain Chester has dropped a few coins in my pocket in return for a taste of my cock, but there are far greater rewards to be had. I tried my hand first as a companion to the ladies of Richmond, who were certainly keen to be "had." They came to the theater and eyed me as I stood at the door; many of them blushed or whispered to their companions as they swished by me in their fancy gowns. Some were quite shameless, and propositioned me directly, inviting me to visit them in the daytime when their husbands were at work. Others took a more roundabout route to the same thing, engaging me at first in earnest talk about the "Negro problem"—the only real problem for them being how they could get their hands on a real live Negro without fatally compromising their social standing. When they realized that I was educated, discreet, and trustworthy, they suggested I might like to take tea with them some afternoon. And the outcome was the same.

Some of the ladies had the good sense to send me away with coin in my pocket; others thought that they had shown quite enough favor by allowing me to have my wicked way with them. For these ladies I had nothing but contempt. They assumed that, because of the color of my skin, I was little more than a ravenous beast who "fed" on white flesh—at least, this was the sort of crap they used to spout while I was fucking them. Perhaps they had spent their girlhoods on Daddy's plantation, driving the slaves crazy by flashing their pink asses at them, too scared to do anything about it for fear of being branded as a nigger-lover. Well, now in the crazy world of wartime, they could scratch that itch with the boy from the theater.

I was never going to get rich servicing the dames of Richmond, and to be honest my heart was never in it; if I wanted to fuck something in a skirt, didn't I have Billy beside me all day long and most nights? He had developed something of a following as a travesty turn at the theater, having been "discovered" by Captain Chester trying on some of the items in the wardrobe. He came on with a painted face, false curls, and a good deal of padding in front and behind, sang a few popular and patriotic songs, and then waited for admirers to turn up at his dressing room. There was never a shortage.

I soon found out where the real money lay in Richmond. One afternoon, while entertaining a very respectable lady named Mrs. Prentiss, who lived in one of the most beautiful houses in town, I was surprised to hear the outer door of the house slamming shut and the sound of a male voice in the hallway.

"Caroline, my dear, are you home?"

At the time, I was taking Caroline from behind over the back of a tapestry-covered easy chair, her skirts hitched up (she had not been wearing underwear), so it would have been quite easy for her simply to stand up, smooth down her clothes, and pretend that nothing more sinister than a cup of tea was being enjoyed. Instead she clamped herself hard around me, clutched her hair in "wild distress" (I had seen this done in plays), and screamed loud enough to be heard all over the house.

"My husband!"

I tried to disengage myself, but it was no use.

"Don't move," she cried, shoving herself back against me. "All is lost!"

I heard Mr. Prentiss's feet ascending the staircase, and the door burst open.

"Caro—oh, my God!"

"Frederick!"

"My God, boy, what are you doing to my wife?"

I thought it best not to say, "Fucking her."

"I am undone!"

Prentiss was carrying a riding crop—although I had not heard the sound of horses' hooves prior to his arrival—and strode toward us. If he had attempted to strike me, I could easily have broken his arm. Instead, however, he used the crop to lift his wife's skirts even further, so that he could see the point of union.

"Oh, I see, I see," he said, in a voice trembling with emotion, "your huge black cock is violating her delicate pink flower…"

I realized that we were acting in a play, and that I too had my role. I pulled as much of my "huge black cock" out of her as I could, so that Prentiss could admire its length and girth, then plunged it back in. Caroline shrieked, rather musically.

"Good God, Caroline, how could you allow this to happen?"

"I don't know, Frederick… He made me…"

"Is this true? You forced my wife to submit to your bestial desires?"

I could think of no reasonable reply to this, and besides was afraid that if I did speak I would start laughing, so instead I withdrew my cock completely and rubbed the head all over Caroline's quivering white buttocks. Prentiss was spellbound.

"Oh, vile, vile... No, don't stop... Oh, the shame, the shame... That's right, slap her with it..."

Prentiss was the typical Richmond gentleman, about 45 years old, stylishly dressed, a hint of the dandy about his striped silk vest and his cream spats. You would have passed him in the street without a second thought, seeing simply a prosperous, settled family man. Now, I realized, there was more behind that facade than the casual observer could guess. I wondered which way this scenario would develop.

"Frederick," whimpered Caroline, who had reached a hand down between her legs and was fingering herself, "can you ever forgive me?"

"You must be punished, my girl."

"Yes."

Prentiss let his riding crop play over the sticky surface of his wife's buttocks, occasionally using it to stroke and tickle my cock. I could see, from the rapt expression on his face, that he would like to be exploring it with more than just his crop. I put my hands on my hips and waved it at him. He looked me in the eyes, held my gaze for a moment, nodded slightly, and then returned to his part.

"I'll teach you to disgrace me in my own home." The riding crop sliced through the air and stung Caroline across the ass. She shrieked.

"No!"

"Again!" *Swish, smack!* went the crop, leaving a red mark on her behind.

"Frederick, I beg you!"

Swish, smack! Swish, smack! Six stinging bites of the crop crisscrossed Caroline's white buttocks with red lines.

"And now, my dear, you must take the rest of your punishment. You want this black man to fuck you?"

"Oh... No, no please..."

"It's too late to ask for mercy now." Prentiss took hold

of my prick with one hand and guided it toward his wife's pussy. I noticed that he took the opportunity to caress it, to feel the weight and heat of it before feeding it to her.

"Here he comes, Caroline." He held her pussy open and guided me in, feeling every inch of me as I slid into her. "How does that feel, Caroline?"

I had a feeling that Prentiss would be finding out for himself how it felt before too long.

"Oh, Frederick. Oh!"

I fucked her for a while, as she and her husband kept up the dialogue. Mr. P had been erect inside his clothes for some time, and I thought it was time he joined in, rather than just flicking his wife with the riding crop and feeling my dick every time he could get a hand in. So I reached over and grabbed his crotch and gave him a good squeeze. His eyes opened wide in surprise as I rubbed and caressed.

"What are you doing? You don't intend to have me as well, do you? In my own home? Oh, you brute!"

I simply winked, and guided his hand back to my wet prick. He was less guarded now in his handling of it, and I could tell that he wanted it all to himself. But there were appearances to be kept up, at least for the time being.

I started to unbutton his fly; this was not easy while a) fucking his wife and b) making sure he was able to handle me on the way out and the way in. But he got the message and finished the job for me. Soon his pants were around his ankles, his shirttails framing a stiff prick of reasonable proportions. He stood for a while, uncertain how best to proceed, so I grabbed him by his handle and drew him toward me. Caroline was oblivious to what was going on behind her and could not see the look of rapture on her husband's face as I masturbated him. I fucked her hard, and kissed Prentiss full on the lips. This was getting interesting.

Caroline started looking around, so Prentiss drew away— but he had that glazed look in his eyes that I had seen so many times before. He would be back for more. I pulled out of his wife, making sure that he had a good feel of my prick as I did so, and pulled Caroline to a standing position.

"Oh, help!" she cried, quite softly. "Two of you! Oh, what is going to happen to me."

"Does she suck?" I asked.

"Oh, I could never... Oh dear..."

I took that as a "yes," and moved around to the other side of the chair. When she saw my dick waving around in her face, she opened her mouth wide, emitted the tiniest of screams to justify the action, and then got to work on me with her lips and tongue. This left her rear end clear for some conjugal attention, and Prentiss plunged in with some enthusiasm. His eyes never left me. Thus arranged, we gave Mrs. Prentiss what she wanted, and what she thoroughly enjoyed, as she soon dropped any pretense to the contrary. When I was on the point of coming, I pulled out of her mouth and finished myself off in full view of the husband, who, I was quite sure, would have given anything to have exchanged places with the wife. I shot a good big load that arced over Caroline's head and landed on her back. Prentiss stared at the gooey white puddles and would, I'm sure, have liked to lick them up—but that would have been a step too far. Instead he increased his pace, fucked his wife good and hard, and came inside her.

We were silent, all three of us, as we rearranged our clothes. Caroline was the first to return to the realm of the conventional.

"Well, Mr. Johnson, it's been a pleasure to see you. I hope you will call again."

"Thank you, ma'am."

"My husband will see you out."

"Thank you, ma'am."

Prentiss held the door open and followed me downstairs. As we shook hands, he pressed a wad of bills on me; I knew better than to look at them, or even to acknowledge the gesture.

I tipped my hat and left.

I judged that Prentiss would leave a decent interval—72 hours, perhaps—before contacting me again, and I was right almost to the minute. Three days later, when I was sweeping up the theater in preparation for another evening's entertainment, the Captain hailed me from door.

"Letter for you, Mr. Johnson."

"Thank you, Captain Chester."

It read as follows.

> Prentiss and Barlow, Attorneys at Law
> Richmond, Virginia
> *Dear Mr. Johnson,*
> I wish to discuss a business proposition that I hope will be of considerable mutual benefit. Would you be so kind as to call on me at home before six o'clock this evening? My wife is visiting relatives and will not return until the morning.
> Yours sincerely,
> Frederick Prentiss

I had not been deceived. I finished my work, told the Captain that I would be out for a couple of hours, and wondered, as I walked the half-mile to Prentiss's house, whether I would be obliged to play the sensual black beast again.

Prentiss was nervous, formal, when he admitted me to the house. It was clear that the servants had been given the day off. He showed me into the drawing room himself, and fiddled around preparing me a glass of lemonade.

"You wanted to talk business, sir," I said, more to break the silence than anything.

"Ah, yes," he said, as if he'd quite forgotten why he invited me. "That I do. Now, of course you understand that what happened with my wife earlier this week was quite...well, quite extraordinary...and most unsuitable... It must never happen again."

"I understand, sir."

"She was very wrong to submit to your...desires."

I was in no mood to play this role again, and fancied that Prentiss would prefer me to be direct. "They were not my desires, Mr. Prentiss, but hers. I hope that I gave her satisfaction."

"Ah. Well, that I don't doubt. The thing is, Johnson..."

"Sir?"

"There are other considerations to be...er..."

"Considered?"

"Quite so."

"And what would they be, sir?"

"My standing in the community..."

"Don't worry about that, sir. I won't breathe a word."

"But it would be most convenient if I could enjoin you to..."

Enjoin? He was certainly taking the long way around.

"Is there something you want from me, Mr. Prentiss?"

"Well, I had the impression that..."

"Yes?"

If he wanted my cock, he was going to have to ask for it.

"That you might be inclined..."

"That I might like men? I do, sir. I prefer them to women."

"Ah."

"As, perhaps, do you."

"Well, I mean to say..."

"And you need someone discreet who will satisfy you in that department, perhaps? Without having to go out looking for it."

"Hmm..."

"So?"

Silence fell. I looked around the room at the rich decoration, the obvious signs of a well-run, expensively run, household, and decided that I was prepared to put up with Prentiss's timidity for a few minutes longer. Anyone who spent time and money on cleaning the chandeliers and polishing the brass in the middle of a war, when there was a shortage of basic foodstuffs, not to mention labor, had to be worth a little patience.

"Ever since my boyhood," Prentiss began, clearing his throat, "I have been conscious of...well, certain needs that can only be satisfied by a fellow man. I love my wife, of course..."

But not well enough, I thought; why else would she be running after stagehands?

"Of course."

"But there are certain needs that a man has... I've been married for twenty years..."

And how many cocks have you tasted in that time, Mr. Southern Gentleman Prentiss? How many times have you spread your legs and let some rough engineer or farmhand fuck that solid butt of yours?

"That's a long time."

"And I love my wife."

As you've said so many times.

"Naturally."

"But I have to have..."

Would he say it?

"I mean I really need...well, you know."

I looked him steadily in the eye. Ask for it, Prentiss, and it's all yours.

"I need your cock."

I smiled, and he breathed a sigh of relief.

"There, it wasn't as hard as I thought. I need your cock. I want to suck it and hold it and..."

"Take it up the ass?"

179

"Yes."

"Then go right ahead."

He was down on his knees in a second, rubbing his face into my groin, which was already well engorged as a result of our interview. He was delighted, and pressed the hardness against his smooth-shaven cheek. I reached down and rubbed his head. He wore his hair short, and he was balding on top—not unattractively. Prentiss was a good-looking man who obviously took care of himself, unlike some of the fat slobs who hung around the Alhambra. When he felt the touch of my hands on his head, he looked up, a puzzled expression on his face.

"We don't have to pretend that we don't both want this to happen," I said. "Let's just enjoy ourselves. You want me, don't you?"

"Yes."

"And I want you."

"You...want me?"

"Sure. Can't you tell?" I pushed my groin forward.

"Can I..."

"Yeah. But first..." I leaned down and kissed him on the mouth, pulling his head in toward mine with a hand at the back of his skull. From that position, we lowered ourselves gently down onto the carpet and lay side by side. We rolled around, we kissed, we tore at each other's clothes.

"Strip for me."

He stood up and did as he was told, revealing a body that was firm and hairy, from the stocky calves right up to the powerful shoulders. I joined him, shedding my clothes as quickly as I could. We faced each other, both our cocks throbbing, and I reached out and took hold of his. I think this was the last thing he was expecting, and he jumped.

"Calm down."

"I didn't expect you to..."

He was as nervous as a rabbit, so I dropped to my knees

180

and started sucking him.

Over the next two hours, we cemented our new friendship in every way we wanted. We both sucked, we both fucked, and we came lying side by side on the couch, arms around each other's shoulders, kissing and masturbating.

When Prentiss saw me off the premises this time, he was much more friendly, and peeled off a considerable number of bills.

"I'd like to see you again, Aaron."

"As often as you like."

"I'd like you to come and stay with me all night sometime."

"Whenever you want."

"Are you real? Or are you a dream? Am I going to wake up when you leave?"

"If you're in any doubt," I said, "just ask your ass. That should remind you."

Life was sweet enough for some time. My income from the theater, from Prentiss, and a handful of other wealthy admirers meant that I was never short of the basic necessities of life. What I didn't spend on food and clothes (and on neither did I squander money) I saved in the bank, an institution in which I had little faith but which was perhaps marginally safer than a tin box under my bed. I had an idea that, when the present situation was resolved and I was free once again to pick up the threads of my life, a decent sum of capital would make for a fine new start. I told myself that all I had to do was wait. The war would end, life would begin. I could go wherever I wanted. Back to Vermont, perhaps, to find Jack and apologize to him for the time that we had wasted...

One night, after the Alhambra's main bill of fare had come to an end, Billy, Charlie, and I were cleaning up the stage when Captain Chester burst into the empty auditorium. "Boys, boys," he shouted, his voice slightly blurred with drink. "Put down those brooms! We have a command performance for a few special guests! No time to lose! Billy, get dressed!"

He hustled us backstage and explained himself quickly; a group of his friends had requested a performance "behind closed doors"—and just as well, for the nature of the performance would have got the Alhambra closed down and our asses hauled into jail if it had been advertised to the public.

"They want to see a sweet young Yankee girl—that's you, Billy, now see if you can get into that muslin dress without ripping the damn thing—raped by a runaway slave—yes, that's you Aaron, you don't need to wear much—and rescued by a gallant Southern soldier. Come on, Charlie, don't stand there catching flies, get into the uniform!"

"And I take it that the gallant Southern soldier then fucks the Yankee girl up the ass."

"Well, that's the general idea."

"How much do we get paid for this?" Charlie asked, always thinking of his wallet.

"I'll see you right, boys. Just put on a good show for my friends."

"Any of them want to see a gallant Southern lad sitting down on a big black cock, by any chance?" I asked.

"Maybe, Aaron, maybe. I wouldn't mind watching that myself. You can take it, can't you, Charlie?"

"God damn, I ain't doing that!"

Charlie seemed to have forgotten what we did on the road together, before arriving in Richmond.

"He can take it, and he'll shoot a bigger load if I'm fucking him," I said. "Do your friends pay by the pint?"

"Enough talk!" Chester said. "Let me get the house settled. You're on in five minutes."

"How do I look?" Billy asked, tying on a straw bonnet with a pretty primrose ribbon.

"Hell, I'd fuck ya!" Charlie said.

"You do anyway, whether I'm dressed as a girl or not."

"Hush your dirty mouth."

I grabbed Charlie by the throat. "Since we got to Richmond, you been talking very high and mighty, young feller," I said, shaking him. "Just remember who your friends are. Now, if I'm going to go out there as the big black buck, we better make sure that I look the part." I hauled my cock out of my pants. "You better get me ready, boy."

I pushed Charlie to his knees and slapped him around his handsome face with my dick. He was soon sucking it with a will, his protestations all forgotten.

We made our way to the wings, and I peeped through a hole in the curtain, specially made for the performers to spy on the audience. There were, perhaps, ten men in the auditorium, all of them well dressed, and Chester was doing the rounds, exchanging a few polite words with each. Then he jumped up onto the stage.

"Gentlemen! I don't think there are any ladies in the house tonight, are there?"

This was greeted with a polite ripple of laughter.

"The Alhambra is very proud to welcome the members of...well, shall we just say of an august society whose name is known throughout America as a byword for generosity and works of charity..."

He went on this vein for a minute or two; Chester really knew how to lay it on thick. I could feel my erection subsiding, so I forced Charlie to his knees again.

"...By special request, the Alhambra is proud to present a tableau of modern life, entitled Virtue in Danger, or the Rape of the Union."

There was a quiet round of applause, and Chester stuck his head around the curtain to make sure that we were ready.

"Get her down on the ground, Johnson!"

Billy and I moved into position—he lay on his back with his stockinged legs kicking in the air as I pumped away between them—and the curtains parted. Billy screamed out in a pretty falsetto—it sounded about as convincing as Mrs. Prentiss's cries of distress—and I laughed what I thought was a dastardly laugh.

Billy landed a stage punch on my jaw, and I rolled off him, making sure that the audience had a good view of my naked nether regions as I did so. I heard a collective intake of breath as my dick, and then my ass, were revealed. Billy scrambled to his feet, picked up his skirts, and ran around the stage; I set off in pursuit, my hard cock bouncing and slapping against my stomach with every step. There was a certain amount of cheering. Finally I "caught" Billy, who swooned in my arms and allowed himself to be carried around the stage, the folds of his skirts cascading down around my prick. I laid him down at the footlights, pawed at his false bosoms for a while, and then stuck one hand down his bodice. I fumbled and grabbed, and then, to the audience's evident delight, pulled out a wad of cotton. My face expressed confusion; my hand went back in, and extracted another wad of cotton. Billy was now flat-chested. He moaned a little in his swoon, threw his head back, and thrust his hips upward.

This time, my hand went under his skirt, pulling up the muslin to reveal a shapely stockinged leg. I went further; at the top of the stocking was a creamy thigh. (Billy had taken to shaving his legs since appearing at the theater.) I gloated more and pumped my prick a few times, to the audience's evident delight. And then, with one triumphant movement, I reached up to "her" crotch—and when my hand made contact with Billy's stiff prick, I registered every shade of shock and dismay I could muster. I lifted the skirt, stuck my head under for a look, and emerged with even greater horror. The audience was laughing—so, positioning Billy so

184

that everyone had the best possible view, I lifted up the skirts and showed them all what I had "found," a very handsome and stiff cock framed by stockings and petticoats.

The men cheered; this was what they had come to see. Some of them were openly masturbating. I played with Billy's cock as if it was the first one I had ever touched, and then, glancing around to make sure that no one could see us (such was my idea), I leaned down and gingerly licked the tip of it. Billy chose that moment to come around from his faint, just as my lips encircled the head of his cock. He shrieked again, still ladylike despite all evidence to the contrary, and made melodramatic gestures of distress. The audience was on its feet to get a good look; hands were reaching out across the footlights to tug at his dress or my boots. I had a feeling we were about to end up at the bottom of a pile of very horny Southern gentry, so I pulled Billy to his feet and we moved upstage.

"Grab me by the skirt," Billy whispered as I set him down again, and he feigned a struggle to escape. I did as he suggested, and the garment came away in my hand, leaving Billy in his ladies' shoes and stockings, a garter belt framing his fine hard cock, his ass bare naked. He screamed and ran; I tore at the bodice, and that too came away. He was naked now apart from those items on his lower body, and the absurd wig of bouncing chestnut ringlets that adorned his head. He ran around the stage, giving everyone a good view of what was he was offering, and then allowed himself to be caught. I roughly turned him so his back was to the auditorium, parted his cheeks and showed the gentlemen his rosebud-pink hole, rubbing my fingers around it in a way they found most exciting.

My cock was still at full attention, and I was looking forward to fucking Billy in front of a room of onlookers, when suddenly there was the sound of a badly played cornet from the wings, and in charged Charlie, evidently impatient at being excluded from the performance for so long. He looked handsome in his gray uniform, and there was a loud cheer from the house.

"Fuck her!" cried a voice, which wasn't exactly the way the plot was meant to develop.

Charlie grasped Billy by one arm, I grasped him by the other, and we tugged him to and fro between us. Eventually Billy collapsed, falling forward with his head in my lap; I lost no time in ramming my cock into his mouth. Charlie drew his sword—fortunately it was only made of painted wood—and brandished it at me. I shook my fists back at him. He made a triumphant pass at me with his weapon, which I clutched under my arm, and I died, with much twitching and groaning, at his feet. Billy never relinquished my cock until I was well and truly "dead."

"Oh!" he squealed, his wig falling over one eye, "My hero! My savior!"

Charlie, who was never one for delaying when there was fun to be had, was already yanking at his belt, and soon his own prick was drawing gasps of admiration from the audience.

I will not itemize every move that made up the rest of our improvised performance. Suffice it to say that, after Charlie had abused Miss Billy for a while, I judged it appropriate to regain consciousness, and the show ended with me up his ass, Charlie down his throat, and three big loads of spunk landing on the bare boards of the stage. From what I could see, several loads had been shot on the faded plush of the auditorium as well.

Such was our life in the theater in Richmond, Virginia, in the summer of 1863, and I was in no hurry for it to end. The war barely touched us. I had more security and more satisfaction of a certain sort in the Alhambra than I had ever known, either with my family or in my subsequent career.

That security was won at a price; I sacrificed my morals and my ideals in return for an easy life and a pocketful of dollars. But that seems a small price to pay, particularly in wartime. Who of us can afford to take the high road, where we're exposed to danger and insult, when the low road is so much safer and more comfortable? Sure, I would never be a shining light to others. I would never live up to the ridiculous, trite truisms that I trotted out for the benefit of poor Jack Edgerton—fool that he was to listen to them. Perhaps if he'd just told me to shut my mouth and mind my business, we could have made some kind of life together in Vermont... But that's all in the past now. The present—with my daily duties at the theater, and my increasing round of nocturnal assignments with Frederick Prentiss and a dozen similarly inclined gentlemen—keeps me busy and well fed. I have friends, I even have a sort of family with Captain Chester, Billy, and Charlie. I do not have love, exactly, but one must expect to go without certain luxuries in such times as these.

XI

BENNETT YOUNG DISMOUNTED, LEAPED UP THE FRONT STEPS of the bank—from my upstairs window I could see the bald spot that no amount of elaborate combing could altogether conceal—and fired his gun twice in the air. The few citizens still in the street took shelter in doorways or peeped out from windows.

"This city is now in the possession of the Confederate States of America!" he yelled, in a voice loud enough to be heard in every building in town. "Resistance is futile." And looking at the gang of desperadoes who rode behind him, about 20 in total, some of whom I recognized, it looked very much as if St. Albans had been invaded.

The gang thundered down Main Street, herding pedestrians onto the village green, where they cowered in a small circle while horsemen galloped around them, much as we are told native Indians do to their captives. There was gunshot and shouting, screams and crashes, but I could see no more.

What happened in St. Albans that day I have pieced together from newspapers, personal accounts, and my own suppositions. I see now that a plot had been hatching directly under my nose, and I was too cockstruck to see it. The web of lies that Young spun around me, from the moment he caught my eye in that hotel in Rutland right up to our final parting, had caught me just as surely as a spider catches a fly. Camp Harmony was nothing but a base for Confederate bandits hell-bent on raiding the unprotected Northern borders, carrying off what booty they could and diverting it back to sustain the Rebel cause in the South. Young's fine talk of "European powers" and "real governments" was nothing but a smoke screen, guaranteed to blind me to the truth. How well he had read me! He knew my vanity—how much I would enjoy the idea of being in on some kind of secret society, making me superior to the ordinary folks who believed what they read in the newspapers. And he counted on my ignorance, the fact that I wouldn't recognize uniforms or names that were bandied around the camp, or even the songs that were sung around the fire, as the badges of the Rebel cause. I had allowed myself to be used as a decoy, the willing little Yankee boy who was sent into town to do Young's business, putting up a respectable face while he plundered and cheated all through the Northern states. And to make sure I asked no questions, he plugged my mouth and my ass with his ever-ready dick. When he suspected that I might be tiring of him, when he saw that I was awaking from my reverie and starting to look around and ask questions, he threw me to the rest of the pack, who fucked all the sense out of me and got me hooked on new thrills, washing away my conscience and dignity in gallons of their hot piss.

While I'd been living at Camp Harmony, happily eating food that had doubtless been stolen from the honest homes and stores of my home state, Young and his gang had been planning the St. Albans raid with the precision of a military operation—and I had been a key component in that shameful plan. The fact that it misfired so badly says much about

Young's own shortcomings as a commander. Just as his elaborate combings and dressings concealed a bald spot of which he was clearly ashamed, his grand military gestures, fancy uniform, and brave talk concealed a lack of strategy and an almost suicidal contempt for common sense. It was some consolation to me that the plot of which I had been the ignorant instrument turned out to be such a fiasco.

Young and his henchmen rode down Main Street, where they divided into three parties. One of them harried the townsfolk on the streets, stealing wallets, jewelry, and any personal effects that might be worth a few dollars to unscrupulous Confederate traders. The women, apparently, screamed and fainted, assuming they were about to be raped, little knowing that in fact it was their menfolk who were in far greater danger. The other two parties headed for the two main banks in town, which they intended to clean out. One of them they found shuttered, locked, and bolted—not because the manager had feared any such raid, but simply because they were closed for some essential plumbing work, due to start on the morrow, which Young could easily have discovered had he paid attention to such mundane difficulties. Thus half the gang's "takings" were slashed at a stroke, and the frustrated party rode around town firing their guns, unsure of what to do next. They broke a few windows and then, apparently, repaired to a local bar, where they drank whiskey and waited for Young's orders.

Young, meanwhile, was faring little better. He and his four companions—Doty, Gregg, Teavis, and Brown—burst into the one remaining bank, which was staffed by only a single teller, a pleasant gentleman named Bishop with whom I had had many dealings (the Northern Rock account was held at that bank). They whipped out revolvers and threatened Bishop's life. Instead of panicking, as doubtless Young would have, had he been in his shoes, Bishop coolly "surrendered" and handed over a bunch of keys to Young.

Whooping and whistling, the gang swarmed over the counter, unlocked a safe, and started stuffing their leather bags with as much money as they could. Estimates of how much they took vary from $50,000 to $200,000. When they left, Bishop immediately closed up the bank with himself inside it, secure in the knowledge that Young, in his greed and hurry, had completely overlooked the main safe (to which Bishop had not given him the key), which contained at least $500,000.

The plan, as detailed in Young's diary, which I later extracted from its hiding place and handed over to the governor, was to meet with the rest of the gang at the railway lines, which they would dynamite before riding out of town, back across the Canadian border, to disappear into the mountains, later making their way south to meet Jefferson Davis's forces and pour money into his shrinking coffers. The gang—many of them, I later learned, escapees from Union jails whom Young had rounded up, seduced, and indoctrinated over the last 12 months—would swell the ranks on the eastern front.

It didn't quite turn out that way. One-third of the gang, those who had been robbing civilians, had ridden to the other side of town, where they thought they might be able to plunder some wealthy houses; they were driven off by armed civilians, some of them women, and suffered terrible injuries. The second party, who had taken shelter in the bar, were late for the rendezvous, and, when they finally emerged, could hardly mount their horses. Whoever was meant to bring the dynamite for the railroad tracks had forgotten to do so, and Young was obliged to do what little damage he could with a crowbar. In the confusion, the gang became increasingly desperate to demonstrate their "control" of St. Albans, and indulged in ridiculous feats of horsemanship, rearing their mounts up on their hind legs or racing up and down Main Street at top speed. Their leather satchels scattered money at every turn, and soon the street was covered in bills, which some of the gang started trying to pick up. Gusts of wind blew the money around like confetti; this I saw for myself, from my window in the Northern Rock office.

Finally, Young gathered as many of his men as could still ride and, realizing that state troopers would soon be on the way, rode out of town. As they left, they threw what looked like packets of cornmeal, but which I later learned were homemade bombs, at all the storefronts; none of them went off as planned. Young intended to leave St. Albans in flames, but managed only to destroy a rickety woodshed into which Teavis accidentally drove his horse.

Less than an hour after the first gunshots, Young disappeared, leaving Caleb Wallace dead, and several wounded, behind him. They crossed the border into Canada as planned, but never made it south. What remained of the gang—many of them seem to have deserted Young after the raid—were arrested in Canada, and the money was recovered. And that was end of Camp Harmony, Bennett H. Young, and a foolish dream from which I had only been awoken by violence.

I had time to reflect on my folly, as I remained locked in the Northern Rock office for much of the rest of the day, until soldiers broke down the doors and found me cowering within. In all honesty, I was in no hurry to be released, knowing that I would face interrogation, suspicion, and shame as an accomplice of Young's gang. And so I sat in Young's expensive swivel chair and meditated on the path that had led me to this shameful place.

It was easy to blame Bennett Young, with his smooth lies, his lack of morals, his insatiable appetite for sex and power. But I could see, even then, before I knew the full scope of what he had done and what he had intended to do, that the real responsibility lay at my door. My love of cock had blinded me to everything else. Whenever questions had formed in my mind, instead of asking them I filled my mouth with a prick. Instead of pursuing the truth, I pursued orgasms. With every mouthful of spunk that I swallowed, I swallowed an even greater load of lies. Young had fucked me, and fucked me over, and I had rolled over and taken it all.

What was I to do now? First, of course, I would have to face the music. But after that? If I managed to persuade the authorities that I was a dupe, that I had in fact committed no crime (had I? I wasn't sure...) and was allowed to go free, where would I go? Who were my friends? If danger awaited me even in Vermont, where I thought I could hide my head and ignore the realities of war, then what would be my fate when cast out into the world, a marked man, friendless and suspected?

Of one thing I was certain as I sat in the office waiting for deliverance: I would never again allow my lust for cock to betray me into such degradation as it had up till now. Better to face danger as part of an army than to expose myself to the ridiculous risks of life as a male whore—for what else had I been? I had believed since the first inklings of manhood, and certainly since my induction at the White Horse Inn, that being the way I was somehow exempted me from the duties of my normal peers. As a lover of men, I was neither a man nor a woman, neither Confederate nor Union, neither abolitionist nor pro-slavery. I believed that, insofar as I believed anything. I never allowed myself the time to reflect; there was always cock to be chased. But now, I saw, my queer brothers were no different, no better, than the rest of humanity. They were not above the law, serving some greater government, the possessors of some secret knowledge. They were just crooks and mercenaries, pure and simple. And if Young and his gang were such low scum, what was I? I, who had built myself up in my own mind as a kind of hero, was lower than the bum begging for pennies around the bars.

So: no more cock. Time for decisions. When the door

was finally kicked in, and four handsome soldiers burst into the room, I didn't even bother to flirt with them—as if they would have been interested anyway. I allowed them to lead me off to jail without a struggle. Just a week before, I would have regarded a prison cell as little more than a playpen. Now it seemed a fitting setting for my utter humiliation. I sat in the corner and spoke to nobody.

I faced a list of charges as long as my arm, and when I was arraigned before the court I had almost resigned myself to execution by firing squad, hanging, burning at the stake... But in fact my life was of little interest to the court; they could see, I suppose, that I was little better than a child led astray by the promise of candy, although perhaps they didn't realize exactly which sweetmeats I preferred. My only use to them was not as a scapegoat but as a source of information, and I happily sang like a canary, giving them the names and descriptions of as many of the gang as I could, and details of Camp Harmony. I led them to Young's diary—typical of the man's incompetence that he would leave it behind in the hotel—and explained as much as I could. I like to think that it was my information that put the gang behind bars and prevented them from taking the money to support the Rebel cause.

After my cooperation with the authorities, it was quite clear to them that I was not really in on the plot, that I had been a victim as much as anything. And yet there still remained the question of what they were going to do with me. They could keep me in prison in St. Albans, at some expense, or they could send me home, they supposed, for my father to deal with. A third alternative I suggested; I could join the army, and go to war, and by my death I could buy back some of the self-respect I had sold at so cheap a price to Bennett Young and the Rebels.

I left St. Albans by train and headed south to Montpelier, my original destination. I did not announce my arrival to my friend James or his family; they would have read of my disgrace in the newspapers, and I was not yet strong enough to see the disappointment in a friend's eyes. Let me regain some worth first, or die trying. Instead I walked straight from the station into the recruiting office and announced that I wanted to fight for my country.

The officer to whom I was handed over was a tall, shaven-headed man of perhaps 30, with tanned skin and the most piercing blue eyes I had ever seen. He sat behind his desk as I was shown into his office, and looked at me in silence for what must have been a minute. I wondered how much he knew about me, whether he recognized my name from the forms I had filled in, and whether he was about to upbraid me for my part in the St. Albans raid. I could not help noticing that he was handsome, with his finely shaped skull covered in the merest dusting of stubble, with his strong jaw and large, mocking mouth. His shoulders were broad, and he wore his uniform with the kind of casual grace to which Young, with his dandified airs, aspired. This man looked at home in his skin in a way that Young never could.

"Edgerton," he said at last, in a tone of voice that confirmed all my worst suspicions.

"Yes, sir."

I braced myself for the onslaught, but it never came.

"You are ready, then, to do your duty?"

"I am."

"I wondered when we would be seeing you."

"Sir?"

He did not explain himself. Perhaps Aaron Johnson had been right; more people than I dreamed of knew of my exploits. Well, I was over that now, over any pride or fear that I had about my "secret" life. As far as I was concerned, my life was over, and any secrets were public property. This officer, his fellow officers, and, for all I knew, every soldier in the Union Army had probably been laughing at my foolish cock-crazed ways for months.

"Do you think you're able to fight, Mr. Edgerton?"

"Yes, sir. At least, I think I am able to die."

"You're of no use to us dead, Edgerton."

"No, sir."

"So you'd better learn how to keep yourself alive. Think you can manage that?"

"I've never fired a gun, sir. I've never been any good at fighting. I'm not much of a man..." I could feel tears rising, my face flushing, and I thought it best to stop talking.

"Let's see if you can at least stand like a soldier," he said, getting up from his desk and walking around me. "Come on. Straighten up. Shoulders back." He placed a hand on each shoulder and pulled them into a more military position. "Stomach in." He reached around, placed his hands on my belly, and pulled it toward my backbone. "Head up." He put a hand under my chin and lifted it.

"That's a bit more like it," he said, continuing his walk. "You could be a credit to the force, Edgerton."

"Yes, sir."

"Say yes, Captain Healey."

"Yes, Captain Healey."

"Good boy."

He paced around to the front and perched on the edge of his desk. He was taller than me, but in this position he had to look up. His eyes were hypnotizing me, so cold, so blue.

"You've taken a few wrong turns in your life, Edgerton. Ain't you?"

"Yes, Captain Healey."

"But we'll let bygones be bygones. The army is one big happy family and nobody is going to ask too many questions in the middle of a war. You understand? You can consider yourself forgiven."

"Thank you, sir."

"At least, as soon as you got those papers in your wallet

that show you're Private John Edgerton of the First Vermont Medical Corps."

Is that what he had in mind for me? Well, I was in no position to argue, although I had a sudden vision of severed limbs and burned faces, which almost made me faint. But I kept my chin up, my chest out.

"Think you can live with that, Edgerton?" Healey had obviously seen the look of disgust flitting across my face.

"Yes, sir. I'll do as I'm told."

"You'll go where you're needed. I understand you're not stupid." He flicked over a pile of papers that, I saw, formed some kind of record of my short and misspent life. "You've been to school. You have an aptitude for learning. You're not going to be much good to us in the front line, but you seem like the kind of boy who can take care of those who are doing the real work. Would you say that's a fair assessment?"

"I don't know, sir. I think I might be a coward."

"That's the first intelligent thing you've said. A knowledge of weakness is the first step to strength." He looked up at me with those piercing blue eyes—and I recognized that one of those moments had just passed between us in which we had reached a new plane of understanding. The "old" me would have said something such as "I'd like to see how strong you are, sir," and licked my lips, knowing that within five minutes, maybe less, I'd be tasting the Captain's hard dick. Instead, I glanced up toward the ceiling, remembering the trouble that such behavior had already got me into.

Healey stood up and was suddenly businesslike.

"I think, given the circumstances, we can bypass the formalities. I have the information I need right here." He patted the pile of papers—among which I saw the discharge notice from St. Albans prison. He consulted a list, running his fingers down the entries. "Yup, yup, that's all fine, mmm-hmm... Oh, well, I guess the only thing we really need to do before we stick you in a uniform is the medical examination."

I gulped. "Sir?"

"Don't worry. It won't take long. And you're in luck—I'm qualified to do it. And I've got nice warm hands." He grinned.

Perhaps I had misread the situation; so long in a world without moral signposts had led me to some pretty foolish conclusions, and this might just be another one of them. But I could not ignore the fact that Captain Healey had a big, wolfish grin on his face as he took off his jacket and rolled up his sleeves. His forearms were thick and tanned, and much hairier than his head.

"Open your mouth, Edgerton." He angled my head toward the window and took a good look at my tongue, teeth, and throat. "Mmm-hmmm...a little wider. Thank you. That all looks nice and fresh."

He ticked something off a list, then started feeling my neck. "Good, good. No swollen glands. Do you feel in good health, generally speaking?"

"Yes, sir."

"Do you get much exercise?"

Most of my exercise had been on my back or on my knees, but I just said, "Yes."

"Can you touch your toes?"

I bent over and placed the palms of my hands on the floor.

"Hmmm, good flexibility." He ticked something else off, and I started to rise. "No, stay there. Let's just feel your spine while you're in that position." He prodded and poked my vertebrae, seemed content, and made another note. "You may now stand up and remove your boots and socks."

I wondered, briefly, if this was standard army procedure, but one look at Healey's face told me not to ask any foolish questions. I squatted and untied my bootlaces, bared my feet.

"Sit down." He gestured to a wooden chair. "Gimme your foot."

He sat once more on the edge of the desk and grabbed my ankle, pulling me toward him. My heel rested on his hard thigh, and he diligently inspected between each toe.

"You've not had a bath in a while, I guess."

I was ashamed of the state of my feet, and it was true, it was some days since I was last able to wash as thoroughly as I would have liked.

"No matter. Nothing wrong down here." He inspected the other foot, and seemed satisfied with that one as well, massaging it, flexing the toes with his fingers, turning the ankle, and cradling the heel. I was starting to relax as the familiar feelings reasserted themselves in my body. My good resolutions were slipping away, I could see that—but this was not my fault. I was only taking orders. If this was a necessary step to my redemption through military service, so be it.

"Now, strip."

I was only taking orders... I pulled off my jacket and shirt.

"Hold it there."

Captain Healey placed a hand over my chest, feeling my heartbeat.

"Hmmm..."

He took my hand, and felt for a pulse at my wrist.

"You're running fast."

"Yes, sir."

"Are you feverish?"

"No, sir."

"Frightened?"

"No, sir."

He dropped my hand. "Raise your arms above your head and hold them there." He felt my armpits, which were slightly damp with sweat. "Good strong muscle tone, Jack." He ran his hands down my sides, allowing them to rise and fall over the ribs, until they rested on my waist. He was standing before me, and I could feel his breath on my throat. I dared not look up into his face.

"Drop your pants."

I knew that if I did so, my erection would be even more obvious than it already was, and I was nervous about Healey's reaction. Had I misread the situation? Would he take this as some kind of unwanted advance and have me thrown back into prison? My hands hesitated at my belt.

"You heard what I said!" he shouted, straight in my face, a vein standing out on his forehead. "Drop your pants right now!"

I did as I was told. I was wearing underwear, but it was loose and stretched through much wearing and washing, and stuck straight out in front where it covered my hard prick.

"That's better," Healey said, still standing so close that the tip of my cock almost brushed his pants. He didn't move. "You'd better learn to take orders, Edgerton. "Now lose the underpants."

This time I did not hesitate, and I kicked the last remaining items of clothing away from me. I stood completely naked, and fully erect, in front of Captain Healey.

"Good boy. You're learning. Now, what's this?" He tapped the end of my dick with his pen, which got smeared with precum.

"That's my cock, sir."

"It's your penis, Edgerton. You're going to have to learn the right names for things if you're going to be working for me. Your penis." He gently took hold of it for emphasis. "And these are not your balls." He moved his hand down and cupped me. "What are they?"

"My testicles, sir."

"Well done." He rolled them around in his fingers. "They feel healthy, Edgerton. When did you last ejaculate?"

"About four days ago, sir."

200

"Four days? At your age I was shooting twice a day. You have a problem in that department?"

"No, sir. But I've been feeling very low."

"You don't look low now, Edgerton. You look pretty... up in the air." My cock was throbbing as he "examined" my balls, and a drop of sticky fluid gathered at the head. "You should try to empty them more regularly than that, Edgerton, it's not healthy to keep it all stored up. I always ensure that I ejaculate at least once a day."

"Thank you, sir. I will, sir."

"Now bend over the desk."

"Sir?"

"I need to examine your anus."

I leaned my elbows on the desk. Healey strode around to the rear.

"Not like that! You look like a schoolgirl at a church picnic!" His boot pushed my right foot to the right, my left foot to the left until they were a yard apart, and he pushed me forward. "That's better. Let the dog see the rabbit."

It was a position to which I was well accustomed, as any reader who has bothered to travel this far with me will know all too well. I rested my head on my forearms and waited for whatever Healey wanted to do to me.

A hand (warm, as he had promised) was placed on either buttock, and they were pried apart to expose my hole. Despite the lack of bathing opportunities, I had been sure to keep my ass clean with cold water and rough paper. Despite my good resolutions, I was keeping myself "nice" just in case of—well, situations like this, I suppose.

Healey was taking his time examining my asshole, and I could hear that he was breathing rather more heavily than before. Well, if he wanted to look at it, I was happy enough to show it. I pushed it out a little bit.

"Good. That all seems to be...in order..." For the first

time he sounded less certain of himself. "Have you ever had any trouble with hemorrhoids?"

"Not as far as I'm aware, sir."

"I'd better check. They're a big problem for so many of our soldiers."

"Yes, sir."

A finger started rubbing and poking my ass; I relaxed my muscles, as I knew well how to do, and it popped in to the first knuckle.

"Seems healthy... Let's see..." The finger delved deeper, and I pushed back against it. Even without a drop of lubrication, not even spit, I could take a good deal without pain. Healey's finger entered me to a depth of maybe two inches, and moved gently in and out.

"Good, all clean and clear," he said, slipping the finger out; I let it go reluctantly. My hard cock was pressing against the edge of the desk, which pushed it back down between my legs; Captain Healey could see that I was even more turned on by his anal prodding.

"Of course, I really ought to check your...er...prostate gland," he said, referring quite pointlessly to his paperwork. "Usually we use a piece of specialized equipment for that, called a proctoscope, a big metal dingus that goes up there and enables us to see if it's swollen or inflamed. But I don't have one here."

"No, sir."

"I can find out everything I need to know by feeling it, of course."

"Then go ahead, sir."

"That will require me to insert at least two fingers quite a long way into your rectum."

"Yes, sir."

"Do you think you can take that, Edgerton?"

"I'll do as I'm told, sir."

"Good. Good boy. Now, in order to do that, I need to

lubricate your rectum with some special cream, otherwise it will be painful for you and there will be too much resistance for me. Do you understand?"

"Yes, sir."

He rummaged around in a desk drawer and produced a small white ceramic pot with a screw lid. It looked and smelled like hair pomade, a product for which Healey could have absolutely no use whatsoever, so I assume that he kept it in his office for just such "medical" purposes. Whatever it was, a large gob of the white, greasy substance on the end of his index and middle finger was soon applied to my asshole, and allowed him to glide in without inconvenience. I sighed, and opened up to him. My cock was oozing, and I made no attempt to hide my pleasure, clenching and loosening my ass around his invading fingers. He enjoyed the ride for a while, and forgot himself enough to finger-fuck me a few times, but then he remembered that he was meant to be examining my prostate and continued his inward passage.

When he reached his goal, and pressed it, I groaned with pleasure.

"Does that hurt, Edgerton?"

"No, sir."

"How does it feel when I press it like this?"

"It feels fine, sir."

"Can you explain how it makes you feel?"

"It makes me want you to do it more, sir."

"I see. Like this?" He pressed more, harder, letting his two fingers slip and slide over the sensitive spot.

"Oh, yes…"

"What would happen if I stuck another finger up there?"

"I…don't know, sir…"

"Think you could take it?"

I knew damn well I could, and a whole lot more, but I

thought it was best to give Healey the impression that I was learning obedience. "Try it, sir."

A third finger joined the other two, and my ass was well and truly stretched. Healey was obviously enjoying it as much as I was, and allowed himself to fuck me that way for much longer.

"You need to ejaculate, Edgerton." He was telling me, rather than asking me. "Do you think you could do it if I keep doing this to you?"

"Yes, sir."

"I need to ejaculate too, Edgerton. I haven't done it yet today."

"Yes, sir…"

"Can you see any solution to the problem?"

"Perhaps…"

"Yes?"

"Perhaps if you stuck your co—your penis up my rectum, sir, we could both ejaculate together."

"You're a smart boy, Edgerton. That's an excellent idea." I looked over my shoulder, and saw him lowering his pants. He placed another gob of grease on the end of his big, hard dick and started slicking it up.

"Let me, sir."

I reached back and smeared the grease all over his dick, enjoying the heat and the girth of it, running my finger along the huge vein that ran from his bush down to the head, bifurcating just before it disappeared. Healey stood with his hands on his hips and let me take my time.

"I'm ready for you now, sir." I guided his prick toward my hungry hole. With so much lubrication, this was going to be a very smooth ride. I leaned over the desk again and prepared to be entered.

He was in me and up me in seconds, the head of his hard cock pressing against my prostate just as his fingers had done. I felt his bush against my buttocks and knew I had taken all he had to give.

"Am I doing well, sir?"

"You're doing fine, boy. If I do this"—he fucked me slowly—"I'll be ready to shoot pretty soon." He was starting, to my great relief, to drop the medical jargon and use the words of the bar and the barracks.

"If it helps, sir, you can fuck me as hard as you like. I can take it."

"Good boy. I'm going to fuck that ass as hard as it's ever been fucked." This I doubted very much, thinking back to some of the use my ass had suffered, but I said nothing. And indeed, the captain had a lot of energy. He pumped in and out of my ass like a piston, and even without touching my cock I knew that I couldn't hold out much longer. Fortunately, the captain wasn't far behind me.

"Oh, fuck, you have a sweet ass," he said, drops of sweat falling from his forehead onto my naked back. "My dick feels so good up there. Oh fuck." He pushed right inside me, and fell onto me, pressing his chest against my shoulder blades. I felt his lips on my neck, his tongue, his teeth.

"Fuck, I'm gonna come inside you, boy. You ready for me?"

"Yes sir."

He pumped harder, faster, and started spewing a great load up into my guts. It felt so good. And, just as he was shuddering into the last few spasms, I managed to squeeze a hand down between my hips and the desk, and grabbed my prick.

"Hold it, boy." He pulled me back, stopped me from touching myself—and kept his prick firmly lodged inside me. "We've got to do this properly."

He withdrew, spun me around and sat me back on the desk, pulling my legs up by the knees. Then he plunged his still hard cock into my wet ass and proceeded to gently fuck me. "This way I can see what you're doing."

I needed no prompting and took hold of my cock. I was determined to give him a show, to keep him inside me for as long as possible, so I didn't tug as hard as I could—that would have put an end to our fun. But, even lightly caressing myself, the sensation was too much. Under Healey's hungry wolf's eyes, I shot a huge load over my stomach. It ran down my sides and into my navel. Such was the intensity of the orgasm that my ass shot his prick out.

We stayed there without moving for a while, both our cocks softening, the spunk running out of my ass and down my body. I assumed that Captain Healey would tell me to get dressed and throw me out. Instead he helped me to my feet, put an arm around my shoulder and ruffled my hair.

"Welcome to the army, Private Edgerton. You're going to make a very good soldier."

XII

I MIGHT HAVE STAYED IN THE ALHAMBRA THEATER FOR THE rest of my life, I suppose, every day sinking a little deeper into a mire of heedless hedonism, had it not been for a clarion call from the very last quarter I expected.

Captain Chester had never struck me as a moral man, certainly not a patriotic one; his only interest seemed to be in keeping himself safe, getting laid, and making as much money as possible. I wouldn't describe him exactly as a war profiteer, but he certainly recognized that, in the siege situation that beset Richmond during that nightmarish phase of the war, there were plenty of people looking for distraction and entertainment—and he did all he could to provide them. The regular business of the Alhambra was doing very well, and there were scarcely ever empty seats. Since Chester's wife had left town to seek refuge with relatives in Tennessee, the Captain had dropped all pretense of preferring women and installed Billy in the vacated marital bed—although they were far from faithful to each other. Billy, indeed, was fast turning into the most popular attraction in town.

The Alhambra's public shows were pretty risqué, with scarcely draped dancing girls and handsome young men showing as much flesh as the Captain deemed advisable. Under the circumstances, nobody was going to bother raiding the Alhambra for indecency; the authorities were otherwise occupied. The private shows, of which I was a regular star, were becoming more and more popular, and I believe that Chester could have turned the Alhambra over entirely to the kind of performances I have described, had it not been for his need to keep up a respectable front. That dozen or so gentlemen who first saw me "rape" Billy soon grew to 20, 30, even 50, all of them paying top dollar for the chance to see some real cock on stage. We the performers did a healthy trade with our growing list of admirers; even Charlie, who still professed to prefer women, realized that there were far greater rewards to be had from men. The three of us were doing well for ourselves. Billy and I were saving; Charlie was spending, dressing like a gentleman, and looking around for a young girl of good family who would bring a decent dowry. Some of his gentleman admirers went so far as proposing their own daughters as prospective wives, on the basis, I suppose, that it was better to retain such "talent" as Charlie's within the family circle. In any case, our prospects were good, and we frequently toasted our success, mindful always of the dire circumstances in which we had met. "What would that sheriff Jed Brown say if he could see us now?" Billy wondered, laughing, more than once, and we'd fall into reminiscing about how clever we were to escape from jail, how funny Jed Brown looked flailing around in a puddle of piss.

One afternoon, as Billy, Charlie, and I were drinking a pot of coffee in the dressing room and recounting our exploits of the previous evening—Billy was showing off a very elegant diamond clip that he'd been given for fucking an old man up the ass while he (Billy) wore full drag—

Captain Chester walked in with more than his usual air of self-importance.

"Boys," he said, "the time has come for all able-bodied men in this here town to do their duty and stand up and be counted."

"Shit," Charlie said, having been comprehensively drained by an extremely greedy married couple the night before, "I don't think I can get it up again before tonight. It's sore enough as it is."

"Not that sort of standing up," Chester said, although he did sneak a peak at Charlie's groin, which Charlie was rubbing in an offhand sort of way. "I mean, we have an opportunity to make something glorious of ourselves by fighting for freedom and truth and the rights of the individual."

This was not Chester's usual idiom, and I wondered to whom he had been speaking. I found out soon enough.

"We've had a visitor, boys, A very fine man from the Fourth Virginia Cavalry. Spoke a lot of good sense about the situation that we find ourselves in during these...er...these turbulent times."

Chester swept the room with a grand gesture, as if here, among the stale costumes, spilled powder, and bitter coffee could be found some symbol of our national conflict.

"What did he want, exactly?" Billy asked, looking suspicious.

"He wanted men, Billy."

"Don't they all. Which one of us does he want? The big black stud, the handsome young gentleman, or the lady-with-a-secret?"

"He wants all of you, and me as well."

"Greedy bastard."

"And he wants all the other men in the theater."

"That I'd like to see," Charlie said, sounding interested for the first time.

"And he's going to have us," Chester said, scowling. I

realized that this was not about servicing the appetites of some opportunistic client.

"In other words," I said, standing up, "you've sold us to the army."

"I wouldn't say sold, Aaron..."

"What were your terms?"

"Now listen to me," Chester said, sitting on a dressing table and lighting a cigar. (His cigars had grown cheaper and fouler as the war dragged on, but he still got them.) "It may not be apparent to you boys, living in the lap of luxury and getting all the cock you can handle—" We groaned, but Chester chopped the air with one commanding hand. "—while you're going from one bed to another, fucking and sucking and making merry, for which I am, by the way, truly grateful, some of us have been dealing with...shall we say, reality? Shall we say politics? Shall we say the fact that there is a war going on under our noses and that it is no longer possible to ignore it?"

"He threatened you, then," I said, looking Chester coolly in the eye. His gaze flicked away from mine for a moment, then returned more resolute.

"Indeed he did, Aaron. That damn recruiting officer told me in no uncertain terms that if I did not provide ten good men for a new company, he would shut the theater down."

"So you saved your own skin," Billy said.

"I saved my skin, sure, and I saved your pretty little white skin as well, Miss Billy," Chester said, throwing a powder puff across the room. It exploded like a tiny smoke bomb. "If he don't get you, then the prison does. Do you know what they do to deserters down here?"

"We ain't deserted from down here, though," Charlie said, sounding scared. Underneath his bravado, he was by far the most cowardly of us three.

"You will have, if you don't join up," Chester said. "This isn't a question of volunteering, boys. This is conscription.

210

You don't have the choice to say 'Yes, please' or 'No, thank you.' If you don't jump to attention pretty damn quick, you get hauled up before the board and you go down. You may think it's fun in one of those military prisons, boys. You might think that your pretty faces and asses and your big stiff dicks will keep you out of trouble. Boys, I'm telling you, they'd kill you pretty damn quick. They might fuck you first, they might fuck you after, but they'd kill you, sure as I'm standing here."

"So we join the army and you get to keep your theater open."

"What do you take me for?" Chester said, puffing out his chest. "Didn't I always tell you I was a captain? I'm coming with you. Now clean yourselves up, make any farewells you need to make, and meet me in the front office in two hours. We're going to war."

Company K of the 4th Virginia Cavalry was made up of every layabout, ne'er-do-well, and miscreant who could be flushed out of the Richmond tenderloin. In addition to us four, there were two more stagehands from the Alhambra, a couple of acrobats and dancers who appeared regularly on the stage (in both the legitimate and the illegitimate shows), and a six-piece band that played the same ragged repertoire whether they were accompanying a plate-spinning act or an all-male butt-fucking orgy. There were a few other faces that I recognized from around town: doormen, barmen, and pot-boys from the bars and whorehouses, some regular drink-ers and clients from the same establishments, even a couple of honest office workers who had, once or twice, saved up enough money to avail themselves of the Alhambra's more exclusive services. In total we were about 20 men, more or less sound in mind and limb, although a less likely fighting force I never did see. Needless to say, mine was the only black face, and I stuck out as we mustered in the city square to be addressed by the recruiting officer. We all tried to look brave, but I noticed a large number of heavy winter coats and mufflers, even though it was a mild day. I suppose that nobody wanted to be seen shivering.

We stood around in a nervous group, talking in undertones, wondering what the next 24 hours would bring, when Chester nudged me in the ribs and nodded toward the steps of city hall. I saw the bright brass buttons of an officer's uniform, I saw a strong, solid silhouette ascend the steps, I admired the gray hair curling neatly over the collar of his gray tunic—

And then he turned around.

Jed Brown. Sheriff Jed Brown, from the prison in Allentown, the man I had last seen covered in spunk and wallowing in piss. Jed Brown, in the uniform of a Confederate officer. I was too shocked to ponder this puzzle; my eyes goggled and my mouth hung open as he began his address.

"Men of Company K!" he began, surveying us all with a cool stare. His eyes passed over my face, stopped, came back, rested on me. I tried to compose myself, to stop catching flies, but he saw my discomfiture and smiled, very slightly. His eyes narrowed, his eyebrows arched a fraction of an inch, and I remembered his last words to me before I fled with Charlie and Billy to freedom: *I'll be looking for you. I'll get you, black bastard.* Well, now he had me. I glanced around at Charlie and Billy, who both looked a greenish shade of white.

Brown's address was impressive. He spoke in even tones about the challenge facing the South, the value of democracy and freedom, the fact that the war was turning in favor of the Confederate cause—which I knew to be untrue, and yet when he said it, you could believe it. His voice was deep and well modulated, his hand gestures sparing but emphatic, and in all he seemed like a well accomplished politician. How he had gone from being a sheriff in Union Allentown to a major in Confederate Virginia I had no idea—but something about his idealistic oratory suggested to me that the Rebels had welcomed a man spurned by the Yankees, and he was properly, volubly grateful. Within ten minutes, he had turned a group of 20 scared, disaffected men into a cheering band of comrades in arms, or soon to be. We marched rather than shuffled out of the square, heading straight toward the army camp just outside town. Some of us, including Charlie, were already dreaming of feats of arms. Few, I suspect, were thinking of the almost certain death toward which we walked with such a spring in our step. One of the musicians produced a small fife from his waistcoat pocket and began a jaunty rendition of "The Bonnie Blue Flag," with which we all joined in. I thought it better to put on a show of obedience, whatever my private thoughts and fears.

Jed Brown stood at the gate of the camp taking the salute from his new recruits as they marched in. I raised my hand to my brow and looked straight ahead, hoping to pass in unnoticed—I had just about as much chance as a chicken passing unnoticed into a fox's den.

"Mr. Johnson, I believe," Brown said, detaining me with a hand on the arm. "We have some unfinished business. You'll report to my tent in ten minutes."

I was in no position to argue; Brown was backed up by two surly-looking men carrying rifles.

"Yes sir."

I had just time to see Charlie and Billy settled, and to allay their immediate fears, telling them that the only alternative to our current position was far, far worse, and that here, at least, we had a chance to use our wits to make life comfortable for ourselves. I left them to the tender mercy of the quartermaster, who was ordering all the new recruits to strip off and hand over their civilian clothes in exchange for uniforms. I looked fondly at those two white asses that I had fucked, and seen fucked, so many times, and then, squaring my shoulders, set off to find Jed Brown's tent.

It wasn't difficult; it was the only tent of any size, and certainly the only one with an armed guard at the entrance. The two men were both sizable brutes, but not unattractive. They barred my way with their rifles and asked for a password. I was about to reply with a particularly choice four-letter password, but bit my tongue. Brown emerged from the tent, his tunic undone, a clean white shirt underneath, his head bare, his face wet.

"Come in, Mr. Johnson. I've just been washing up. You get so dirty in these damn camps."

"Yes, sir."

I stepped into the tent; it was furnished with a desk, a couch, a bed, a proper wooden floor spread with rugs—all of it, I suspected, appropriated or stolen. There were some fancy bits and pieces hung from the ropes—a birdcage with no bird in it, a handful of horse brass ornaments, a wicker basket filled with artificial flowers. There were files and boxes of documents stacked in crazy piles and no discernible order, there were bills and posters rolled up, some of them crushed and muddied. This was not the tent of an efficient recruiting officer, but rather a showy opportunist. I felt right at home.

"I wasn't so clean and tidy last time you saw me, was I, Johnson?"

"No, sir."

He chuckled; things were not going to be as bad as I had feared.

"Do you have any idea how much trouble you and your little friends got me into that day?"

"I have a shrewd idea."

"Handcuffed, naked, in my own jailhouse. Stinking of piss and cum. How do you think that went down with the good citizens of Allentown?"

"Like a cup of cold vomit, I imagine."

"You'd be right. I should have you executed for that, Johnson."

"What would be the charge this time, sir? Not vagrancy again, I guess."

"Treason."

"Treason against whom, exactly? As I recall, sir, you weren't quite such a hot-blooded Rebel as you are now."

"Careful what you say," Brown said, drying his handsome, lined face on a towel. "I'm your commanding officer now. I can do with you whatever I like."

"No change there, then."

"I can make life nice for you and your friends, Johnson, or I can make it sheer hell. Which is it to be?"

"I've lived through good times and I've lived through bad times," I said, facing him squarely. "On the whole, I prefer the good times."

"Smart boy."

"So what do I have to do?"

"First of all, you have to promise me that you won't breathe a word to anyone in this camp that we've met before, and under what circumstances. And your boys had better keep their mouths shut too, at least in that respect."

"That I can ensure."

"Secondly, you can put together a team of the best men— or the least bad—and organize them into a decent police force. Think you can manage that?"

"Shouldn't be a problem. What are we policing?"

"In the first instance, Richmond town. You may not know this, Johnson, but we're in for a hungry winter—the corn's running low, Jefferson Davis isn't quite the tactician we're supposed to believe, and the coffers are empty. The Yankees have cut off his supplies from the bandits in the North. When the good folk of Richmond find out that they're going to go hungry, they're going to get very, very mad. I need someone with a strong arm and a cool head to keep them in order. Think you can manage that?"

"I reckon I can."

"And there's a few other jobs that need doing around the place."

"Name them, sir."

"Well, first of all, you can wipe that goddamn insolent smirk off your face."

I cleared my throat and tried to look serious.

"Secondly... Well, God damn it, I don't have to ask, do I?" He sunk to his knees on the rug before me, and started unbuttoning my pants. Within a few seconds, I was fucking his mouth.

My interview with Jed Brown set the tone for the weeks to come; there was a great deal of sucking and fucking in Company K. Even those who were not naturally that way inclined fell into what they called "bad habits," although they would occasionally break out of the camp and attempt to rape local women, in order to reassert their masculinity, I suppose. Brown dealt harshly with them before delivering them to the authorities. One such disciplinary hearing, which I was obliged to attend, involved the two miscreants being fucked in turn with fingers, dicks, and, finally, some very large vegetable squash, being forced to come while these large fruits were up their asses and then being tied to posts in the center of the camp with signs reading LATRINE and USE ME hung above their heads. You can bet that every last man in camp pissed on that unhappy pair, and more than a few used their mouths for quick, brutal relief.

My job, apart from giving Jed Brown my cock whenever he required it, was the policing of Richmond; I formed a small patrol of eight men who took turns walking the streets of the city throughout the day and the night, breaking up meetings and reminding the citizens that they were under constant observation. I hated doing it, and I felt sorry for the townsfolk, who were clearly experiencing hardships that they never believed they would suffer, but it was better for all that they should be dissuaded from open riot, even by the use of threats and force. My worst nightmare was that Company K would ride through the streets of Richmond firing at will, so I endured the threats and the insults (most of them related to the color of my skin) that rained down on me every time I led my patrol into town.

You will be wondering, no doubt, how a black man was ever accepted into the Confederate Army, but in truth I was not alone. By this stage in the war, the Confederates were accepting anything with two arms and two legs; there was even talk of some women's companies being formed in the more backward parts of Georgia. Black men—most of them freed slaves or runaways—were promised all sorts of rewards and privilege if they would set aside their objection to the slave trade and lend their muscle to the Confederate cause. Of course, none of them ever got what they thought they deserved; they were cheated into service, and fought for an administration that would gladly deprive them of their most basic rights. But for many of them—and I include myself—the army offered regular food, a small amount of pay, a roof over one's head, the companionship of one's equals, and, above all, freedom from the kind of dangers that we would have encountered on our own. Given the treatment that was meted out to me in the abolitionist North, I was in no hurry to find out how the good ol' boys of the South would deal with me if they found me stealing eggs from their chicken coops. No, on the whole it was better to wear a uniform and carry a gun, even if they matched badly with my black face.

When we weren't patrolling Richmond, we spent our time in the camp—and a tedious, degrading life it was. Little wonder that the men were easily persuaded to engage in acts that would have disgusted them in civilian life; there was nothing else to do, apart from drink, gamble, or swear. We had little money, so card games could become heated and violent over a matter of a few cents, or, when cents were scarce, over beads, tobacco, or even pebbles, whatever was the currency of the day. I saw (and separated) men who had come to blows, holding knives at each other's throats, because they suspected one another of cheating in these paltry contests.

It was not difficult to persuade such men into vice, and within a couple of weeks in the camp I was as big a whoremaster as Captain Chester (who managed to translate his fictional captaincy into fact, and swaggered around in his uniform like a real officer). I used my dick on every young mouth and ass in camp, and I even allowed myself to be fucked if I took a liking to a particular soldier—and I liked plenty of 'em. Company K was much like the Alhambra Theater, and very soon I was comfortable and reluctant to leave.

The only real opposition that I encountered in my early army career was from the small but very vocal religious contingent. There was no official pastor in the camp, but there were one or two officers who set themselves up as ministers, preachers, or priests, and who spent their every waking hour persuading the men that they were wrong to fall into the sin of Sodom. They despised the drinking of strong liquor, they abhorred the corrupting influence of tobacco, they forswore gambling and fornication, but it was for unnatural vice that they reserved the finest flower of their rhetoric. In fact, the only subject on which I never heard them preach was war, of which they seemed on the whole to be in favor.

I lost track of time, fucking and sucking my nights and days away. It was, in some ways, the happiest time of my life. There was good comradeship in the tents of Company K, as well as good sex, and I learned that the men of the South were not always the intolerant, prejudiced slavers that I had known them to be. They were just men, whatever the color of their skin and the condition to which they had been born. Many of them were disillusioned with the war, uncertain of the cause for which they were fighting—if cause there was, other than money and power for a small group of men far remote from the mud and blood of battle. We all had the same dreams, the same hopes, the same fears, and the same appetites, even if we expressed them in different ways. We bled if we were pricked, we laughed if we were tickled, and we came if we were rubbed the right way. Many of them learned that an ass could give just as much pleasure as a pussy, and there were plenty who found more love and trust in that camp than they had ever known at home.

One thing we never talked of, though, was home, or hope, or the future. Whenever those subjects came up, our eyes turned to our boots, or we stared into the fire, and we dropped into silence until someone started singing, or told an obscene joke, or someone (often me) got out his dick and offered it to anyone who wanted to suck it. We fucked away the blues, whenever they threatened to envelop us, and a happier way of dealing with the vicissitudes of life I have yet to find.

Men found many different ways to excuse, explain, or disguise their enjoyment of sex with their fellow men. Some, for instance, would sit around the tent bragging about their women, how they'd met such a one in town, how they had another one back home, a sweet Southern belle who would do anything you asked her to, or a pretty octaroon girl who would meet them down by the river, or the mother of a friend who invited them around to fix the gutters, and so on and so forth. The tales were familiar to us all, but they gave some credibility to the inevitable complaint "God damn it, I'm so horny I could fuck anything that moved" and the rubbing of the crotch. Then cocks would come out, and there would be much laughter and backslapping, often developing into a dick-measuring contest, with the "judge" kneeling between the two erect weapons, holding them together, rubbing them, and eventually sucking them. There were plenty in the camp who were quick to volunteer for these duties, and they were sought-after tentmates.

There was a great deal of casual contact in the latrines, and around them. We were lucky; we had a medical officer who understood the dangers of diarrhea and dysentery, and ensured that we had new latrine trenches dug outside the perimeter of the circle of tents. We had all heard tales of camps where the latrines or "sinks" were so vile that men ended up pissing and shitting outside, or even in, their tents and spreading disease that way. We had fresh trenches with boards across them, which enabled a man to squat when necessary, and we could wash ourselves in a nearby stream which flowed away from the camp, away from the town. (God help anyone who lived down that way who was using the stream for water!) Often in the latrines one would see men hanging around long after they had finished and cleaned up, idly playing with their dicks until someone came and joined them. From there, it was easy to slip away into the darkness of the woods that backed the camp for a little mutual enjoyment; on warm nights, the dry, leaf-strewn floor of the woods was covered in pairs of lovers.

The washhouse was another happy hunting ground for those less wary of discovery, and what started off as an innocent offer to help a buddy wash his back often turned into mutual masturbation or more. As the weeks passed, it became common to find men fucking in the washhouse, until Jed Brown put out an order forbidding it on the ground of hygiene. After that, the men went to certain tents that were known, in the language of the camp, as "happy houses." Needless to say, mine was the happiest of all, though it was a nuisance if you wanted to sleep.

My favorite memory from Company K's camp days was given to me by a young man whom I befriended shortly after arrival, a dark-haired, heavyset lad from rural Carroll County who had the reputation of being a simpleton because he couldn't read. He was, in all other respects, a typical, healthy young farm boy who enjoyed kicking a ball around the yard, climbing and falling out of trees, drinking too much liquor, and singing sentimental songs about mothers. I'd seen him watching me a few times during parade or at meals, and I couldn't figure out if he despised me for the color of my skin or wanted me to take his cherry; frequently the two things went together. But one night he approached me as I sat on a stool at the entrance to my tent, scribbling in my diary.

"You always writing, mistuh," he said, in his drawling accent.

"Yep. Beats playing cards or getting drunk."

"I bet it does."

"You want something, son?"

He looked at me from under his heavy brows. He can't have been more than 20, but he had the heavy beard growth and the pronounced features of a man ten, 15 years older. I noticed that the vee of his open-necked shirt was filled with thick black hair.

"The other fellows say I'm stupid because I can't read and write."

"Do they say so?"

"Yeah, and I guess they're right."

"You don't seem stupid to me."

"Well, I don't seem stupid to myself when I'm sitting alone and thinking, and when I'm talking about stuff, but when it comes to books and such I guess I'm a dunce."

"Maybe you were never taught right."

"I was taught all right, with a strap over my hand every time I got a word wrong."

"That ain't no way to teach a child."

"How'd you learn to read and write, mistuh?"

"Does it surprise you, kid?"

"Where I come from, the niggers don't go to school."

221

I drew breath to berate him for using a word that had always been offensive to my ears, but changed my mind.

"They teach you that word, son?"

"Yeah."

"Well, don't use it again around me, or I will beat your white ass from here to Mexico. Understand?"

"Yes, sir."

"Now come and sit by me." I pulled up a stool and patted it. He sat obediently, his hands pressed awkwardly between his knees. I turned the page of my notebook and wrote in large, clear letters the word *cat*.

"What does that say?"

He followed the letters with his fingers. "Cat."

"Good boy. Now try this." I wrote again.

"Cow."

"Good. Now this."

"Fu–oh, I ain't never seen that word writ down before!" He laughed, and I nudged him hard in the ribs, and he toppled off his stool.

"So why do you come to me asking me how I learned to read and write, boy?"

"Because I figured that a nig—I mean, a black man like you wouldn't be so quick to judge me, mistuh."

"That's a good enough answer, boy, and I admire your honesty." That wasn't all I admired about him; as he sprawled on the ground laughing, red in the face, I had the opportunity to assess his strong legs, chunky ass, and strong torso.

"What's your name, boy?"

"Howard, sir."

"That your Christian name or your family name?"

"Christian name. Family name is Porter."

"Pleased to meet you, Howard Porter. I'm Aaron Johnson." I wrote our two names, HOWARD and AARON, in my notebook. His finger traced the two As at the beginning of Aaron with a certain amount of wonder.

"Aaron, like in the Bible? The brother of Moses?"

"You know your Bible, Howard?"

"Sure. I love the Bible stories. Aaron made a Golden Calf and the Israelites bowed down before it."

"So you're not stupid, then."

"I guess not... I wish you could teach me to read."

I could teach you a few tricks, baby, I thought, but reading wouldn't be at the top of my list. But looking into his trusting, bashful face, so masculine but so boyish, I didn't have the heart to take advantage of his trusting ways.

"I'll do my best. At least I won't hit you with a strap."

"Thanks, mistuh."

"Call me Aaron." And feel the power of my rod, I almost added.

"Aaron. Are we going to be friends?"

"Sure. Why not."

"Because most of the guys don't want to be seen with a idiot."

"You aren't an idiot," I said, hoping that this wasn't going to be the extent of our conversation.

"I got a letter today," Howard said, drawing a small white package from his jacket pocket. "Don't know what to do with it."

"Where's it from? Home?"

"My sweetheart, Emily. I know what her handwriting looks like. See? It's pretty, isn't it? Look at the way she writes my name, all them curls and such. Almost as pretty as she is."

"What's it say, Howard?"

"Don't know. Haven't opened it." He dropped it on the ground. "Can't read it."

I picked it up and flicked off a bit of mud that had stuck to the envelope. "You want me to...?"

Howard's face lit up. "Would you? I mean, really? I couldn't ask anyone else, because they'd make up lies and

223

stuff to make a fool of me. They'd say she'd run off and married a circus freak or she'd born me a child or something."

"Did you and her...do things that could make a child?"

"Sure. The night I left town to join the army. She let me."

"How was it?"

"It was the greatest time of my life," he said, with a serious expression on his handsome face. "At least I done that once before I die."

"Are you sure you want me to read it? It might be bad news."

"I'm sure."

I opened the envelope and drew out two sheets of fine blue writing paper; it looked so incongruous in the filth and masculine squalor of the camp. It was covered with the same elaborate penmanship that I'd seen on the envelope, and I already had an idea that Howard's sweetheart was never going to make him a happy man.

"Dear Howard," I read.

"Emily writes that beautifully, don't she?"

"Yes, she certainly does. Shall I go on?"

"Yep."

"I hope this letter finds you well. Everything here is much the same, we have had some lovely flowers in the garden and no end of party invitations. I danced at the Mason's ball with four different partners and everyone said that I was the prettiest girl at the dance."

"They got that right," Howard said. "She's the prettiest girl in the world."

"Howard, if you keep interrupting I won't be able to read you the rest of the letter."

"Sorry, Aaron. I'll keep quiet."

He composed himself into a thoughtful posture, and I continued.

"Mama and Papa have been visiting all over the county

and Papa has done some wonderful business deals so we shall have new dresses and shoes and maybe even a new pony. I am so looking forward to Thanksgiving and Christmas and all the parties that we shall have where I can show them off."

This did not sound like the letter that a real sweetheart would have written, and I began to wonder if Emily had simply dallied with Howard—who, after all, was physically impressive—and was now about to drop him. I hesitated to read on, and Howard glanced up at me.

I continued, "Well, I see that I have covered nearly two sheets of paper and Papa says that we must limit the amount we write so I shall close now. It remains only to say that I hope you did not misinterpret the friendship I showed toward you in those last weeks you were at home, when I took pity on you and allowed intimacies that no gentleman would ever have taken advantage of."

I was having some difficulty following this, and glanced over at Howard. He was scowling and staring at the ground.

"Please do not try to contact me again, as I am engaged to be married and I would not like any complications to arise. Yours truly, Emily Willison."

A tear dropped from Howard's eye and splashed on his boot.

"I'm sorry, Howard. I really am," I said.

"Oh, it's all right," he said, wiping his eye with his sleeve. "I always knew she was too good for me."

"She's no good, Howard. She's treated you—"

"Don't say that!" he shouted, and scrambled to his feet. "You don't know her. She's an angel."

I let him stomp around for a minute, then he returned and sat beside me—a little closer this time.

"I guess I knew that this would happen. Her such a fine young lady and me just a—"

"There's nothing wrong with you, son. You're a good

man, a strong man. Look at this letter," I said, picking it up again. "She shows no real concern for you. She doesn't care that you've gone to war; you might as well have gone on a picnic for all that she's bothered. She's only interested in showing off her new finery, and bragging about how many men she's danced with, while you're risking your life to protect the likes of her and her family."

I was warming to my theme, and suddenly noticed that Howard was leaning against me, resting his head on my shoulder and silently crying. I put an arm around him and held him close.

"What am I going to do now? She was the only friend I had."

"She's not worthy of you."

"Now I'm on my own."

"Nonsense. Look around you! The camp is full of fine fellows; all of them would be honored to be your friend."

"They ain't. They call me a fool."

"Well I don't call you a fool. As far as I'm concerned, you're one of the best men I've met. And if you want, you can pick up your kit and you can move yourself right in here beside me.

"You're just saying that."

In answer, I kissed the top of his head, just where the dark hair parted at the crown. He looked up at me, puzzled.

"Why would you be so kind to me?"

"Because someone was kind to me once, when I needed a friend." I was thinking of Jack Edgerton when I said this; I hadn't thought of him for weeks. Had he really been a friend? Had I been a friend to him? I would have to think about that later.

"You're a good man, Aaron Johnson." He looked directly into my eyes, and his lips parted. It was too much to resist, and I kissed him, caressing his stubbly face with my fingertips. Someone whistled from nearby, and I heard ribald

226

laughter, but I didn't care; I was only interested in comforting Howard, and if this was the way he wanted it...

Of course, I'd been hard in my pants ever since he sat down beside me; the thought of helping this handsome, serious young man with his reading, and of breaking the news that he'd been jilted by a heartless girl, was most appealing to my lower nature, as it put him so completely in my power. Now, however, I wasn't just interested in skewering his hairy white butt on my cock. I wanted to do that, of course—but I also wanted our relations to mean something, to impress upon Howard the fact that I really cared for him, rather than just the pleasure that could be had from various conjunctions of our sexual organs.

We lay back on the ground, our feet still sticking out of the tent, but our upper bodies concealed by canvas as far as the knee. At first he seemed stunned by my kisses, and lay passively in my arms—but then, quite suddenly, he began to return them, his tongue pressing into my mouth, his lips devouring mine. His fingers delved into my hair, into my shirt. I grabbed him by the ass and drew our groins together; when he felt our hard cocks making contact he jerked and gasped.

"I never knew it could be like this."

"You mean with another man?"

"Oh, no... I seen what goes on around the camp, and once or twice I let them, you know, play with my thing."

He wasn't a virgin, then.

"But I never heard about kissing and holding and...loving and such."

"How does it feel?"

Again, that serious, thoughtful expression.

"Pretty good."

That was all the encouragement I needed, and I started to undress him. As each item of clothing came off, his body was revealed as even more magnificent than I had imagined;

he was a young man used to physical labor, a stranger to vanity, whose hard, dense, hairy body was made for pleasure. I could not help pitying Miss Emily Willison, who had forfeited her chance of a lifetime of making love to Howard Porter.

Finally I had him naked, his hard cock pointing straight up to his belly button, resting on a dense mat of hair. Black hair covered his body from the neckline downward, forming whorls over his nipples, tapering into a line down his stomach, then fanning out again over his groin and thighs. I could not resist, and I dived into one armpit, kissing and licking as I went. Howard's hips bucked, so I grabbed his thick cock and squeezed. He stuck his fingers into my hair and held on as my mouth explored his chest, his stomach, then further down...

"I want to feel your skin," he said.

"Go ahead."

"Stand up."

I stood, and he undressed me as a valet undresses his master before bedtime. He unfastened my shirt, drew it over my head, and laid it neatly on the chair. He undid my belt, unbuttoned my fly, peeled down my pants. I kicked off my boots and allowed him to pull my pants over my feet; now I was as naked as him. He was kneeling, I was standing, and there was only one obvious course of events.

It happened. He kissed the tip of my cock, looking up at me for permission. I smiled, caressed his faced, and drew him toward me.

Howard Porter learned how to suck cock that day, how to take it without gagging and how to adjust his pace to suit me. He learned how to lie back and receive it as well, and, despite his initial aversion, he learned to enjoy the feeling of a tongue and a finger or two up his ass. I kept him going for as long as I could, but it was obvious that the boy needed to come—and I cradled him in my arms, kissing him pas-

228

sionately while I jerked his stiff cock to a messy climax. I don't think he'd come in a while; there was enough there to repopulate the Commonwealth of Virginia.

He took a while to come around from the slumber he'd fallen into—but he didn't run away as I'd feared he might. Instead he resumed sucking my cock, and by the time I was ready to come, he too was hard again.

"Go and get your things," I told him. "You're staying with me from now on."

He dressed reluctantly and kissed me for so long that I thought I'd never get him out. And tonight, Howard Porter, you're going to learn to take more than a finger up that hairy little ass of yours, I thought, as I watched him walking across the camp. He had a spring in his step.

With Howard as my companion, life in Company K was even sweeter than before. But, of course, it all came to an end soon enough. Captain Chester came into my tent one day with tears in his eyes and announced that Company K, and indeed the whole of the 4th Virginia Cavalry, was going into battle.

"Where are we going?"

"I don't know. South." He was pale, his hands were shaking. He fumbled as he lit one of his foul cigars.

"Are you frightened, Captain Chester?"

"Frightened, boy? Not on your life." His voice cracked a little, and he would not look me in the eye, but I admired his bravado.

Howard was lying naked on my blanket, picking twigs and blades of grass from his densely matted chest. (I'd just taken him for a "stroll" in the woods.) "I'm not frightened," Howard said. "I joined up to fight. What else is war about?"

Captain Chester and I looked at each other. War, for both of us, had been about opportunity, about hiding from reality, about turning a profit and getting our dicks sucked. War had been about young, normal men like Howard doing things that they would never have done in peacetime, and that they would deny for the rest of their lives, except perhaps in their solitary reveries. War had seen the world turned upside down—a Negro fighting for the slave owners, a boy like Billy acting like a woman, a Union sheriff transformed into a Confederate officer. Our camp was that crazy world in microcosm. I had found myself a lover, a companion both of my bed and of my heart, whom I was teaching to read and write and fuck and suck. Captain Chester had put his talents to good use, while Captain Jed Brown had worked his way through every young man in the camp, enjoying his authority and handing out a unique form of "discipline." Billy was living almost full-time as a "woman" now, having been taken up by a visiting major who exempted him from active service—in the normal sense of the word—and kept him as other men would keep a mistress, showering him with gifts in return for sexual favors. There was only one crucial difference, Billy told me one night—and that was that the general enjoyed being fucked just as much as he enjoyed fucking. "He's got everything he needs in one package, he says," Billy remarked. "Now he says he'll never need to cheat again."

But, to the major's dismay, Billy folded up his finery on the day we were mobilized, locked his jewelry and his money in a case, packed a trunk with his skirts and wigs, and said, "And they won't come out again until the war is over."

We paraded at dawn to receive our marching orders. Jed Brown was more impressive than ever; he may have been playing a role, but he played it well.

"Men of Company K. And ladies!"

This got a laugh and set us at our ease; all of us, at one time or another in the last few weeks, had taken the lady's part.

"We move out today, bound for the Shenandoah Valley.

The Yankees are burning the corn, burning the houses, killing folk, killing the cattle. We must do all we can to stop them. We may not be many, we may not be strong, but we are all together, are we not?"

There was a faint cheer.

"We are brothers in arms. We have been together, here in this camp, for long enough now. We have worked together, trained together, fought together—"

"And fucked together!" This, of course, was Charlie.

"And fucked together, yes," Jed Brown said, "and I know of no man who hasn't become a better soldier for learning to take it up the ass. Am I right?"

This time the cheer was anything but faint.

"So let's march with pride in our hearts and friends on either side. Who would dare to cross the men of Company K?"

There was much more in the same vein, and much cheering and whistling, much shaking of hands and kissing, much slapping of backs and asses. We marched out of town with the old Alhambra band at our head, playing "Dixie." Our hearts were light though our packs were heavy. I had Howard at my side, and I told him that I would not let anything happen to him.

And so we set out for the Shenandoah Valley, each of us stifling in our hearts the fear that we might never return alive.

XIII

MY MEDICAL TRAINING WAS BASIC, TO SAY THE LEAST, AND
was frequently interrupted by the attentions of Captain Healey, who regarded me as his personal property and fucked
me whenever he liked. I was an unwilling and unresponsive
lover, but I dared not refuse him in case he decided—as he
frequently threatened—to turn me over to the police for my
part in the St. Albans raid. He had a whole string of charges
that, he said, would land me in a military prison for the rest
of my life, if I didn't cooperate.

Under Healey's tutelage, I began to see how sex, which
I had always regarded as a pleasant and harmless pastime,
could become a form of abuse, an expression of corrupted power. At one time, not so very long ago, the idea of
"corrupted power" would have excited me, particularly if
it involved a brutally handsome, bald, muscular man in an
officer's uniform who simply wanted to fuck my ass and
mouth. It was the sort of thing I dreamed about back home
in Bishopstown, jacking myself off to sleep with visions of
domination just such as that which I was now experiencing.

But the dream was very different from the reality. Healey didn't care if he hurt me, or if I wasn't in the mood to be fucked. He didn't even care if my ass was in no fit state to be fucked due to its more natural function as an egress for excrement. He reveled in my discomfort, and if I fouled his prick he used it as an excuse to degrade me even further. I was obliged to submit, and thankfully I was always able to perform efficiently enough to get the ordeal over with quickly, but I came to hate Healey and what he was doing to me as much as I have ever hated anyone in my life. I had ample opportunity to kill him, or to betray him to the authorities, but I knew that it would have made life worse for me. So I suffered in silence.

The one thing that sustained me during this time was my rapid advance in medical studies. As a medical orderly, I was expected to do little more than roll bandages, empty slop buckets, carry the wounded and sick, and occasionally hold down a soldier while his leg or arm was amputated. All of this I learned to do in the field hospital to which I was initially posted, down in Baltimore, which we reached after a three-week march from Vermont.

I did all my work without complaint, and it soon became apparent to the overstretched doctors and nurses that I was intelligent enough to do more than mop and carry. I was taken under the wing of a nurse named Jenny Wallace, a brave, strong-shouldered farm girl who had overcome no end of opposition to obtain work at the hospital. Most of the nursing was left to badly trained soldiers such as me, or to recovering patients with little idea of hygiene, let alone how to treat sickness or injury. Jenny had been training as a nurse before the war began, and decided to put her training to some use. "I thought my ugly face would be a protection against what Daddy called man's baser instincts," she told me, "but I've realized that most men, even those who are near to dying, aren't too fussy about what a woman looks like, as long as she's a woman." Jenny was homely enough, it's true, but she had kind eyes and a beautiful smile which would have made any man of sense fall in love with her. She'd developed a wide range of techniques for thwarting unwanted attentions from the men, patients and doctors as well as men of other ranks; some of these techniques were purely verbal, while others involved a swift knee in the balls. I used a few myself to stave off unwanted suitors, and I wished I had the guts to kick Healey in the nuts the next time he started pawing me.

After a few weeks working alongside Jenny, I was a pretty proficient nurse myself. I could clean and bandage even quite serious wounds, and I found that I was not as squeamish as I feared. I could remove bullets or shards of metal from bleeding flesh, I could pack burns with soothing creams, I could hold down a screaming man while the doctors performed hideous but lifesaving operations on him. I quickly conquered my repugnance for blood, vomit, shit, and pus; I suppose my recent way of life had counteracted the delicacy of my upbringing. I learned the properties of various medicines and could prepare sedatives or antiseptic washes. I knew how to administer the drugs that would help a man in a fever, and for those who were beyond such help I learned the arts of making them comfortable as they awaited the inevitable end. I saw many young men die in that hospital, and consoled myself with the fact that I had eased their final moments. Many of them commissioned me to write letters home, or pressed into my hand tokens of loved ones, parents, friends. They allowed me intimacies that they were afraid of allowing to Nurse Jenny, so I often had to help wounded men go to the bathroom, or wash them if they had messed themselves. I didn't mind. I saw it as penance for a life almost entirely wasted in selfish folly.

For once in my life, I had no idle time in which to seek pleasure or trouble. I worked every hour I could, partly because the need around me was so great, partly because it kept me from the attentions of Captain Healey, who, despite his autocratic pretensions, could hardly remove a nurse from the wards just because he wanted to fuck him. I often worked for 16 hours at a stretch, which allowed me two hours for other military duties, two hours in which to submit to Healey's desires, and, if I was lucky, four hours in which to sleep. I lost weight, my muscles wasted away, and my skin took on the gray tone of exhaustion. My hair fell out even more rapidly; after a couple of months, I had a definite bald patch on top of my head. I was no longer the pretty boy who had turned heads in the White Horse.

When the call came for volunteers to proceed to the front in Virginia, I did not hesitate. Captain Healey tried to stop me from leaving—he had no desire to get his head blown off, he said, and he almost pleaded with me to change my mind. I suppose, in his way, he had grown fond of me, or had at least grown accustomed to the skills that I practiced on him. I had learned those skills in the heat of passion, even of love—now I reproduced them coldly, with hate in my heart. I did not want to associate those feelings of physical joy with anger, spite, and pain ever again, and if that meant losing my life in the service of the sick and dying, it didn't seem such a bad exchange. Healey tried appealing to my sentimental streak, which he rightly guessed was a mile wide, and he even told me that he loved me. I did not believe him. No man could do the things he had done—things I do not care to remember, much less write down—to someone he loved. When I told him this, he reverted to his true character and started threatening me again. I went straight to his superior officers and told them that I was eager to be released for active service. They signed my papers right away.

We were marching to the aid of Union forces that had been severely beaten by Confederate troops under General Early, at Kernstown, just south of Winchester. I knew little of the tactics of the operation, and understood less; it seemed to me, from what I could glean, that both sides were swinging up and down the mountains and valleys of the area inflicting terrible losses on each other with no advantage to be gained in any direction. Mine, however, was not to reason why; mine was but to patch up the wounded and comfort the dying.

For much of the summer of 1864, I worked at the field hospital near Winchester. Our own position was dangerous enough to begin with, as Early's forces were still running amok in the valley, ambushing our men and coming perilously close to the hospital; I often wondered who had given the order for the medical corps to be established in such a vulnerable position. All this changed, however, when General Grant sent us General Sheridan. News spread fast that this was the man who would end the war, at whatever cost. In the hospital, we braced ourselves for hard work, and in private I prayed that both sides would somehow manage to lose each other in the labyrinth of hills and gullies that characterized the area. It was a beautiful country—as beautiful in its own way as the landscape of my childhood. But as time went by it was increasingly marked by war, by fire, by death. Sheridan arrived with one mission in mind: to beat Early into submission, and to turn the Shenandoah Valley into a barren waste.

Wounded men came into the hospital in considerable numbers every day, although they assured us that they had inflicted far greater damage than they'd sustained. Early's men, they said, were cowards who would run rather than fight, but by the look of the wounded there were enough of Early's men who would stand their ground rather than let the Yankees pass unchallenged. I did all that I could to help them, but with the massive numbers of sick and dying still unmoved after the Battle of Kernstown, it was all we could do to prevent disease from wiping out all of us.

236

With each intake we heard new tales from the front line, some of it obviously bragging, as soldiers' tales are apt to be—I learned to sift the truth from the fact—and some of it very strange. There's a superstitious streak in your average fighting man, always ready to see some supernatural influence at work in the battlefield, and we heard many tales of angels coming through the smoke to carry the dying off to heaven, much as in the myths of the ancient races. And again and again I heard news of a "black devil" who fought harder and more fiercely than any other Rebel, who "rose from hell" to inflict terrible injuries before disappearing with a whiff of sulfur. I gave these tales little credence, but they became the currency of the sickroom and troubled the fever dreams of many an injured man. The Black Devil became as real a figure of the times as General Lee or Jefferson Davis.

Work, and the horrors I witnessed, made me into an automaton, which was a blessing in disguise. When I slept, I slept like a dead man, absolutely unconscious until I awoke—suddenly, totally awake—and started working again. When I saw my face in the shaving mirror I was skinny and pale. I had always looked younger than my years; now I looked older. Perhaps all the depravity of the last few years was catching up with me at last—which would be ironic, as I was now to all intents and purposes celibate. My only intimate contact was on the wards. I cleaned and cared for the men in my charge—all colors and ages and shapes and sizes—with as much fortitude as I could muster. Sometimes, they wanted comfort of a more carnal nature and would force my hand down onto a stiff cock. Once, I would have taken advantage of the situation; now I just took a leaf out of Nurse Jenny's book and rapped any upstanding member with a cold metal spatula which I carried in my belt for just such occasions. That soon took the pep out of them.

For all my good intentions, I could not prevent myself from becoming fond of some of the men—I realized that mine was essentially a sentimental nature, looking to give and receive love, which is what had led me into so many ridiculous situations in the past. I had mistaken fucking for love, and had given too much of myself, to the wrong people, as a result. Most of the men I processed as a butcher would process meat, but there were a few who touched me in a different way.

One I will never forget came to us from one of the Zouave regiments that had fought their way down the Potomac and were now dispersed among other units. He was a dark, handsome New Yorker, with a typical gruff East Coast accent, dark thinning hair, and a thick moustache—he reminded me a great deal of the railroad workers who used to fuck me at the White Horse. He had been badly injured by flying shrapnel and came to us delirious with fever, his Zouave uniform in tatters. He had lost the fez that characterized those most elegant of soldiers, but retained the tight-fitting jacket, the baggy pantaloons, the white leggings with their leather cuffs, and of course the wide, long sash that is the pride of the Zouave soldier. It was all filthy and badly torn, revealing large expanses of tanned, hairy thigh, chest, and stomach. His injuries were mostly concentrated on the right arm, which had taken a bullet in the elbow, smashing the bones to splinters. Before he recovered from his delirium, he was hurried into the operating theater, and his arm was amputated just below the shoulder. He hardly seemed to feel the pain, but tossed on his bed in terrible nightmares, occasionally screaming out. I did all I could to make him comfortable, and prayed that gangrene had not already set in.

For two weeks I nursed him through fever, dripping water into his mouth on a sponge, feeding him when possible with soup, providing him with the means to urinate and defecate, washing him, and even trimming his hair and moustache. I tried shaving him, but it was too painful for him, and soon he had grown a beard that almost matched the moustache in thickness and splendor. It had been my job, when he first came into my care, to cut away the remnants of his splendid Zouave uniform, and to clean up the lesser cuts and lacerations. What was revealed, as the tatters came away, was a body of immense strength and elegance, the skin brown, the hair jet black. I washed him in clean water, and allowed myself to delight in the beauty of his form, which seemed like a light in all that darkness.

His name was Michael Kardashian—he was of Armenian extraction. All this he told me when, one grim day like any other, he suddenly awoke from his fever, sat up in bed, and asked for food. By some miracle, he had survived the amputation, the fever, and the malnutrition of the last weeks, and apart from a certain haggardness, he looked as healthy as anyone in the hospital. I brought him water, and he caught me by the arm. "You're the one, aren't you? The one who took care of me?"

I said that I was.

"I owe you my life."

"I'm sorry about your…"

"My arm? Well, I'm alive, no? There's nothing that my right hand could do that my left hand can't."

I helped him eat, shave, and wash, but he was impatient to learn to be self-sufficient. He was clumsy, slopping water into his bed as he attempted to clean himself, and I had to scold him, but we always ended up laughing. I was able to give him a little privacy by hanging sheets around his bed, while he struggled to perform the most basic functions "without an audience," as he put it. He never minded me being there.

I knew that Michael was well on the road to recovery when, during one of these washing sessions, he developed an erection. I'd had ample opportunity to see his cock when he was ill, and I had tried not to be too interested in its size and girth, even when (as frequently happened with fever patients) it became spontaneously, rigidly erect. Now, however, as I was washing his back, I noticed that he was trying to keep his knees together. He was sitting up in bed, and it looked like a most uncomfortable position.

"You can lie back now, Michael."

"No, I can't."

"Why not?"

He grinned. "I'm embarrassed."

"You've never been embarrassed before—oh. I see." He lay back, and his dick bounced up to lie against his hairy stomach. It reached up to his belly button.

"I guess you've seen it all before." With his left hand, he was idly rubbing the hair on his chest.

"Yes, I sure have."

"Don't suppose you could…give me a helping hand? I know I said that my left hand could do as well as my right, but—"

"You know I can't do that, Michael."

"Aw, come on. Help a man out. Just let me feel alive for a while. Let me feel like someone cares for me."

It was hard to resist, and he was very, very hard. With every beat of his heart, his dick pulsed on its mat of hair.

"Please?" His eyes were wet, his lips slightly parted. I put down the wet cloth and rested a hand on his groin. The heat that came off him was tremendous, and I worried that he was becoming feverish again. But the moment I touched him he sighed, closed his eyes, and looked immediately ten years younger. I let my fingers encircle his cock—they barely met around it, it was so thick—and started to jack him off. I did not want to overexcite him, as he was still a sick man, but I could see from the look on his face that this was doing him nothing but good. Or was I once again deluding myself?

With his remaining hand, he caressed my arm, reaching up to my shoulder, catching me by the collar, and pulling me toward him. When we kissed, his beard and moustache felt rough on my face—but his lips were soft, and his tongue even softer. He moaned slightly, the sound muffled by our joined mouths, and started spurting all over his hairy belly. When he had finished, I cleaned him up, held him for a while, dressed him, and changed the sheets. This happened many more times, and Michael told me frequently that he loved me and would never forget me. It went no further, but it was enough. After a month, he was well enough to leave the hospital and return to New York. He was no longer fit for active service, and I hope that he saw out the rest of the war in safety, surrounded by people who cared for him as much as I did.

I lived in a continuous present, untroubled by memories of the past or hopes and fears for the future, until one night I was visited by an unwelcome dream. I was back home in Vermont—how long ago and far away that seemed!—surrounded by the trees in their summer finery, the stream babbling along through our garden, my sisters and my parents sitting around me, smiling and laughing. I smelled the honeysuckle that grew wild in the hedge, and the savory smell of a roast chicken that my father was about to carve. I felt myself loved and embraced, as I had once been, but now it was so painful I almost cried out, as if someone had touched me on a wound.

And then the scene darkened; the stream ran cloudy, and black with blood. The leaves withered from the trees, my family faded away with their hands over their faces, and all was silent but for the throb of a heartbeat—mine, I suppose. Smoke filled the air, made my eyes water, made me choke and retch. The garden disappeared, and I was no longer at home, no longer in any place that I knew. The red glow of fire illuminated the scene, one figure looming from the confusion, growing nearer and larger, a dark silhouette that was part of the smoke, part of the fire. It came nearer to me, smelling of blood and decay, and just as I was about to scream I recognized the face of Aaron Johnson.

I awoke with a start, convinced that the ward was on fire. But all was well; the only noises were the groans of the fever patients, the sobbing of the dying men, the occasional scream from the operating theater—noises that were so common I no longer heard them, as one does not hear birdsong in the woods.

I rose, even though I was not on duty, washed my face in cold water, and went to see if I could be of assistance anywhere. There was always too much to do, and never enough people to do it, so my offer was not refused, even though Nurse Jenny looked at me as if she'd seen a ghost.

However busy I made myself, I could not stop thinking about Aaron. I had been so proud, so sure of getting him, so angry when he avoided me. For a long time it had rankled with me like unfinished business, and I actually resented the high tone he'd taken with me, the pompous pronouncements on the right way to live our lives. Oh, how I'd tried to undermine him, to bring him down to my level! I thought, back then and for a long time afterward, that being queer excused me from the need to live a decent life. I thought that we were by our very nature outsiders, that we had been condemned by society to live beyond the pale and that our revenge would be to live exactly as we pleased. But life had taught me a few hard lessons—there was no sphere of existence into which questions of good and bad did not come. A man is not judged by his preferences, or the names he calls himself, but by his actions to others. Aaron had told me this a hundred times, and he tried to make me live right. I laughed at him, and when he turned away I found consolation with the first dick I could get my hands on.

Well, he was right, and I was wrong. And if I had utterly forfeited the right to call myself his friend, not only by the way I treated him back in Vermont but in the damnably foolish way I'd chosen to live since, I was well rewarded for it now. Perhaps, by hard work and self-sacrifice, I could one day purge myself of the shame that, I felt, had driven us apart. He would never know, of course; wherever Aaron Johnson was, he sure as hell wasn't thinking of me, and he would never need a fool like Jack Edgerton in his life.

I knew that it was a foolish dream, my dream of Aaron Johnson and how things might have been, but it gave me comfort and enabled me to be a better nurse. I allowed myself to think of him as my lover—my distant, absent, wholly ideal lover. And by thinking of myself as his, I kept away from others. So this was how my life would end, I thought, and I was not distressed.

What I had feared finally came about: the hospital was swept by dysentery, and the patients started dying by the dozen. I was no longer afraid of death or dead bodies, but the scale of the epidemic alarmed me. I was carrying out one or two a day, then four, then ten. We could not dispose of the bodies except in mass graves over which we were obliged to shovel quicklime in order to speed the process of decay and to contain the infection. I assumed that I would come down with the symptoms at any minute, as the level of hygiene was rudimentary at best, but every day I awoke with nothing worse than a headache and a dry mouth. I did not even develop diarrhea. I remained, to my dull astonishment, in relatively rude health.

The hospital had to be closed down, and those who were not dying were transferred to safer, cleaner destinations. I could have gone with them but chose to stay. I volunteered instead to staff a new, makeshift field hospital even closer to the battle lines. If Death would not find me here, then surely it would find me there.

Getting out of the hospital and back on the road did me powerful good. For weeks, even months, the furthest I had been from the dead and dying was around behind the hospital building—once a fine family home, appropriated from its owners—where I had disposed of soiled materials and, all too frequently, corpses. Now I was outdoors again, sleeping under canvas as we moved south to our new, perilous position. It was more dangerous than I knew; during September, Early's Confederates skirted our position and fought a bloody battle at Winchester, leaving us effectively surrounded by the enemy—though, whether by luck or planning, they did not pay us any attention. Our new base was near Fisher's Hill—and it was here that one of the bloodiest battles of the campaign would be fought.

I do not intend to go into details of that engagement—I am not a military historian, and I know nothing of the tactics and planning that resulted in that ghastly bloodbath. I heard much from my colleagues and patients about the strange formation of the Shenandoah Valley which made it possible for armies to circle each other without meeting, however much they may have wanted to. There was much talk of bandits roaming the area, snipers picking off people at random, and our status as noncombatants was no protection. However, we proceeded through the countryside unmolested.

And what countryside it was. Where once had stood trees and houses, where once the Shenandoah meandered through a paradisial landscape, now there was mud and ash, the blackened stumps of tree trunks, the ruins of houses. Cattle roamed through this nightmare scene, their udders full and distended, searching for grass and bellowing in pain. Chickens ran around, scattered from destroyed farmyards, pecking contentedly for grain; more common were the crows that clustered around dying livestock and dead humans. We even saw children wandering through that manmade hell, and took them to safety whenever we could.

Our destination was just outside the town of Strasburg, which had been badly knocked about by Sheridan's men.

We took over an old school, pitched tents around it, and transformed the interior into the best infirmary we could, which was not much. We were given an armed guard, but the town was empty. We heard that Sheridan was planning a major confrontation with the enemy any day now, and we hurried to do all that we could in the time we had. Nurse Jenny worked by my side, as strong and capable as any man and much cooler in a crisis. I suppose we were brave, but we didn't think much about it. We both expected death, and perhaps, for our own different reasons, we both wanted it.

Before we were ready to receive them, sick and wounded men were arriving in scores. Sheridan had been skirmishing up and down the valleys, attacking Early's forces wherever he found them, but they weren't ready to give up yet and gave as good as they got, sometimes better. Even here there was talk of the Black Devil, who had sent many a good Yankee boy to his maker. Those who were not seriously wounded we bandaged up and pressed into service; many a soldier was transformed into a porter or an orderly or even a nurse after being under Jenny's and my command for a few days.

Suddenly, the steady trickle of admissions became a wave, and that was when we knew that Sheridan and his fellow generals had put into practice his plan to destroy the lingering resistance in Virginia and lay waste the country. The battle of Fisher's Hill and its incendiary aftermath quickly became a national scandal, and it nearly brought me the death I had expected for so long.

I will not waste words describing what I saw and did in the hospital that day, or the day after. I did all that I could, and I saw things that no man should ever see. Perhaps I helped a few, but there was often nothing that I could do. But every man who came in, however badly injured, was proud to report that the losses on the other side were infinitely greater than ours. I found this to be of no comfort whatsoever.

The battle was declared over, and the last of the wounded were stretchered in to be patched up, sawn up, or buried, as best the doctors could. Jenny and I were exhausted, and she was sick, vomiting all the time; I felt sure she would die. And then, suddenly, as we thought we had reached the very bottom of the pit of hell, we were under attack. Through the stench of blood and shit and puke, I smelled smoke. This time it was no dream; the hospital was on fire.

I ran outside and saw that our tents were flaming. A few dark figures were running around the camp, some of them our comrades, others the insurgents who had set the fire. They were running toward the building, and there was nothing I could do to stop them. This time it was no party; war had found me at last. I was unarmed; the guards had all the weapons, and they were, as yet, unaware of the attack. I sounded the alarm, ringing the old school bell as loud and hard as I could, until I became conscious of bullets whizzing past my ears. I ran back into the ward, where I saw Nurse Jenny trying to calm a delirious soldier while the Rebels poured in through a window, upturning beds and cutting throats. I grabbed Jenny, dragged her away from the bedside and back through what had once been the kitchen. Unable to rescue any of our belongings, or to equip ourselves with the most basic necessities of life, we fled the scene. Jenny fell, and when I turned back to find her she was gone.

I had no choice but to save my own skin; we were surrounded by uncontrolled Rebel forces, themselves cut off from the lines of command, who were meting out to the "invaders" (as they saw us) the same kind of treatment that Sheridan was unleashing across the whole Shenandoah Valley region. The hospital was on fire, the roof had already collapsed onto the operating theater, and it looked as if the same would happen to the ward. I stood for a moment, indecisive, knowing that I should go back and save as many men as I could—and then I saw a gray-uniformed soldier charging toward me with a knife. I ducked behind the bins where we stored soiled dressings and linen until they could be burned and held my breath, not just for fear of detection but because of the vile smell. The bins had not been emptied for weeks, and they were now a breeding ground for maggots.

The soldier ran past, thank God—he had not seen me, or did not think me worth dirtying his blade for. I knew that I could scramble over the old perimeter fence into the woods, where at least there would be hiding places and the chance of surviving the attack. My better self told me to stand my ground, to die protecting the vulnerable—but instinct took over, and I ran. By the time I reached the trees, I was soaked with the cold sweat of terror.

The woods had been burned months before, when the Confederates had driven the Federals out of the valley the first time, and I thought that nobody was likely to pay too much attention to what now amounted to a few stacks of standing charcoal. The dust that rose from the charred forest floor was fine and choking, and within seconds my hands and face were black, the ash sticking to the sweat and forming a weird mask. I kept on running, almost blinded, and the sounds of screaming and shooting started to fade.

There was a stream in the woods that flowed through Strasburg and then joined the North Fork of the river a little further below, and it was toward this that I headed, thinking I could follow its course to some kind of shelter and at least wash my eyes. But when I reached it, the water ran foul, dyed black with the burning upstream, the surface greasy with what I could only assume was oil, or maybe blood. I did not care to find out by getting much nearer; polluted streams like this were dangerous sources of infection.

I kept a few feet between myself and the water, but followed the course downward to what I presumed was a safer part of the valley, away from the fighting. Rounding a bend, I pulled up short, took in a scene of desolation, and vomited.

The ground was covered with corpses, perhaps 20 of them in a small clearing, laid out as they had fallen, some of them touching, some of them isolated, spread-eagled. There was no time to turn away, to stop myself from seeing the fact that they were little more than children. The filthy remnants of their gray uniforms proclaimed them Confederate soldiers, but their smooth, beardless faces betrayed the truth—none of them was more than 16 years of age. Had it really come to this—that we would send our children to fight for a cause the rights and wrongs of which we had long since forgotten?

One of them moved; he was not dead. I ran to him, saw that he was badly injured but, perhaps, not fatally, and instantly set about trying to stanch the blood that flowed from a wound in his leg. I tore my shirt to form a tourniquet around his upper thigh, pressed the edges of the wound together—it was clean enough, thank God—and packed it down with what remained of my shirt. If only I had water! The boy would die of dehydration if not from loss of blood. But I had come away from the hospital with nothing but the clothes I stood up in, and I could do nothing to slake his thirst. After all I had given to men, and taken from them, I had not even a drop of water to save the life of a dying child. I cradled his head in my lap, and wept—for myself, as much as for him. A tear fell onto his lips, and his tongue—miraculously clean and pink—reached out to take it.

The sound of crashing from near the stream brought me back to the danger of my situation, and I had barely time to look up before a huge dark figure bore down on me, as if it had materialized from the burned earth. It was as black as soot, as huge as a tree trunk, its arms stretched out as if to sweep me and the boy up and drag us down to hell. A gun waved in one hand, a knife in the other. As the man ran through the ash, a fine gray dust rose up around him, like smoke. I remembered those feverish tales of the Black Devil and composed myself for death. I could not even stand to fight him; to have done so would have meant dropping the boy in the dust, which I could not do. And so I bowed my head, muttered a quick prayer, and braced myself for the blow.

It never came. There was a crash, a cloud of choking ash, and the Black Devil fell on the ground, a foot in front of me, like an ox that has been poleaxed, a tree that has been felled. I lifted the filthy head to one side, so that he would not choke to death in the ash, and I saw his face.

It was Aaron Johnson.

PART FOUR:

Hot Valley

XIV

HIS SKIN WAS BLACK, BUT THAT SIGNIFIED NOTHING; MY SKIN was black, the dying boy's skin was black, everything was black in that burnt valley. But as I looked at the eyes, the lids fluttering as he struggled to remain conscious, I saw that the lines around them were black too, unlike the tracery of dirty white wrinkles and tearstains that surrounded mine and the boy's. I recognized in an instant the thick, cropped hair, the strongly molded skull, the firm jaw, the full lips—and I knew that this was Aaron Johnson, thrown at my feet, vomited up by the war, delivered to me as if by some miraculous courier. The years between us disappeared, and for a moment we were back in Vermont, riding over the mountains, bathing in the streams, the war a distant rumble that could be easily ignored in the eternal summer of my youth.

But now the war could not be ignored. Aaron was sick, maybe wounded, maybe dying. The boy in my lap, too, would bleed to death unless I could treat him. I had no water, no equipment, barely any strength in my limbs, certainly not enough to carry two men to safety. I grabbed Aaron by the shoulder of his filthy tunic, pulled him toward me, and rolled him over. He sighed, a huge, deep sigh, as if he was falling into the most contented sleep in a feather bed with his beloved by his side. I could not let him sleep; I feared there would be no awakening. It was all-important to me that Aaron Johnson did not die—more important than saving my own life, or finding my way home, or having a future after the war. All that mattered was that he did not slip away before I had a chance to tell him—what? That he had been right all along, way back then in a land and time that seemed as remote as a fairy tale? That I had learned my lesson the hard way? That I had tasted life's cup to the bitterest dregs? That I loved him? Did I love him, after all? Is that what was making my throat close up, my chest heave, and my eyes water? Or was it the smoke, the ash, the fear, and the stench of death in that desolate place?

Still cradling the boy in my lap, I leaned over Aaron and felt his brow; it was burning. I knew that fever was rife, the dreaded yellow jack that was wiping out hundreds if not thousands throughout the war zones. His face looked gaunt; he could easily be ill. But I didn't care. He must not die, that was all. I wanted, somehow, to give him life. My tears splashed down onto his skin, making little clearings in the soot where his beautiful brown skin showed through. Without thinking what I was doing, heedless of possible infection and against all my medical training, I bent down and kissed him on the lips. If he was going to die, I might as well follow him—that, I suppose, was my thinking, although it was not a conscious thought. I only wanted to impart something of my life to his.

It was like kissing a corpse—but then, miraculously, his lips twitched and parted, and the kiss was returned, weakly but unmistakably. Aaron Johnson was alive, and kissing me. If we had both died then, I should not have complained.

But we did not die. After Aaron had crashed to the ground, the valley had gone eerily quiet, so quiet that I could hear myself breathing, and the struggling breath of the boy in my lap. I came to my senses and realized that fate had given us a chance—the attentions of the war were engaged elsewhere, and if I could get these two to safety we might yet survive. Of one thing I was certain—I was not going to run.

"Please wake up, Aaron," I murmured, my lips still hovering around his. "Please. I need your strength now." His eyelids opened a little, I saw his pupils—thank God he did not have the pale, fading look of death in those eyes—and he smiled.

"Jack."

"Yes, Aaron, it's me, Jack."

"You found me."

I thought he might be delirious.

"I need you to wake up, Aaron, and help me. We're in danger here. We've got to get away. Can you open your eyes for me?"

"Jack... I knew you'd find me..." His voice faded, like a man falling asleep.

"Don't leave me like this, Aaron. You've got to wake up. We're in danger. Please, Aaron, help me."

I kissed him again, the tears rolling down my cheeks and into our mingling lips. He smiled slightly and seemed on the verge of dreamland.

"No! You must not fall asleep!" I shouted, shook him by the shoulder, slapped him around the face. The boy in my lap sensed the movement, and groaned in pain. The situation was hopeless; we were all surely going to die here together.

"God damn you, Aaron Johnson!" I shouted. "Wake up!"

My voice sounded strange in that quiet landscape, muffled by the soft ash that covered everything like black snow. A crow flapped overhead, waiting for its meal. Not long now, little brother, I thought.

And then Aaron's eyes opened. I had seen this happen in the hospital—the moment of lucidity that comes directly before the end. I held my breath, waiting for the death rattle, but it did not come. Aaron's eyes focused on mine, and he breathed normally.

"Still the same old Jack Edgerton," he said, with a scowl. "Always telling other people what to do."

"You're awake!"

"How could I sleep, with all that racket? The question is, am I really alive?"

"You're alive, all right."

"This isn't another dream? I haven't gone to heaven?"

"You call this heaven?" I looked around at the black ground, the burnt trees, the corpses and crows.

"Well, you're here. That's good enough for me, Jack."

I didn't have time to think about what this meant, particularly as the boy was groaning in what sounded like serious agony.

"We've got to move. Can you stand?"

"No... Let's stay here. I'm afraid that if I wake up properly, you'll disappear. Kiss me again..."

I kissed him again, and would have sunk into death in that kiss, but for the crying of the boy. "Please, Aaron. Just try for me. Get up. I won't leave you, I promise. I'm not a dream. I'm real. Look at me. Do I look like a dream?"

His eyes focused again, taking in my face.

"No. You look like hell."

"Thanks a lot. Now get yourself up on your feet and help me carry this kid."

Aaron struggled up, obviously in great pain, and was almost sick—but he swallowed it, braced himself, and stood shakily erect. "Fuck. Where are we?"

"Somewhere in the Shenandoah Valley."

"Oh, that wasn't a dream, then. Or a nightmare."

When he was standing, I could see what a sorry state he was in, his limbs crisscrossed with improvised bandages, his clothes black with dried blood.

"What happened to you?"

"There's no time for that now. We've got to hide. Come on, get him to his feet."

Between us, we managed to raise the dying boy and support him on our shoulders. He was shorter than the two of us, and if we stood up straight we could keep his feet from dragging in the dirt. I could see how much pain and effort this was costing Aaron, but he overcame it and led us toward the thickest part of the burnt forest.

"There's a cave and a spring," he said. "Come on."

How we made it to that place of safety I do not understand; perhaps the hand of God was guiding us. Fires were burning all around us—small fires, dying down for lack of fuel, a few flickering tongues of flame springing from the black ash like crocus bursting through the late snows of Vermont. Smoke was everywhere, hanging over the valley like a morning mist, permeating our clothes, our hair, our lungs. Every so often we heard the sharp whiz of a bullet from a sniper somewhere close at hand. Were they shooting at us? I didn't know. There was nowhere to shelter, no cover from their fire. The bullets came randomly, from different directions, occasionally hitting a burnt tree, occasionally landing in the soft ash with a weird, muffled "whumph." All we could do was pursue the shortest course across that burning field of death, hoping not to catch a bullet ourselves. I might survive a flesh wound, but for Aaron and the boy, it would mean certain death.

The seconds seemed like minutes, the minutes like hours, but I suppose we covered little more than half a mile before we reached the extent of the fire. Suddenly, the trees were green rather than black, the grass unscorched. Scrubby bushes became thickets and then woods; here, at last, was some shelter. Aaron led us through a thicket, the branches scratching our faces; I had to hoist the boy over my shoulder like a sack of corn. And then Aaron ducked down behind a bush and disappeared from view. A large rock concealed the mouth of a small cave in the hillside. I managed to push the boy through and followed him into the darkness.

We rested for a while, hearing only our own breathing and the faint tinkle of water. We could no longer hear the bullets. We were safe, crouching together in the blissful dark and dampness. After the hell of the burning valley, this tiny cave with its wet rocky floor seemed like heaven. Aaron rested his head on my chest, the boy lay in my lap. I sat, cradling them both, loving them both. War had brought us together, perhaps to die but at least for a moment to love and care for each other. Aaron worked my shirt open and rested against my bare chest, kissing it and licking it. I stroked his hair, felt the powerful muscles of his neck and shoulders, smelled the sweat and dirt on his body.

We could not stay like this for long. For one thing, the boy was in a bad way—and I wasn't too happy about Aaron's condition either. As for myself, I knew that I was badly dehydrated, but that was about all; I seemed to have escaped without even a scratch. The hospital must have burned down, all the patients must be dead, God knows what had happened to Jenny—but Jack Edgerton had nothing more to complain of than a dirty face.

I roused Aaron. "What do we do now?"

"Further in," he said. "Water."

I could see nothing, but there was an unmistakable sound of water from not so far away. I groped my way in and found that the ground sloped down, allowing just enough room for a man to squeeze under the stone of the roof. Trusting to the Providence that had kept me safe so far, I wriggled through, leaving Aaron and the boy together in the mouth of the cave. I slid down a sandy slope and landed softly in a pile of leaves. I could tell from the echoes that I was in a larger chamber, but I could see nothing; it was pitch-dark. I could hear the water, lapping and dripping. I could smell it.

But there were other things in there apart from leaves and

water. My hand came to rest on a cold metallic object—a rifle, I quickly realized. And there were sticks in a pile, and something sharp that turned out to be a knife. I continued to explore with my fingers and found the one thing I hoped to find—a box of matches. They were slightly damp, and it took a few attempts before I finally lit one. It sputtered into life, then burned steadily, enough to show me that I was in a roughly circular chamber about eight feet in diameter, with a pool of fresh, bubbling water and the makings of a rudimentary camp. This must be where Aaron had been hiding out, making his raids on the Yankee troops, earning himself the reputation—for who else could it be?—of the Black Devil.

I collected a few of the drier leaves and sticks and made a loose pile as far from the water as possible. The entrance tunnel would act like a chimney; I prayed that the smoke would not betray our presence. But there was enough smoke in the valley already; another wisp would not make too much difference. I struck the match, held it to the edge of one curled brown leaf and watched the flame lick its way along. Fire, which had seemed so ghastly on the outside, here seemed like the key to life itself.

When the sticks had caught, I called to Aaron to come down. There was no response, and I feared that he had lost consciousness again. I called again, and now there was a groan and the sound of shifting. The boy's legs appeared in the tunnel, and I caught them, lowering him into the cave. Aaron followed him.

"All the comforts of home," he said, before collapsing at the side of the pool and drinking his fill. I cupped my hands, filled them with water, and brought them to the boy's mouth. His lips opened, and the water ran in. Perhaps we could save his life.

The fire burned steadily, warming and lighting the cave. I could see enough to dress the boy's wounds and make him comfortable on the smooth sandy floor. He slept, but now his breath was gentle and regular. He had lost a lot of blood, but he might make it; he was young and strong. I smoothed his hair away from his face and caressed his smooth, beardless cheek. He was so young, so young...

"Cadet brigade," Aaron said, propping himself up on one arm. "Virginia Military Institute. Some of the bravest soldiers I've ever seen."

"He's a child."

"He's a vicious child," Aaron said. "They bite and scratch like cats."

He looked so peaceful, sleeping there on the floor, his head on a rolled-up sack, a few leaves piled over him for warmth.

"And you, Aaron." I hardly knew what to say; *How have you been?* seemed inadequate.

"Yes, me. Well, what's left of me. They took a few chunks out of me." He pointed to his patchwork of filthy bandages.

"I'd better take a look at those."

"Yeah. I think some of them have gone bad. They smell like death."

It was true; Aaron was exuding an unwholesome, putrid smell, suggesting that infection was gaining a foothold. I knew what to do. I could clean and, if necessary, cauterize his wounds. It would hurt him, but it might save his life.

"Don't worry," I said, sounding as cheerful as possible. "Luckily for you, I'm a trained nurse."

"No shit," he said, laughing and groaning. "Aren't you full of surprises, little Jack."

"And aren't you full of crap, Aaron Johnson. Now you just lie back there and let me take a look at this." I started to pull his shirt away from his shoulders; it adhered in places, stuck to the skin with dried blood. He winced.

"Always trying to get my clothes off, Jack. Some things never change."

"Yeah, and this time you're going to lie back and shut up and let me do what I want to do."

"Oh, baby," he said, "whatever's left, you're welcome to it. Ouch! Fuck, Jack!" A strip of burned skin came away with his shirt; the flesh underneath was raw and wet but, from what I could see, quite wholesome.

"How have you stayed alive, Aaron?" I said, cleaning the wound with a handkerchief dipped in water. "You should have died a thousand times, by the look of it."

"They took everything else from me, but they couldn't take my life."

His hand dug into my leg; he was obviously in agony but bearing it with fortitude. He stared into my face throughout.

"They took my friend…" There were tears rolling down his face, whether from physical pain or the pain of bereavement I could not tell. "Only boy who ever cared for me, for myself. Howard Porter. Stood by me, took the bullet that was meant for me, fought like a tiger to stay alive but died in my arms."

"When was this?" I tried not to look in his eyes, knowing that the pain I'd see there would distract me from my task.

"I don't know. A week. A month. How do you tell day from night when everything is black and burning? Sometimes the smoke and the fire seemed like we were in hell—"

"Hold still now. This is going to hurt."

I'd found a large splinter of metal buried in a wound on his back, near the kidneys; had it penetrated any further, he would have died quickly. As it was, the wound was dirty, stinking, unable to heal. Aaron bit down hard on his wrist and I yanked the metal out of him, knowing from my experience in the hospital that one short unbearable blast of pain was easier to survive than the slow agony of a more cautious approach. He screamed and passed out. While he was unconscious, I probed the wound and found there were no more fragments, I cut away some of the infected tissue, and then, heating the blade of the knife in the fire, cauterized the ghastly graying flesh. The smell was foul but was soon carried away with the smoke from the fire through our chimney. Aaron didn't stir, and I thanked God that he had been spared this horror. If he survived this, he had a chance.

I cut away the rest of his clothes, trying not to disturb his sleep, and converted any shred of fabric that was not positively filthy into a bandage. At last he was naked, the dressings forming a map of pain on his huge black body. The firelight showed every contour, every bone, every muscle, every scar. I had him now as I had so often wanted him—vulnerable, at my mercy. I kissed his mouth, his neck, his chest, his nipples. Resting my head on his stomach, I felt his shallow breathing. I buried my face in his soft, wiry bush, and inhaled his odor. Finally, I kissed his cock, placed my hand over it, lay down by his side, and tried to keep him warm. And so we all slept.

A sickly light was filtering through the tunnel when I awoke. I had no idea what time it was. My mouth was dry, and I was cold; the fire had gone out, leaving a damp smoky smell behind it. My arms were around Aaron, my leg thrown over his. He was still warm, breathing, alive. I disentangled myself, crawled over to the boy, terrified that he had died in the night—but he too was warm and breathing.

Aaron's wounds were still terribly raw and would cause him a lot of pain, but he was not feverish and there was no further danger of blood poisoning or gangrene. If I could keep him clean, warm, and hydrated, he would survive. The boy was weak, but if he was as much of a fighter as Aaron said, he might make it. I did not want to give another meal to the crows if I could possibly help it.

I drank a little from the spring. It was good water, bubbling up clean and fresh from the ground. Just a few yards away, the stream would be polluted, but here it seemed like a miraculous gift.

Drinking made me realize that I was hungry; I had not eaten in a long while. If we did not have food, then all the nursing care in the world would go to waste; we'd starve to death in that cave. I scrabbled around in Aaron's stores, but could find nothing edible. There was no choice—I'd have to go out and scavenge. I pulled the boy as gently as I could across the floor and placed him beside Aaron. They could keep each other warm while I was away.

The world outside was as silent and desolate as before. There was no sound of sniper fire, no crackling of burning trees, just the dead echoless air and the occasional call of the carrion crows. Beyond the trees I could see the black landscape of death; I headed away from that, into the small green living patch that had, like us, survived the onslaught. Somewhere in those few square yards there must be something that we could eat.

I found berries—wild blueberries, I suppose they were, or something like it, on a low bush near the ground. I picked as many as I could. There were dandelion leaves, quite clean, on a grassy mound; they would make a salad or a soup. I dug around in a patch of wild garlic, harvesting the little onionlike bulbs, and found a little patch of sorrel. And then, at the top of a tree, I saw a large, fat pigeon, staring stupidly at me, occasionally making little cooing noises. I hated doing it, but I climbed that tree, shooed the bird away, and pulled from its nest three fat squabs. I had dinner.

I killed and cleaned the birds outside the cave, wrapped the bodies in dandelion leaves, and took them back down into our little home. Aaron and the boy were still as I had left them, sleeping. I lit a fire, set some water to boil in a blackened pot, threw in the garlic bulbs, the sorrel leaves, and the squabs. Soon the cave smelled of food. I took the pan off the fire. Aaron had awoken and lay watching me, one arm around the sleeping boy, the other crooked behind his head.

"How do you feel?"

"Alive."

"Hungry?"

"Yeah."

"Much pain?"

"Yeah. Much pain."

"Any fever?"

"No. Just feel like I've been run over by a freight train."

"Oh, is that all? What are you complaining about, then?"

"Come here. Kiss me again."

I did as I was told, leaning over him and kissing him on the mouth. His tongue found mine, and we melted into each other. His body felt warm and dry, no longer clammy as it had been before. His cock, resting on his thigh, stirred to life. I squeezed it.

"That'll keep till later. We don't want to corrupt Sleeping Beauty."

"I don't imagine he's as innocent as he looks," Aaron said, squeezing the sleeping boy around the shoulders. "But let's not shatter our illusions just yet. I'd like to get him back to his mama in one piece."

"Okay, you need to sit up and get some clothes on."

"Clothes? I don't see no clothes. What I had on you got off me, you sly dog."

"Got a blanket?"

"No. There's a big old coat somewhere, found it lying on the field. That'll have to do." He reached into the recesses of the cave and threw a filthy overcoat around his shoulders like a cape.

"Will he wake up, do you think?"

"We need to feed him," I said.

"Come on then, small fry," Aaron said, shaking the boy gently. "Chow time."

It took a bit of doing, but eventually the boy opened his eyes and looked around him.

"I'm starving," he said.

"There speaks a true Virginian," Aaron said. "Always thinking of his belly. Can you sit up?"

The boy struggled, and wobbled, but with a little help he managed to prop himself against the cave wall. He asked no questions, just glanced around him, taking in the naked black man swathed in a cape and bandages, me with my filthy face and tattered clothes, the fire, and above all the food.

I passed him the can, which was now cool enough to hold, and he started shoveling it in.

"Hey, these things got bones!" he said, spitting out a handful of stewed baby pigeon.

"Chew the fucking thing, don't swallow it whole. Didn't your mama teach you no manners, boy? And say thank-you to the cook."

"Thank you, mister," the boy said, holding the baby bird and picking off the meat. I passed the can to Aaron, and he passed it to me, so between us we made, I thought, a reasonable job of breakfast, or whatever this meal might be called. After a few drafts of water, we all felt a great deal better.

"Where am I?" the boy asked, wiping his mouth and belching.

"We're in the Shenandoah Valley."

"Who are you?"

"Friends," I said.

"You're a Yankee," he said, scowling.

"I am."

"Fucking bastard."

Aaron lifted a huge hand as if to swat him but arrested the movement in midair. The boy cringed.

"This fucking Yankee bastard saved your ass, you ungrateful little shit," Aaron said.

"And who the fuck are you?"

"Told you they were little cats, didn't I, Jack? I am the

Black Devil. Did you never hear of me?"

The boy's eyes widened. "The Black Devil? Come on. That's just a story."

"Well, you better believe that story, boy. And don't think that I wouldn't eat a nice little chicken like you in one mouthful, gobble gobble gobble!" He bugged his eyes and made faces at the boy as one would at a child. The kid laughed, half in fear, half in delight.

"You a Yankee too?"

"No," said Aaron.

"You ain't a Confederate."

"Why not?"

"You're a nigger." He said it with such blank simplicity that it was hard to argue with his logic. I feared that Aaron would lose his temper, but he remained calm and reasoning.

"I ain't Confederate, and I ain't Union."

"You gotta be one or the other."

"Well, not me."

"What about him?" The boy jerked a thumb toward me.

"He is my friend."

"Yeah, I bet he is." The boy made simpering gestures, and spoke with a lisp. "I seen you two fooling around like sweethearts."

"You better mind your own business."

"I heard about your type. Queers, you are. A Yankee queer, a nigger queer—"

Aaron raised his hand; at full strength, he could have knocked the boy out with one swat. But instead he let it fall into his lap, and sighed.

"Yeah, a Yankee queer and a nigger queer who just happened to save your dumb ass."

"I didn't ask you to."

This time, Aaron was really incensed, his face twitching. His arm shot out lightning fast and grabbed the boy by the throat. But his voice was calm.

"Now, you're going to say thank-you to Mr. Edgerton for saving your life."

"Thank you," the boy said, grudgingly, struggling for breath.

"Thank you, sir," Aaron corrected. The boy repeated the word, like an unwilling scholar at his lesson.

"And you're going to say how much you enjoyed the delicious meal he just gave you. Or do you want me to stick my hand down your dirty little throat and bring it back up for you?"

"Th—thank you for my food... Sir."

"That's better. Now wash your dirty face and leave the grown-ups in peace."

"Hey, don't treat me like a—"

Aaron aimed a wet handkerchief, and it caught the boy in the open mouth. We both laughed at him.

"What's your name?" I asked the boy.

"Lee."

"Like the General, huh?" Johnson said, smiling, trying to make peace.

"Yeah. Damn right."

"Now listen, Cadet Lee," I said, "I've got to take care of this man's wounds, do you understand? It's not going to be very pretty, and I don't want you throwing up all over me. So why don't you take a walk, go and find us some more to eat, and come back in an hour."

"I ain't stupid. You're going to steal my stuff."

"What stuff?" Aaron said. "You've got nothing but the clothes you came in."

"I got money," he said proudly, "rolled up in the toe of my boot. You can't have it."

I resented the implication that I was a thief, especially from one whose life I had taken such pains to save. "Take your goddam boots with you, Lee, and see if you can find somewhere out there to spend your dollars. And if you find a bar, bring me back a bottle of whiskey. If they'll sell it to a child."

"Go on, kid," Aaron said, laughing. "Beat it."

Lee crawled out of the cave—by his energy you would never have guessed how close he'd come to death—and for the first time, Aaron and I were alone. I made myself busy with the boiling water, tearing bandages and dressings, conscious that he was watching my every move.

"Jack."

"Yes, Aaron?" My voice was too high, too bright.

"How did you find me?"

"You just...appeared."

"Did you ever think about me?"

"Of course I did."

"What did you think of me, Jack?"

"I thought of you as the friend that I had lost."

"Yes."

"And I thought of you as someone I should have treated better than I did." I felt tears stinging my eyes as I remembered my stupidity and arrogance.

"Yes. And did you think of me in other ways?"

I stopped fussing with the fire. "I thought, often, that you were the man I should have loved."

"Ah." He closed his eyes. "Then it was all worthwhile."

"What?"

"All this. The death, the war, the pain, and the waste of time. It brought us back together again, didn't it? And now we're ready, aren't we Jack?"

"Ready, Aaron?"

"Ready to love each other."

"Yes. We are. We're ready."

I knelt by him, took his hand, held it to my heart, which was beating so hard I could swear it echoed in that cave. I kissed the fingers, rubbed my face against his palm.

"At last," I said, feeling, in that strange hole in the

ground, beside the tiny fire and the magical spring, that I had finally come home.

I wanted so badly to give myself to him, to take him for myself, to express through the union of our bodies all the fear and hope and pain and love of the last months and years— and I could tell, from glancing down at his body where the overcoat fell open around his hips, that he was ready to do the same. His cock was hugely, magnificently erect.

"I want you so badly, Jack."

"I'm yours. But we must wait. You're not as strong as you think you are. If we...do it now, your wounds will open."

"I don't care. I want you."

"Well, I do care, and for once in my life I'm putting good sense first. I want you more than I've ever wanted anything. I want this"—I took hold of his cock, which jumped at my touch—"inside me. But more than anything, I want you to get better and live a long, long time."

"With you, Jack?"

"With me. Forever."

"That's enough for me."

He lay back, and I held his cock for a while, resisting the temptation to jerk it back to full hardness. And then I cleaned and dressed his wounds as best I could.

I wanted nothing more than to lie naked with Aaron, for the first and—who knew?—possibly the last time, so I stripped myself of my clothes, laid them over us, and wrapped the coat around us both. We kissed sleepily, our hard cocks pressed against each other, and within a few moments I came, unexpectedly but copiously, all over his thigh. He kissed me throughout, and we fell asleep as the sperm glued us together.

Lee did not return; neither of us was surprised. We both knew that he would have run like a rabbit straight to the Rebel Army, or would have caught a bullet somewhere in the burning valley. Either way, we would not see him again. And if he had survived, we were in danger. He would repay me for saving his life by betraying us, the Yankee queer and the nigger queer. So Aaron and I stamped out the embers of the fire, rolled up everything that we could in the coat, and dressed ourselves in an odd assortment of tatters. We would need to find better protection before nightfall, but we had enough to get us away from the valley and into the nearest village. At least we could not be recognized as either Rebel or Yankee—the clothes we had were so filthy, and so distressed, that they could no longer be called uniforms. Aaron wore a blackened shirt, the tails torn away to make dressings, and an old piece of sackcloth wrapped around his waist like a skirt. I still had my pants, and I improvised a tunic from another sack in which I cut a hole to poke my head through. We looked like a couple of scarecrows from a very badly tended melon patch.

We crawled from the cave and threaded our way through the trees away from the dead valley. There were other figures on the move, furtive and blackened like us; now we all stood out against the untouched green of the woods. But none of us wanted confrontation. In this deserted world, we were no longer fighting a war. We were no longer enemies. We were simply fugitives, clinging to life, fearing each other, and keeping our distance. That suited me fine.

A patrol of Confederate soldiers burst into the woods; we avoided them by crouching behind a rocky outcrop, holding our breath, ready to play dead if they got too close. They passed by so close we could hear the squeaking of their boots. They marched like automata, left, right, left, right, from who knows where to who knows where. Perhaps their mission was to round up deserters or pick off Union snipers; whatever it was, they had forgotten it, in that land of death.

Finally, as night fell, we saw the outlying buildings of a

small village. We reached a farm, and found a bed of straw in one of the barns—obviously Sheridan's troops had not yet reached this far—and we slept in one another's arms, exhausted, thanking God for giving us one clear day together.

XV

THE FARM WAS DESERTED, THE FARMERS EITHER DEAD OR fled, so we holed up for a few days while Aaron rested and recovered. I raided the farmhouse for clean cloths to turn into bandages—there was a well-stocked linen closet that had been untouched by soldiers—and we ate well, thanks to the abandoned livestock. Chickens were living wild in the woods, and I soon found their nests, so we had fresh eggs every day. One or two of the chickens themselves ended up in the pot. A goat gave us milk, and we ate apples from a small orchard. I used the farmhouse kitchen, and we drank fresh water from the pump in the yard, but at night we slept in the barn, where we were harder to find and whence it was easier to make a silent escape, if necessary. We knew that, sooner or later, a foraging party would find the farm and raid it to feed the starving Rebel soldiers. And it was also likely that they were searching for us, if Cadet Lee had got through the valley alive. Aaron was now wanted by both sides—the Yankees would love to string up the Black Devil for all to see, and the Rebels would arrest him as a deserter.

And if Lee had been telling them tales, they would all want to kill us because we were queer.

But, for all the danger, I was reluctant to leave. There at the farm we were warm and dry and well fed. Aaron could rest and allow his wounds to heal; for all his courage in the face of pain, he was a very sick man, and the infections had left him weak. I knew that if we went out on the road again too soon, sleeping rough and eating only rarely, he would catch the first fever going, and I would lose him. As long as there was no immediate danger, I insisted that we stay in the barn, buried in hay, wrapped in blankets, our stomachs full and our bodies warm.

We slept together, of course, our limbs entwined, kissing and talking and dreaming—and perhaps it was that, more than anything, that made me unwilling to leave our little home. I knew it was a fool's paradise, and that to linger longer was inviting danger, but to sleep beside the man I loved, to feel his heart beating and his strength returning, was hard to give up.

As we lay together one evening, savoring the silence all around us, Aaron instructed me to dig into our few possessions and pull out a filthy oilcloth bag. I had seen it when we were in the cave and assumed it contained money; Aaron guarded it as if it was precious.

"Open it, and read it. I'm going to sleep."

He nestled into my side as I drew out a wad of dirty paper, tied with a piece of string. As Aaron's breathing slowed and steadied, I read of his journey from Vermont, his career in Richmond, and his transformation into the Black Devil. This last phase of the narrative disturbed me particularly—I had not allowed myself to think of the sufferings he had undergone—but it was illuminated at the end by a declaration that took my breath away.

"Marched south for four days," began the first of a series of scrappy, sporadic notes.

The boys are footsore, hungry, and scared. Some of them are sick. Charlie has deserted; they say he ran off with the governor's wife but who knows if we'll ever see him alive again? I hope to God he is safe. Billy and Chester are together as man and wife, although Billy has been obliged to abandon his preferred wardrobe for a while. I stay close to Howard, and we are a great comfort to each other. When he is too tired to go on, I carry him. At night, when we rest for a few hours before dawn, too tired to sleep, certainly too tired to fuck, I hold him and caress him and try to allay his fears. He rewards me with the warmth of his young body and the most complete trust and gratitude that I have ever known.

The next few pages detailed the horrors of military life, with which I was only too familiar. The fatigue, the fear, the hunger, and above all the stalking specter of disease. The men of Company K started falling prey to strange fevers, and there was no one to nurse them. Many were left to die where they fell by the roadside or were found stiff and cold in the gray light of dawn.

We were ambushed at 3am just outside Yellow Tavern. Surrounded by 100, maybe more, Yankee soldiers, with guns trained on us as we rested. Taken captive without a chance to fight. Now in prison camp, I do not know where. Howard took a bullet.

The next entry was barely legible.

Nursed Howard through four days of fever, unable to secure medicine or clean water or food.

Could only hold him and watch him fade away.
He died in my arms this morning, and the body
was taken from me.

This was the last entry in that particular bundle; I could only
imagine how Aaron felt, to have lost a friend so dear.

One final sheet of paper remained, covered on both sides
in a script so tiny that I could barely make it out.

The prison chaplain visited me two days after
Howard's death. A Boston man, he told me,
smooth faced and broad shouldered, one of those
'muscular Christians' that used to go about trying to convert the dark races when I was a kid.
But he seemed friendly and genuinely concerned
that I had lost my friend. "You did your best to
look after him," he said, smiling. I replied that
there was not much I could do, as the boy had
been denied proper medical attention and left to
die like a dog. Then he asked me, "What are you
fighting for, brother?" This, I thought, was where
he would try to convert me to the Yankee cause—
and in truth I might as well be fighting for them
as for anyone else. I told him that I was fighting
for my own survival, nothing more.

"And you see where that has brought you?" I
wanted to take a swing at him for implying that
somehow I was to blame for my current sorry
condition—but then I realized that he was right.
Why was I fighting for the Rebels—those Southern gentlemen who hated me and denied me my
rights? Why was I fighting at all? This was not my
struggle. I joined Company K because I had no
choice, because of loyalty to a band of rogues and
thieves and vagabonds. I was not ashamed of that

loyalty, but was it worth all this death?

"What is really important to you, Aaron Johnson?" asked the chaplain. "Liberty," I replied, for want of anything better to say. "Liberty," he repeated, looking straight into my eyes. "That's a lovely word, but what does it mean? The freedom to buy and sell, the freedom to live and die, the freedom to love and hate?" "The freedom to love and live as I please," I said. "And is this how you please?"

He left me, and I fell into a troubled doze, thinking about what he had said. Liberty? What had I meant when I said that? To love and live as I please? Well, to love as I please, yes, that was important, but have I ever really loved, or been loved? Howard, for instance, taken from me by a greedy death... We were lovers, in one sense of the word, but only because the war had thrown us together and he needed someone stronger than him to take his fears away. In gratitude, and perhaps for the pleasure of the moment, he had given himself to me, but I was not what he wanted. And all those others, those who had bought my love in Richmond, those who had fought with me or betrayed me along the way—that was not love. I scoured my memory for one man that I could honestly say I had loved, and who had loved me in return, and I found nothing.

And then I remembered Jack Edgerton. All those thousands of years ago in Vermont, in the cold bright clean air of Vermont, the woods and the streams, and his laughing face, his self-important airs, his foolish belief that we could have whatever we wanted, his arrogance and innocence and joy of life; yes, Jack had loved me, not wisely but really, truly. And I had pushed him away. Yes, my reasons were sound, my reasons for everything were always sound, but perhaps reason was not what I wanted anymore but liberty, as I had told the chaplain. Jack was like me, a lover of men. If we could find each other again, and find liberty, far away from the war and the people who knew us, then perhaps I might live again…

Tears ran down my cheeks. Aaron believed that I had loved him, way back in Vermont when all we seemed to do was fight. Perhaps he was right. Perhaps I had loved him from the first moment. Desired him, certainly, as I did now; my cock was as stiff as an iron bar inside my pants. And yes, I loved him now, more than I had loved anyone. Had he guessed back then what it took me so long to realize? Could he be so certain, that a love like mine could sustain him in his most desperate hour? I felt ashamed, unworthy, but above all exhilarated.

They started executing prisoners yesterday. I saw the chaplain saying prayers as some of the boys were marched out to the woods to be shot. I stole a knife from the cookhouse, cut the throat of one of the guards, stole his gun, and ran from the camp. It was so easy. Regained Rebel lines within five hours. Gave news of the fate of Company K. As I have no papers, they did not believe that I was a soldier. They would have taken me into custody again. Having just escaped from a Federal prison camp, I have no desire to walk straight into a Confederate one. I ran again, stole a horse, joined a gang of foragers who were only too happy to add my strength and courage to theirs. We camped out in the woods. There is one

young man in the group, blond like Jack, who
sucks my cock when the rest of the gang is asleep
and the woods are dark.

I looked down at Aaron, sleeping peacefully beside me, and
I envied that young blond man who had done to him the
things that I had never done. I wanted so badly to make love
to him, in the fullest way possible, but I was still frightened
that the violence of my passion might kill him.

The notes went on.

We reached a farmhouse where a woman and a
teenage boy met us on the porch with guns. The
men fanned out and aimed their weapons, ready
to slaughter the mother and her son for the price
of a hot meal and a bed for the night. "We're
on your side!" said the mother, waving her gun
wildly in the air; I doubted if she could hit a cow
at five paces. The boy was visibly shaking; neither
of them stood a chance.

"Shut the fuck up,"' snapped Tilbury, our
ringleader, a mean son of a bitch with a scarred
face and a sick delight in violence. He cocked his
rifle and leveled it at the boy's head.

"You see your little baby die first, bitch, then
you follow him to heaven."

Tilbury never knew what hit him; I was
standing behind him, and simply swung my rifle
around and blew his head off. It exploded like a
watermelon.

"Anyone else?" I cocked again, ready to fire.
The rest of the gang slipped away into the trees.
The blond boy, my cocksucker of a few nights,
ran with them.

"You need to leave here. Take water and blankets and get away," I said to the woman. "They will be back. Hurry."

"But this is our home."

"Not anymore, it's not."

I turned my back and walked away fast, unable to bear the look of sorrow on her face. I had saved her life, perhaps for a day, or a week. And my life? How long a purchase did I have on that?

There followed a pitiful account of Aaron's life as a fugitive from both sides, trapped like a wolf in a cage as the battle closed in around him in the Shenandoah Valley, struggling to survive from day to day, using his strength, courage, and cunning to win out in every confrontation he had with the soldiers of either side. This was when he earned the name Black Devil, that semimythical creature who inspired dread in the Union forces and who seemed, to them, like the embodiment of a crazy vengeance for all the wrongs they were inflicting on the innocent civilians of Virginia. But Aaron fought for neither side, only for his own survival. The final entry showed the state to which he had fallen before I found him.

> I know I will die soon, either in my cave like an old black bear, or out in the burning desolation. My time has come and I will find liberty in heaven. Now I want only peace and death. If I could live my life again I would ride as fast as I can to Jack's side and tell him that I love him, but that I know will never be. Even if he is alive I can never find him. I pray that he is safe from harm.

That was all. Aaron slept quietly beside me; I lay and wept as quietly as I could, so as not to wake him. I wept for all his pain and suffering, and for the sheer joy of loving him.

279

We stayed at the farm for four nights, after which I was sat-isfied that Aaron's wounds were healing properly and that there was no longer any danger of infection. We packed up in the morning, and I handed him back the cloth bag con-taining his papers.

"You read them, then."

"I did."

There was an awkward moment of silence, as if we both knew too much and could not find the words in which to say how we felt.

"Aaron..."

"Jack..."

"No, you first."

"No, I insist."

"Did you really love me back in Vermont? When I was such a stupid little bastard?"

"I did."

"And do you still believe that we have the chance of a life together?"

"It's the only thing that kept me alive in these last few weeks."

"I see."

"And you, Jack." He looked sad. "You're young. You have a family, a future in Vermont. You must get back there, I un-derstand. You don't want to be shackled to a man like me."

I could think of nothing to say. Tears came to my eyes, and I tried to speak, but I was choking.

"It's all right," Aaron said. "You don't have to explain. I'm just grateful for everything you've done for me. I'll never forget your kindness, Jack."

"Oh shut up, you ass," I said, bursting into sobs like a child. "Don't you know that I love you every bit as much as you love me? For Christ's sake, what do I have to do to prove it?"

"Well, for starters," he said, drawing me toward him, "you could take care of this."

280

He was hard inside his pants. I touched it, felt its heat and size, but my fingers sprang away almost instantly.

"We can't. You're not well enough."

"Jack, if you don't suck my dick right now, my balls are going to explode, and then I'll die anyway. So just do what I ask, for once, will you?"

And so he lay back in the hay, one massive arm behind his head, the other reaching down so he could caress my head, and I finally did what I had wanted to do ever since I first laid eyes on Aaron Johnson. I unbuttoned his fly, pushed his pants down to his thighs, and took him between my lips. Neither of us spoke or made much noise apart from the occasional sigh or soft moan. His cock fitted into my mouth and throat as if they had been cast from the same mold. I knew exactly how to touch him and where, and he responded exactly as I knew he would. Just as I began to think how much I wanted to taste his cum in my mouth, he started spewing load after load into me. I swallowed every drop. And then, as his cock grew soft in my mouth, he undid my pants, took my hard dick in his hand, and brought me off. I came all over his fingers, and he licked them clean.

It was not the wildest sex I had had, nor in a sense the most exciting—but this simple act in the dry shelter of an abandoned barn meant more to me than every crazy fuck of my life. I knew that I was his for life, and he mine.

When we had arrived at the barn, it seemed like fall, mild and damp. Suddenly, within a few hours of leaving the shelter, it turned to winter. A cold east wind blew up, carrying with it the promise of snow. We could not afford to go near settlements—they were still under attack from Rebel foragers, desperate to feed the starving scattered troops by taking whatever they could, at whatever cost. We could see, to the south, an enclosing ring of fire as Sheridan's troops brought their campaign of devastation further down into the valley.

Even that tiny green oasis where I had first dwelled with Aaron in the cave must now be reduced to ash.

We headed for the hills, knowing that the greatest danger up there was cold and starvation; those enemies we could at least face in a fair struggle. If we were caught in the valley by either army, we would surely die. And so we followed the high ground back north, into what was now Union territory; you could tell by the smoke rising from the scorched earth.

We trekked north for a week as the weather turned colder and colder. We had blankets and frequently found a cave or an abandoned building in which to sleep, but I could tell that this rough living was taking its toll on Aaron. He was still far from well, despite his protestations to the contrary, and he was visibly losing weight. He could march doggedly for hours at a time, but at a terrible cost. We skirted Richmond and headed toward Maryland, keeping to the high ground, avoiding human contact. Where exactly we were headed, neither of us really knew. Away from the fighting, that was the only way I could frame it in my mind. Away from the burning and the death. But toward what? Canada?

One night we rested in a half-burned house that must once have been home to a family; there were scattered items of clothing, and broken children's toys on the floor. Everything else of value had been taken or burned. It sufficed for us; the walls were standing, and there was a stretch of unfallen roof, which would at least protect us from the wind and the frost that were now becoming a nightly feature. We made a bed from our blankets, and I lit a fire; this was our routine.

Aaron was sick and falling into a fever. I boiled water and tried to feed him cornmeal porridge, but he would not eat.

"Jack," he said, his voice alarmingly weak. "If I die—"

"You're not going to die."

"If I die, you must promise me that you'll head back home to Vermont."

"There's no home for me there."

"Promise me, Jack. Your parents love you. Your sisters need you."

"There's no home for me without you, Aaron. You know that."

"I love you, Jack. But I think our time came too late." He started coughing; I had heard that cough before in hospital wards, and I didn't like it.

"Don't be silly," I said, just as I had said to a hundred patients before. "You've just got a cold. You'll be fine." I bustled around, preparing some food, like a bad-tempered housewife.

"Come here and hold me," Aaron said. He was shivering, and his face looked gray.

I held him close and felt the bones through his skin. We had never made love again after that one morning in the barn, and I feared that I would never know his body as I had seen it and imagined it so many times before. Eventually he slept, and I sat awake, listening to every sound around us. His breathing was irregular, occasionally disturbed by a soft choking sound from the back of this throat. I could tell that his lungs were filling up with fluid. If I could not get him to a hospital soon, he would die.

I drifted off to sleep and dreamed a jumbled parade of images, some painfully happy, others horrific, all of them the dreary mental refuse of war, fear, and exhaustion. I suppose I must have been a little feverish myself, because when I awoke all my senses seemed supercharged. Aaron's breathing was as loud as cannon fire, the smell of soot and mold in the house was nauseating—and there was something else, something that should not have been there. I sat up, my mouth dry and my head aching, and listened as hard as I could. I heard beetles scuttling across the floor, I heard an owl screech in the woods—and I heard the sound of horse's hooves. Just one horse, I thought, but it was one too many.

I jumped up, threw the blanket over Aaron, and tiptoed to the glassless window. It was a moonlit night, and I could clearly see the silhouette of a horse peacefully champing the grass outside the house. Had the smoke of our fire been seen?

A twig snapped, and I swung around. There was a faint scratching at the door—hardly a door anymore, just a few broken planks of wood that I had secured with a boulder. It opened a little, and a gloved hand appeared around the frame.

It was then that the cold air hit me—I was only wearing my underclothes—and I started to shiver violently, from fear and fever as well as the temperature, I suppose. A spasm shook me from shoulders to hips, and I lost my head, leaped for the door with a cry just as a booted foot kicked it open. I threw myself on the figure that stood in the door, and we rolled on the floor, scratching, biting, and kicking each other.

I was hysterical, and I fought like a demon. My opponent was strong, but not strong enough to fend off a man who is about to lose everything—not just his life, but his love as well. I fought my way on top, pinned the flailing arms down with my knees, grabbed the head by the hair, and was about to pound it into the floor—when I realized that this was a woman.

I sat up in shock, and the moonlight hit her straight in the face. Our eyes met. It was Jenny Wallace.

I greeted her with joy.

When I awoke, it was light. I was under a blanket. I could smell something like cloves or cinnamon. I looked wildly around for Aaron and saw the figure of Jenny sitting over him, administering something to him in a cup. I lay back and must have passed out again.

How long I stayed in that state I do not know. I have fragmentary memories of light and dark, of dark figures passing around me, of strange tastes in my mouth and a terrible aching in my elbows and knees. There were times when I thought I was lying in water, other times when I seemed to be suffocating. I saw faces of dying men, the horrors of the hospital, my parents, Bennett Young, Captain Healey, Aaron...

And then I awoke in a room I did not recognize, with white walls, and light streaming through a window. I panicked for a moment, but then I was swept by a feeling of joy—the fever had gone, and I was alive. And there, slumbering in a chair by my beside, wrapped in a coat, was Aaron. I tried to speak, but my voice came out as a strange little whisper. My lips were cracked, and my tongue felt shriveled. I knew the symptoms, and I realized how close I had come to death. But I was alive, so was Aaron. We had survived hell.

I let him sleep, and fed my eyes on him. He looked well. His face had filled out again. There were deep lines where once his cheeks had been smooth, and some gray among the black of his hair, but that only made him more beautiful to me.

The door opened, and in came Jenny Wallace, dressed as I remembered her, in a blue dress with a white pinafore. She came to the bed, took my hand, and smiled.

"Well, look who's back."

"Hi, Jenny."

"We nearly lost you."

"I know. I've been ill, haven't I?"

"Oh honey," she chuckled, "you have no idea. Without him you'd have died a week ago."

"What do you mean? Where am I?"

"You're in Richmond, in the hospital."

"Richmond?" I must have looked and sounded very stupid. Jenny laughed a deep, throaty laugh.

"It's in Virginia, sweetheart, or were you playing hooky when they taught geography at school?"

"I know where it is, but how the hell did we get here?"

"He carried you most of the way. No wonder he's tired."

"But he was sick…"

And so Jenny told me the whole story: how she'd found me and Aaron in the burned-out house, nursed us through four days of desperate fever, from which Aaron had recovered first. I had worsened, however, and could no longer survive the rigors of the outdoor life. They braved the last skirmishes of the war to get to Richmond, now in Union hands, where Jenny knew there was a hospital that had survived the burning and was now tending the sick and wounded of both sides.

"This war will come to an end soon enough, honey," she said, "although we still have battles to fight."

"What do you mean?"

"The likes of you and Aaron, and me for that matter, won't be welcome in these re-united States for a long time."

"And how did you find us? Why were you there?"

"You were walking straight into a Yankee trap. They were patrolling through the woods and hills, looking for Rebel stragglers. There was a medical corps sent out but they didn't want us there, they lost us as quickly as they could, and most of them rode back north as soon as it was safe to do so. I couldn't do that, Jack. You know me. I always like to stick around if there's trouble."

"You were up there on your own?"

"Yep."

"Weren't you frightened?"

"Come on, honey, no soldier is going to come running when he sees this face, is he? I ain't exactly one of those pretty little Southern girls."

"How did you get out of the hospital?"

"Don't ask me that, Jack."

"Why not?"

"I'm ashamed. I ran away."

"So did I."

I took her hand, and we held each other in silence for a few minutes. Aaron shifted, snorted, and woke up. When he saw that I was conscious, he jumped from his chair and nearly fell over backward.

"Jack!"

"Yes, he's alive and he's awake. And I think I'd better leave you two lovebirds together."

She withdrew from the room, and Aaron threw himself on me.

"Hey, careful! I'm still...oof!...weak!"

"Jack, oh God, Jack. You're alive. Oh, thank God."

Aaron broke down and cried his heart out. I rested my hands on his head and let him weep. It did us both good.

He lay beside me (the bed was not made for two grown men, and creaked complainingly), his arm around my shoulders.

"As soon as you're well, we're going north, Jack."

"Why?"

"So you can see your family."

"I don't care about my family. I've got everything I need right here."

"You may say that now, boy, but when you were in that fever you cried out for your mama and your daddy just like everyone else. So we're going up there together and you're going to tell them that you love them."

"And what if they don't want to see me?"

"Take it from me, they will."

"I don't want to go."

"I know you don't. But I'll be beside you and we'll face them together. We'll face everything together from now on."

A week later, Jenny said, reluctantly, that I was well enough to travel, so we took the train north from Richmond.

We were dressed in new clothes, with new boots on our feet; Aaron's savings from his days at the Alhambra had survived the war, and they amounted to a fair fortune. I was astonished by the splendor of the apparel that he secured, but he just said that there were a few businessmen in town who owed him a favor. I grimaced, thinking of all the men who had had him in the past.

"A good deal is a good deal, Jack. And don't you worry, there's only one ass that I'm interested in from now on."

He stood at the mirror, admiring himself in his new tweed jacket. He looked very fine.

"And whose ass would that be, I wonder?"

"Well, it's a pretty little white ass that ain't a thousand miles from here."

"It's yours whenever you want it, Aaron."

"Soon, baby. It will be soon. When you can prove to me that you're well enough to run a mile, then you're well enough to be fucked."

I knew he was right—and I was willing to wait. War had taught me one thing, and that was not to waste the good times. These strange days of recovery were the happiest of my life, and I did not need Aaron's cock up my ass to believe that he loved me. I wanted it, of course, but only when the time was right.

"This your boy?" the porter on the train asked.

"No," I said, handing him my luggage. "I'm his boy. Now just put this in our berth."

We trundled gently along the East Coast, through Washington to Baltimore, north to Philadelphia, and then the long journey to Albany, where we stopped for two days to rest up before the final leg of the journey into Vermont, and home.

"I feel like I could run a mile, Aaron," I said, as we laid our bags down on the hotel bed. It was a small room, but clean and cozy enough. We'd slept in worse conditions.

"Prove it to me."

"Come on, then. Let's go out."

"You're not just saying that because you—"

"What do you think? I'd walk through fire to get that thing up my ass."

"Baby, you've already done that, remember?"

We strolled around the town, arm in arm, heedless of the stares of the bourgeois couples. A few of them called us names, but nobody approached us; we'd all grown accustomed to strange sights in wartime, and people were more tolerant, at least for a while. Soon we gained the countryside.

"All right, show me what you're made of."

I jogged along the path, conscious of how weak my legs were, how little accustomed my lungs to breathing deeply. But it felt wonderful to be outside, active, alive again—and strange to be free from the fear of imminent death. Up here the countryside was barely marked by the war—there had been a few Rebel incursions, but compared to Virginia this was the Garden of Eden. I ran gently along for as long as I could, then stopped and caught my breath.

"That wasn't a mile."

"Give me a chance."

Aaron put an arm around my shoulders and kissed me on the mouth, the neck. "You'd better get a move on."

I picked up my feet again and trotted along; Aaron was behind me.

"That ass looks pretty good from here."

"Think how much better it'll look with your cock sticking into it."

"Still the same old Jack Edgerton, waving his tail at every stallion in sight."

"There's only one stallion I'm interested in riding now."

We jogged along contentedly; I could feel my strength returning, not to mention the blood rushing to my lower regions.

"Well, you've tried a few mounts, so I guess you're ready for a thoroughbred."

"Yeah, and you've had a few jockeys."

"I guess we've both been as bad as each other," Aaron said, swatting my ass.

"I was never bad. I was always very, very good."

"Hmmm...I reckon that's a mile. Come on."

It was nothing like that far, but I didn't complain; I was ready to fuck right there in the field.

"No," Aaron said. "I've spent too much of my life sleeping and screwing in the dirt. I want a bed for once."

We turned around and walked back to town. The landlady of the boarding house eyed us darkly as we climbed the stairs.

"My friend needs rest," Aaron said.

"I ain't finished cleaning yet."

"It'll wait. Go out and buy yourself some ribbons." He tossed her a few coins, and she was out of the house like a rabbit out of a trap.

When we got to the room, we both became bashful. We busied ourselves getting out of our coats and boots, folding things up and putting them away far more neatly than was our habit. I realized—and I'm sure Aaron did too—that this was the beginning of something that we had both dreamed of, and perhaps avoided thinking about, for a long time. This was not a recreational fuck, taken for the pleasure of the moment, forgotten the moment after. This was not a pragmatic fuck, engineered in order to gain power over another or to escape from an awkward situation. This was the culmination of many months of growing affection, spiced by our initial hostility, our misunderstandings, our long separation, our growing awareness of our need for each other, our dreamlike reunion, and our fear of death. What we were about to do would express all of that, as well as the enormous lust that we felt for each other. I was not sure if I was man enough for the job, and I fiddled around with a shirt button that suddenly seemed hugely important.

Aaron took the lead.

"Turn around, Jack."

I turned to face him—and there he stood, his chest bare, his huge arms open.

"Come to me, boy."

I rushed into his arms as if I was coming home for the first time. Our lips, chests, stomachs, and groins all met in a rush.

"Are you ready for me, Jack? Because I am ready for you."

There was very little preamble to our union, none of the teasing and exploring that sometimes preceded a fuck. We had all the time in the world for that. The important thing now was that we were joined as completely as possible. I lay back and raised my legs, pulling my ass cheeks apart.

Aaron spat into his hand, slicked up his cock, and positioned the head at the entrance to my ass. We stared into each other's eyes for many long seconds.

"Go," I said.

He pressed into me, and I yielded to him. He started fucking me right away, which was what we both wanted. It didn't take long before he was speeding up, and my hips were bucking, my ass tightening around his hard dick. When we were both ready to come, he cocked an eyebrow, and I nodded my head. As he pumped my ass full of his seed, I shot mine all over my stomach, chest, and neck. He lay on top of me, still inside me, and we kissed until we slept.

At last we were together.

XVI

THE FIRST SERIOUS SNOW OF WINTER WAS FALLING AS WE approached Bishopstown, and it was only with some difficulty that the train got through. I realized that this was not going to be a flying visit; we would be stuck there for days, if not weeks. Aaron thought, on the whole, that this was a good idea, that it would give us both time to rest and recuperate and to build bridges with my family.

Bishopstown looked eerily unchanged as we stepped down from the train. The war had never touched it. Raids into the Northern states were rare—and indeed the events at St. Albans, in which I had been an unwitting participant, were sufficiently remarkable to have passed into the stuff of local legend. The porter told us some long, rambling story about how the Rebels had "murdered folk in their beds," which I knew was not true, but it seemed to cause him a good deal of vicarious pleasure, so I did not disabuse him. Aaron and I caught each other's eye and smiled. What point was there in trying to tell the people of Bishopstown of the horrors that we had witnessed at first hand? They would never believe us.

We booked ourselves into a hotel on Main Street, a well-groomed new business where once had been a struggling dry goods store. The building had been completely renovated; obviously there was money in Bishopstown, war or no war. It was called the Bishopstown Inn, and the brass plaque above the door read "Mr. Michael Sheehan, proprietor and landlord." I had barely time to wonder if I was seeing things, when a stylishly dressed, handsome, middle-aged man with splendid blond whiskers stepped up to welcome us.

"Gentlemen, can I be of—Jesus Christ! Jack Edgerton!"

It was my old friend, my first fuck, Mick from the White Horse, back from the war and transformed into a prosperous New England businessman. I burst out laughing. "Well, I guess this is what you call coming full circle! Mick, this is Aaron Johnson."

"Who could forget you? Welcome home, Jack! Have you come to stay?"

I looked at Aaron. "I don't know yet. Have you got a room for us?"

"Have I got a room for you? You're getting the bridal suite, boys. And this is on the house. It's not every day I get to welcome the best piece of ass in the Union."

"Amen to that," Aaron said, laughing.

"So you two finally got together, then?"

"What do you mean?" I asked.

"Jack, from the moment you and Aaron clapped eyes on each other, I knew there was no room for poor old Mick or any other man in your life."

"You did?"

"You didn't know it, but everyone else did. Everyone else with eyes in their head, that is."

"I guess we knew it too," Aaron said, "but we were too proud and too dumb to admit it."

"Well, that's all in the past. You stay here for as long as you like. And with the way that sky's looking, it could be a while. You're my guests. Here, I'll get Sandy to show you up."

Sandy was the porter, a boy of about 19 in a neat little uniform that showed off his rear end to good advantage.

"Hey, Jack," Aaron said, "looks like you might have some competition in the ass department."

"Yeah, he's pretty good," Mick said, casting an affectionate eye up and down Sandy's trim form. "I've got no complaints."

Sandy grinned and winked and took us upstairs.

When we were alone, I suddenly felt anxious.

"I'm not sure if I can go through with this, Aaron. It's been such a long time since I've seen my folks, and so much has changed."

"Sure you can. They're your flesh and blood. They love you, and you love them."

"Make love to me first."

"Hey, come on. You can't turn up at the house all bandy-legged and smelling of cock."

"Yes, I can." I pushed him back onto the bed and started undoing his pants. He was already erect when I pulled his cock out, and I took my time sucking him off until he rewarded me with a mouthful of spunk.

"There, now I'm ready," I said.

"Sure you don't want me to...?"

"No," I said, adjusting the bulge in my pants. "It'll keep for later."

"You bet," Aaron said, licking his lips. "That's mine tonight. Now come on, wipe your mouth and let's get going."

"Now?"

"Now. No more delays. Let's get on with life."

The road out of town looked uncared for, the brambles overgrowing the pathway, fallen branches lying in the way, half-concealed by snow. It would not be safe for a carriage

294

to navigate. My father had always contributed to the up-keep of the road, and it worried me to see it so dilapi-dated. But the state of the road was nothing compared to the state of the house, which looked like Sleeping Beauty's castle. The fence and gates were overgrown with ivy and brambles, the gravel drive had turned to mud and slush, and the house itself had the forlorn, dirty look of neglect. My heart leaped into my mouth; what had happened to my family?

We stood at the door; the paint was peeling and the brass tarnished. I knocked, the familiar rat-a-tat-tat that all family members used. There was silence within, and then, finally, a slow tread coming down the hall. The door inched open, and a pale face peered out. My older sister, Margaret.

"Yes?"

"It's me."

"Jack."

Silence; neither of us knew what to say. I was shaking, already convinced that something awful had happened to my parents. Margaret looked old and exhausted.

"You'd better come in," she said at length. Aaron put a hand on my shoulder, squeezed it reassuringly, and pro-pelled me in.

"We thought you were dead."

"Well, I'm not," I said, attempting a laugh, which turned into something more like a hiccup. "Where are Mother and Father?"

"Upstairs. They don't come down much anymore."

"Are they sick?"

"They took it very hard when we lost Jane."

"Lost..."

"You don't know, of course. Well, I guess you wouldn't, doing whatever it is you've been doing. " She looked at me with thin-lipped disapproval. "Jane is dead."

"What? How?"

"She went down to New York City to join some kind of Abolitionist League."

"What happened?" I had visions of riots, violence, my sister attacked by a gang of pro-slavery thugs.

"She was run down by a trolley. Go on, laugh."

For an awful moment, I wanted to laugh, and Margaret must have seen it on my face, but I managed to control myself. "When did this happen?"

"About six months after you left us. We know you didn't go to Montpelier. Your friend James told us all about that."

"Well, I was...misled."

"James has been very kind to our family. He visited frequently. He helped Father a great deal after he lost the business."

"The Hydropathic Establishment? It's closed?"

"You wouldn't know about that either. While you've been running around enjoying yourself, things have been difficult here."

I drew breath to answer her back, but again I felt Aaron's hand on my shoulder, and I exhaled. "I'm sorry to hear that, Margaret. Will you please tell me what happened?"

"Mr. Windridge," she said. "He disappeared one day. Daddy discovered that he'd embezzled thousands of dollars from the company. There was nothing left but a mountain of debts. He was ruined. He's bankrupt now, and he can't show his face..." Margaret's voice cracked and squeaked, and she pressed a handkerchief to her mouth.

"I must see them."

"I'm not sure that's a good idea, Jack."

"Why not?"

"I don't think they've forgiven you."

"For what? For running away? My life hasn't been easy either, you know." I wanted to tell her all I had seen, all I had suffered.

"No," she said, shaking her head. "For the disgrace you

brought on the family. You"—here she looked at Aaron—
"and your friends."

"I see."

"They never mention your name. It's as if you were dead
too. We lost Jane, and then it seemed we'd lost you, and the
house is like a mausoleum—" She burst into tears. "Oh,
Jack, why did you leave us? How could you let me face it all
on my own?"

I put my arms around her, but she was as rigid as a poker.

"No. No, I'm all right. I'll go up and tell them it's you.
Perhaps you had better see them before you go."

"Go?" I said. "I'm going nowhere. We're staying here
until we've all sat down and talked things through."

"Jack, please don't," Margaret said, looking terrified.

"Why not? They can't keep pretending I'm dead, just because I choose to live my life the way I want. I nearly died
out there, and I'm not going back to being half alive ever
again. Aaron and I—"

Margaret put her hands over her ears. "Don't tell me! I
don't want to hear!"

"What are you so afraid of, Margaret? Scared of hearing
the truth?"

"Don't be cruel to your sister," Aaron said, in low tones.
"She's been through enough. Miss Margaret,"—he held
out his hand to her, and she nervously took it—"you and I
will talk later, when you've had a chance to compose yourself. Now, Jack, you calm yourself down, and get ready to
see your parents. And remember to treat them with some
respect."

Words like these would have sent me flying off the handle
before, but now I loved Aaron, and I was prepared to see that
he was right. I took a few deep breaths as Margaret climbed
the stairs. Aaron and I held hands and waited for a sign.

"Jack?" came my mother's voice from above. "Is that
really you? Jack?"

I flew up the stairs, two at a time, and threw myself at my mother's feet.

We did not return to the hotel until nightfall, and it was with a heavy heart that I climbed the stairs to our room. I did not even respond to Mick's hearty greeting, or the winks and smiles of Sandy, the porter; I needed to be alone with Aaron.

He understood and held me until I was ready to speak.

"What have I done?"

"You've done nothing wrong."

"I left them and they needed me."

"Jack, everyone has to leave home."

"Margaret didn't."

"And look what's happened to her. We had a talk, your sister Margaret and I. She has secrets that she's terrified the world will find out."

"Secrets? What do you mean? She had a baby?"

Aaron laughed. "No! Don't you see? You're not the only one in the family."

I must have looked very stupid. Aaron grabbed my chin and kissed me. "No, Jack. She's like us. She's...well, she's never going to get married, put it like that."

"You mean she prefers girls? Oh, my God!"

I had never seriously considered the possibility that others in my family might be as interesting as I was, and I wasn't sure that I liked the competition.

"She told you this?"

"Reluctantly."

"You mean, you just asked her?"

"I guessed a long time ago."

"How on earth—"

"Call it an instinct. I knew plenty of girls like that at home."

"I only ever read about those things," I said, realizing how ridiculous this sounded, and how angry I would be if

298

someone said it of me.

"On the contrary," Aaron said. "You lived with it for the first twenty-one years of your life. Now, what about your parents?"

I told him everything I had learned—of the collapse of the business, the shame of bankruptcy, the final blow of Jane's death, and their gradual retreat into the house, which they had not left now for months, becoming entirely dependent on Margaret and occasional visits from my old friend James, who rode down from Montpelier ostensibly to help my father with his accounts, but in fact to make a few discreet improvements to their way of life without seeming to be too obviously charitable. They were egotistical in their misery, ready to blame everyone but themselves for their grief, barely able to listen to anything I tried to tell them about my own life.

"You must understand them, Jack. They suffered some terrible blows."

"So have I. So have you."

"But we're young and we're—what shall I say? We're more ready to adapt than they are. I guess that's what comes of growing up as an outsider. You see the world for what it really is—a thousand possibilities, a thousand shades of gray. To people like your folks, the world is a simple picture in black and white. And when something goes wrong, they can't bend with the wind. They fall. You've got to make allowances."

"Why? Do they make allowances for me?"

"Now who's being selfish? They gave you life, Jack. They raised you, and they didn't do such a bad job. I mean, once you learn to stop thinking only of yourself, you might make a half-decent human being. Now come here and let me see if I can cheer you up a bit."

He undressed me slowly, taking his time, kissing every inch of my skin. Gradually I relaxed, saw the sense of his words, and responded to the pleasure. This time, he sucked me dry and swallowed every drop. The sensation as he entered me, my cock still hypersensitive from my recent orgasm, my ass still twitching, was like nothing I had ever experienced. My troubles were washed away in an overwhelming, almost unbearable sensation of surrender.

Over the next few days we faced some tough decisions. My parents were glad I was alive, but after the first flush of relief wore off it was replaced by a grim refusal to accept my decision to live openly with another man as my lover. "Couldn't you tell the world he's your servant?" my mother suggested. I realized that she was trying, within the limitations of her understanding, to be helpful, and I said only that I thought, on balance, that I could not.

The financial situation was not as dreadful as I had feared. Windridge had been apprehended in Georgia, whither he'd fled to join some hard-core slave owners whose idea of fun was to drink a skinful of liquor and go out nigger-hunting. The police caught up with him in Savannah and confiscated all his funds. Much of that money made its way back to my parents, and although it was clear that they would never go back into business—my father's spirit was broken, and he saw himself as an old man—they had more than enough to live comfortably, either in the house at Bishopstown or anywhere they chose.

Margaret was torn between a sense of duty to our parents and a very natural desire to get out of Bishopstown, as I had done, and start living her life. Aaron, whom she respected far more than me, suggested that she might do worse than to travel with us for a while. She refused at first, out of a sense of decorum more than anything, but day by day the seed grew in her mind and soon she was asking us when we thought the snow would have melted enough to allow for our departure.

But where were we to go? I had no desire to stay in Vermont, beautiful as it was, even in its winter mantle. The town where I had grown up was no place for me. Mick and Sandy might make a go of it; Mick had a sound business sense, and had profited from the impermanence of wartime to establish himself as a trustworthy manager and a bold entrepreneur; he would soon become one of the leading citizens of Bishopstown and nobody would remember the days when he hung around at the White Horse, fucking boys in the shithouse. But for Aaron and me? Vermont may have been the most liberal of states, but I suspected that it was not yet ready for a mixed-race same-sex couple living openly, as we were determined to do. Where could we go, to live without shame or fear?

Aaron, as ever, was ahead of me. While I was recovering from fever in the hospital at Richmond, he had reestablished contact with his former employer and lover, Captain Chester, who had survived the war and returned to the Alhambra Theater, with Billy at his side. The theater had been burned down, but out of the ashes (and the insurance money) they had built a "cabaret," or so they called it, where the Captain served liquor and Billy, who was now living permanently as a woman, provided a program of entertainment. Aaron showed me a letter form the captain which described in great detail just how talented and charming Billy was, and how much they satisfied each other in bed—and how he was convinced that they were going to be run out of town any day soon. "Virginia is too backward for the truly advanced theatrical arts," he said. "We're going to try our luck in California. Why don't you join us?"

California—and specifically San Francisco—had a laissez-faire reputation that appealed to us both. And, as we sat in my parents' sitting room, sipping tea and trying to make polite conversation, watching the melting snow dripping from the eaves, we began to think that relocating to a sunnier climate might not be such a bad idea. "I'm sick of having to unwrap you from all these layers of clothes," Aaron said when he stripped me for action in our hotel room that night. "I want you naked all the time."

We had to say a proper farewell to Bishopstown, to Vermont, my family, the East, and everything that it meant, and the opportunity came when James arrived in town as soon as the roads were clear to visit my father. Margaret had written to tell him of my arrival, but he had not responded, and I feared that my former friend had turned into a prim little Episcopalian. When I saw him getting down from his horse, I suspected that he had not. James had always been a good-looking boy, shorter and darker than me, with a slightly meek air about him that belied his passion in the dormitory. He wore gold-rimmed glasses to correct his short sight, which gave him a studious air. Although we had only been lovers for a short while, and had never done much more than some mutual masturbation and cautious sucking, I well remembered his tight, athletic body, his marble skin, and his strong, hairy legs; I used to joke that he had the legs of a coal miner grafted onto the body of a ballet dancer. The man who stepped up to me with his hand extended was altogether more confident, although the glasses were still in place, and there was something endearingly boyish about the smile.

"Jack," he said, as we shook. "Where have you been, you rogue? You broke my sister's heart when you disappeared like that. Mine too, I might add."

"I was sidetracked."

"And this must be Aaron." He took Aaron's hand, and any fears I may have had that James would ignore or patronize him—as many New Englanders did—were washed away.

"Pleased to meet you, James."

Their hands stayed joined for a little longer than was

strictly necessary, and I could see that James's eyes were sparkling.

"How is your family, James?" I asked.

"Fine, just fine, thank you. I have a wonderful wife and a fine young boy."

"I'm delighted to hear it."

"You'll dine with us tonight at the hotel, I trust," Aaron said.

"It would be my pleasure."

I bet it would, you dirty little bastard, I thought, experiencing a rare stab of jealousy. Aaron gave me one of his special looks, and I bit my tongue.

I watched James that afternoon, talking cheerfully to my parents, allaying their financial fears, saying how pleased they must be to see me alive and happy, and once again I felt that nagging worm of jealousy gnawing at my heart. Why could James, a relative stranger, enjoy their trust and respect when I could not? Well, he was married, a respectable banker, what my father would call "a pillar of society." I longed to tell them that he used to suck my dick, that he was gagging to get his lips around Aaron's rod, that we were as likely as not to spend the night fucking each other's brains out—but to what end? To chip away at another of the fragile props of my parents' wrecked lives?

We drank too much tea, and left the house at six.

"I think I owe you a huge debt of gratitude," I said to James as we walked down the road, our breath steaming in the cold night air.

"Think nothing of it."

"But I do. And I must also apologize for being such a thoughtless fool. When I left home I didn't know—"

"You don't have to explain. Come on, I'm hungry."

"But I want you to understand. I want to pay you back for everything you've done for my family."

"As you wish. But let's eat first."

303

I was about to reply, but then I noticed that James was grinning, and Aaron even more, and I realized that sometimes the best way of expressing your gratitude is to share your blessings.

That last night in Bishopstown was the end of one part of my life, and the beginning of another. Mick seated us in a chambre privée, the sort of place where businessmen would entertain their secretaries without fear of discovery. The table was set for three, but I insisted that Mick join us. He said it would be his pleasure, but he could not in all conscience leave Sandy out—they shared everything else, he said. And so we were five at the table, and a fine, jovial crew we were. Mick's staff was discreet and efficient, leaving each new course outside the room with a light tap on the door, after which they withdrew.

And it was just as well that they did, as our enjoyment could not wait until the meal was served. We managed, I think, to get through the soup without incident, although I wondered if it was necessary for Aaron to spend quite so long helping James with his napkin. And then, when the entrées arrived, all hell broke loose. Aaron, in helping himself to potatoes, "accidentally" allowed one yellow, buttery spheroid to fall into his lap. He pushed his chair back and said, "God damn. Look what I've done."

"I'll help you, sir," Sandy said, jumping up and rushing to Aaron's side. He knelt, retrieved the errant vegetable, and started dabbing at the butter on the front of Aaron's pants.

"You'd better get those pants off, Mr. Johnson," Mick said. "We can have them sponged clean and ready for you by morning."

In response, Aaron extended one booted leg and rested it on Sandy's knee. Sandy knew his place and started drawing the boot off. He was a freckle-faced, red-haired boy with a crooked smile and bright blue eyes—and I could imagine how much Aaron was enjoying his attentions. James's eyes were fixed on Aaron's crotch, like a rabbit staring at a snake, and I could see that there was no point in getting upset about other men wanting a piece of the action. There was plenty to go around.

Mick stood up and raised a glass of claret. He took a swig, and then very deliberately poured the remains down the front of my shirt.

"Now look what's happened," he said.

I allowed him to remove my shirt. "You're hairier than you used to be," he said, running a hand over my chest and stomach. "Thinner on top, but a lot thicker down here." He started sucking on my tit, which was wet with wine. I looked over at Aaron, who was now barefoot; Sandy was helping him out of his pants, and James was kissing him. I decided to throw caution to the wind one more time, grabbed Mick's head, and pushed it downward.

Over the course of the next hour, we tried just about every combination that five men with dirty minds can come up with. Mick fucked me on the table, pouring wine into my mouth and over my chest, licking it off. Aaron had two mouths working over his cock and balls, then allowed James and Sandy to take turns sitting on his prick, while he sucked and fondled the other to keep them both hard. Then the two older men made James, Sandy, and me lie in a circle, each sucking and being sucked, while they watched and jerked off, occasionally pressing their own thick dicks together for comparison. There wasn't much to judge between them in size, but the contrast in color inspired us all.

When dessert was served, we all ganged up on James, who had proved once again that marriage doesn't necessarily mean an exclusive preference for women, and pelted him with the cream, custard, jam, and sponge cake confection that had been so carefully prepared by Mick's chefs. It seemed a terrible waste of good food, but it was worth it to see James naked and messy, laughing hysterically, his hard cock bobbing and his hairy ass and legs slicked up with the sticky mess. Then we four licked him clean—and I mean clean. There wasn't a crevice in his body that our tongues did not go.

"I've just realized," I said, as I lapped hungrily at his ass, "that I never did get around to fucking you, James."

"You never did," he replied, disengaging himself from Mick's mouth; his face looked sore from stubble burn, a feeling I knew well.

"I don't think I can leave Vermont without remedying that."

"I don't think you can."

And so I pushed my hard dick into him; a handful of cream made a very efficient lubricant. The others watched and encouraged us for a while, and then got down to the serious business of getting two very large cocks into one very tight asshole. And so we fucked each other for the rest of the night, pausing only for a recuperative brandy before repairing to the bridal suite. I very much doubt that it has seen such a honeymoon since.

The rest of my tale is quickly told. Aaron and I said our farewells in the morning. We set off in a horse and carriage to say farewell to my parents, and to collect Margaret—she had decided, after all, to travel west with us, and to find out if she could begin a new life. There were tears and painful silences as we took leave of our mother and father, but we all knew in our hearts that it was a relief to part.

We rode south with our few possessions, the roads getting clearer and the air warmer with every passing mile. Hotels and inns along the way accepted us as a married couple with a servant and allocated rooms accordingly. We did not argue, but made our own arrangements discreetly and to everyone's satisfaction.

We reached Richmond within two weeks and were greet-ed by Captain Chester and Billy, who joined their wagon to ours and prepared for the difficult, dangerous journey west. We knew that the road was fraught with dangers, but after what we had all experienced before, it seemed like an adven-ture rather than a threat.

There was one more addition to our party. We paid a call on the hospital and found Jenny Wallace struggling to run her wards under the bullying eye of a doctor who seemed disposed to make as much money as possible out of her hard work. It did not take much to persuade her to abandon her post—particularly not when she clapped eyes on my sister Margaret.

And so we set off west, three men, three ladies—Billy was at least as ladylike as Margaret, and a good deal more so than Jenny—and left it all behind us. But we would never forget, least of all Aaron and I, the ties that were forged in the heat of that burning hell of the Shenandoah Valley.

About the Author

JAMES LEAR WAS BORN IN SINGAPORE, EXPENSIVELY educated in England, and has worked in the theater and the British intelligence services. After a misunderstanding with the authorities, he has lived quietly in London, where he devotes his time to writing and helping local youth.

Hot Valley is his fourth novel. Other titles include *The Back Passage* (Cleis Press 2006), *The Low Road,* and *The Palace of Varieties.* Find out more at www.myspace.com/jameslearfiction.